DIE ON YOUR FEET

TITLES BY SG WONG

Lola Starke Series

Die On Your Feet
In For A Pound (August 2015)
Out Like A Lion (2016)

DIE ON YOUR FEET

A LOLA STARKE NOVEL

SG Wong

SG Wong
PO Box 67064 Meadowlark RPO
Edmonton, AB T5R 5Y3
www.sgwong.com

Publisher's Note: This is a work of fiction. Names, characters, places, and incidents are a product of the author's imagination. Locales and public names are sometimes used for atmospheric purposes. Any resemblance to actual people, living or dead, or to businesses, companies, events, institutions, or locales is completely coincidental.

Book Layout ©2013 BookDesignTemplates.com
Cover Design by little h design works

Die On Your Feet /SG Wong. -- 1st print ed.
ISBN 978-0-9940880-0-0

For my father
Wong Lui
(1935 - 2000)

It is better to die on your feet than to live on your knees.

—EURIPIDES, *Orestia*

ONE

Lola glanced at the clock on her desk, calculating whether she could stop in at home before driving to the Aunties' place. She thought about it a minute too long.

The office buzzer sounded. Lola picked herself up from her chair and walked out to the waiting area.

The man just crossing the threshold was tall, thin, dressed in light grey wool. He held a grey trilby in his slender fingers. His light green eyes contrasted enticingly with his coffee-colored skin. He shook Lola's hand firmly and introduced himself:

"Bodewell Arbogast."

She raised an eyebrow.

"My mother believed in portents." His smile was confident and easy.

Lola motioned for him to enter her office and take a seat. He unbuttoned his suit jacket to do so, reaching inside to pull out a slim silver case. He offered a dark cigarette.

"We have the same taste for exotics, Mr. Arbogast." Lola fetched her own Egyptian cigarette from the inlaid box atop her desk and let him light her up.

"A good omen?" he asked with another smile. They were soon nestled in a vivid blue haze.

"What can I do for you, Mr. Arbogast?"

"I was given your name by Mrs. Bing. She said you were discreet and efficient." Lola nodded. He sat forward intently. "My best friend is missing. Joseph Josephson. Everyone calls him Sunny Joe." Arbogast reached a slender hand into a breast pocket and extracted a photograph.

Lola added to the smoky air as she leaned forward to accept it. She studied the smiling face, the light hair, the gaunt cheeks. She noted the snappy line of his collar. "Is there a particular reason you're not telling the police your story?"

Arbogast didn't hide his displeasure. "They're not interested in a former felon. They don't care where he is. They'd just as soon wait for him to show up, dead or otherwise. That's how they'd help me." He blew out an angry plume of smoke.

"What sort of crime are we talking here?"

"Petty theft. He was a heroin addict. But that was years ago. He's been straight three years." He seemed pretty proud of himself. "Look, Miss Starke, I know Sunny's no angel, but he's not back on the needle. I know it. He's my best friend." Arbogast's conviction willed his statement to be truth.

"Mr. Arbogast, I'm not in the business of giving false hope. I'm going to ask you some questions and then I'll tell you if I'll help."

It seemed straightforward. The two men were roommates, in a house down by the old Southern citrus groves. Josephson had been missing four days now. Arbogast had done a little telephone sleuthing, but had come up empty. No one had seen Sunny Joe recently. At the very least, no one was telling.

Lola nodded gravely here and there, then and now, as Arbogast told his tale. Her expression gave away no judgments. That wasn't the case with her constant companion.

"That's it?" Aubrey's tone was outraged.

Lola gave no outward sign of change. She wasn't in the habit of conversing with her Ghost in front of strangers. It wasn't polite, as only she could hear him, of course. As a rule, Lola tried her damnedest to pretend Aubrey didn't haunt her every waking moment.

So, instead of saying something rude to Aubrey, she repeated her question to Arbogast: "And you tried his employer? He hasn't been sent out on the road?"

Arbogast shook his head impatiently: "Sunny isn't a traveling salesman, Miss Starke." He crushed out his cigarette in an ebony bowl on the desk, mashing until the ember was completely extinguished. He lit another with quick, jerky motions. "Listen, I know how it sounds. You think he's gone back to his old habit." He shook his head. "You don't know us. We're close. He wouldn't keep anything from me."

"Exactly why he'd disappear if he had," said Aubrey.

"Let me be honest with you, Mr. Arbogast," Lola said. "This isn't my sort of case. File a missing persons report with the police and see what they can do for you. It's their job."

"No, absolutely not. They won't help me. If I hire you, I can guarantee you'll work on it. Lillian, Mrs. Bing, was completely forthcoming about your fees. I can match what you made with her."

Aubrey whistled incredulously: "You charged Bing through the roof. He's gotta be hiding something from you."

Lola brushed at an ear impatiently. Her face betrayed annoyance for a split second before subsiding into casual lines. "I'm not in the business of deluding people, Mr. Arbogast. I agree with the police on this one." She raised a hand to stop his objections. "It's common sense. Your friend has a history with heroin. He's vanished, you say.

He's got no tomato to run away with, no family to run to. If this disappearance is something more sinister, that's also a police job."

"Yes, yes, I know how it sounds. But I'm telling you. I would know. This is something else entirely, but it doesn't feel good. I'm willing to pay you to satisfy my intuition. Why turn down honest money?"

Lola sized up the tall man in silence. Aubrey buzzed in her ear, insistent she refuse. The slightest of twitches raised her lips at the ends.

"All right, Mr. Arbogast, I'll take you on." His smile was immediate and filled with relief. "But you should still file that report with the police. That will ensure Mr. Josephson will be tagged if he resurfaces." She held up a hand again. "'If', Mr. Arbogast. As I said, I don't dole out false hope. Now, about my fees."

They settled on a retainer, with per diem and expenses. Lola didn't come cheap. Arbogast didn't bat an eye at the amounts. She scanned his card as he passed it over, but it was blank except for his name and a phone number, Oleander 5972. That had to be the house.

"What about an alternate, say, your work telephone?" Lola asked.

Arbogast shook his head. "It's not convenient at work. They discourage personal calls." He paused to fix her with a sharp look. "I'd prefer regular updates, Miss Starke."

"My kind of work doesn't lend itself to being by the phone regularly, Mr. Arbogast. Let me call you when I have something to update. I've done this before. I won't leave you hanging." Arbogast looked dubious. Lola pressed for more details: Josephson's place of employment, his favorite places, his friends, his last reliable whereabouts. She finished with the tough stuff.

"What about Ghosts? Is Mr. Josephson haunted?"

Arbogast waved his hand dismissively: "Lucille, his sister. But I wouldn't put much store in her. She was never the strong one, just the follower."

"She was obviously strong enough to become a Ghost," Aubrey said.

Lola continued. "His heroin suppliers? Do you know them?"

Arbogast looked her coolly in the eye: "That's not relevant, Miss Starke."

"That's up to me, Mr. Arbogast. I'm the gumshoe. You can tell me now or I can waste time finding it out on my own."

He shook his head, clenched his jaw. "I don't know."

Lola placed a finger on his newly signed cheque. "I make the rules, Mr. Arbogast. If you don't like them, you can take your game somewhere else." She pushed the piece of paper toward him.

Arbogast stared at the cheque in silence. He chewed absently at his lower lip, fingered a suit button. Something in that sleek noggin of his clicked. He straightened his shoulders and reached for his hat. He stood, aimed an imperious gaze downward.

"Keep it. You'll earn it." He tipped his hat and strode out. Lola remained as she was, listened to the click of the outer door closing. Arbogast kept up his long stride to the elevator. The clang of the bell and a bright greeting from Billy, the lift boy. Then, silence as the box descended and another wayward client left in a swirl of dark thoughts.

Aubrey got straight to the point: "His story stinks worse than a drunk on Saturday night. You're taking on trouble with this one, Lola."

That slight twitch of her lips.

"He'll either be loaded or dead or both, probably in an alley behind one of these joints. Or he might be in jail already. One could hope, for Arbogast's sake, if for no other reason." Lola pushed away from the desk and stood in one smooth movement. "Time to go. Traffic to East Town'll be murder."

Buses and train cars were filled with people, everyone wearing that same tired expression, no one looking anyone else in the eyes. The cars thinned out along Fisher. Lola snagged a spot just shy of the corner of Seventh. The Aunties lived on top of a two-storey walk-up, just east of Eighth. The pedestrians were mainly Chinese here, but there were plenty of other *gwai* out and about on a warm spring evening. East Town was a big tourist stop. The city's Gaming Commission made sure of that. Exotic foods, cheap souvenirs, mah-jongg parlors. The loudest, flashiest shops were two blocks south, on Kwan. There was a garish gate at Sixth and Kwan: two bright red columns joined at the top with a faux bamboo roof covering the requisite dragon-and-phoenix show. The nightclubs started west of the Gate, along Sixth. The better quality ones, like Silver Swan or Jade, had the prettier girls and stiffer drinks. The floor shows were usually Chinese musicians playing some classical pieces, including zither and erhu, during dinner and then more modern dance numbers afterwards. Those bands were often mixed. Most tourists didn't want to know what the low-end clubs served.

Fisher was noticeably more low-key. The shops were slightly darker; the sidewalks had a little more grime. The people were quieter. There were no nightclubs or mah-jongg places on Fisher. Just average shops full of foodstuffs or newspapers or straw hats. But there was also a Healer, and she drew a different kind of crowd. Not a lot of tourists looking for luck wanted to see the sick and dying. But the Ha family had lived here long before the Gaming Commission came along. Betta was the third Conjurer in the family to run her business out of this shopfront. The Aunties lived above; something about a healer living below being the kind of luck they appreciated.

There was a silent bell above Betta's door. It flicked on a tiny green bulb in her back treatment room. It wasn't necessary this time, though, since Betta was sitting in her window. She smiled as she watched Lola coming down the street. She was already standing by the time Lola entered the little shop. The women exchanged hugs. Lola felt how sharp Betta's shoulders were getting, but she remained silent.

"You're getting too skinny, Betta," said Aubrey. "You should go upstairs to eat more often. The gods know they've always got food to spare."

Betta smiled prettily. She couldn't help it. She was a beautiful woman. Her dark eyes sparkled as she addressed the air just behind Lola. "If that's your idea of charm, I don't want to know what cranky looks like."

"Are you *sure* he's not an old woman?" Lola asked Betta.

The Healer smiled wearily. "Are you sure you want to know?"

"Touché." Lola looked around her at the front room. Every magazine was in its place, every cushion and chair. The window seat still had a slight dip where Betta had been sitting. "Done for the day?"

Betta shook her head. "One more."

"Come up when you're done," Aubrey said. "You could do with the company."

Her smile faltered. "I think I'll turn in for the night after this one."

Lola moved forward to hug her again, but Aubrey wasn't finished. "Cancer?"

Betta's face tightened and her smile faded. Lola's voice was flat. "Zip it, Aubrey."

"It's all right, Lola," Betta said, stroking the younger woman's arm. "I know why he's asking." She turned to him, presumably by the window now. "Yes, a cancer patient. And yes, I find those treatments wearing." She tried another smile. It peeked out weakly. "You know I'd love to join in tonight, but I'm not much of a player anyway."

Lola embraced Betta again. Her words were light. They didn't match her expression. "Don't take him too seriously. Aubrey's just playing private dick again." When Lola pulled back, Betta's smile had smoothed out again. "See you later."

The building was small; there was no grand lobby. Betta worked in the store front and lived in the back. Her front door faced east, at right angles to her large window onto the street. The stairs to the Aunties' flat were at right angles to the door. Force of habit had Lola looking into their mailbox, just inside the outer door, before heading up. It was locked. Nothing was visible through the slot.

Lola climbed the steep stairs and caught her breath at the landing before the Aunties' door. Her knock was greeted by the sound of brisk slippered feet. She smiled, knowing it was Viola. The door opened to reveal a petite Chinese woman, wearing tailored grey slacks and a pinstriped lilac blouse with white collar. A fuchsia scarf served as a belt around her tiny waist. Her diamond studs winked as she tucked her chin-length hair behind her ears. She ushered Lola inside and greeted Aubrey as though she knew exactly where he was standing.

Lola exchanged a kiss and hug: "Sorry I'm late. Last-minute client."

"Like father, like daughter. Butch was never on time." Viola waited as Lola slid her feet into house slippers, then linked arms and led the way down the short hall. "Have you eaten? I made cold noodles."

They passed two bedrooms on the right, a bathroom across to the left, and walked through an archway into the airy main living space. The dining area was directly ahead, the living room to the right. Windows lined both spaces along two walls, but only the windows along the street had a view. The others looked out on a very narrow space and the neighbouring building's brick exterior. The kitchen was visible from here as well, separated from the dining area by a long counter.

The windows were open to the warm evening air. A fan whirred industriously from the corner by the mah-jongg table. The street noises were subdued.

Two women sat on opposing sides of the living room, each holding up sections of the evening's paper.

Veronica was on the long sofa. She'd tucked her legs beneath her, the skirt of her pale green dress snugged tight against her calves. Her slippers were perfectly aligned to one another, sitting perpendicular to the sofa. The sun behind her picked out the silver amidst the white of her hair. She had it in a tight bun. Veronica never wore makeup anymore, but her face was younger now than when she had been a stage performer. Her age spots looked like freckles. She spoke through the paper: "It's unhealthy and you know it. An unhealthy obsession."

Across from her, Vivian rattled her newspapers in response. "I know no such thing. That's purely an opinion of *yours*." She frowned. In contrast to Veronica's sleek elegance, Vivian had chopped her thick black hair too short. Her face was smooth, unlined, and perfectly round. Her lips were dark red at the moment She wore a lavender blouse with puffed short sleeves. Her long legs, in black slacks, were crossed gracefully in front of her. One slipper dangled carelessly from a suspended foot.

Viola squeezed Lola's hand as she announced: "Lola and Aubrey are here." Then she released the younger woman and went toward the kitchen. Lola went forward to greet Vivian and Veronica, in that order. Vivian was much more likely to hold grudges.

Viola came back from the kitchen and laid a place at the dining table. Veronica was still reading her paper: "Have you eaten, Lola? Auntie Vi made noodles."

"Ahem," replied Viola. Veronica looked up.

"Oh good," said the latter without sarcasm. She gave Lola a critical once-over. "You're losing too much weight."

Vivian snorted: "Those damn foreign cigarettes. Bloody living on them now?"

Lola watched Vivian fit a holder with a cigarillo, long red fingertips immaculate as ever. "Cigarettes and men, Auntie Viv. Don't forget the men."

"Your father would've had something to say about them." Viv's tone was sharp.

Aubrey laughed. Lola washed her hands at the kitchen sink and returned to the dining room. Viola placed a bowl of noodles and a cup of tea on the table. Lola dug in. Viola sat with her as she ate. She smiled and started to say something, but Vivian broke in first.

"Lola, who was this client that made you late tonight?"

"You know she can't tell you that," Veronica said.

"Yes, I *know* that, Vee, but she doesn't have to tell me her client's name. I just want to know what's the case. Is that an *unhealthy obsession* too?"

Lola exchanged a glance with Viola, who shook her head and pursed her lips. Around a mouthful of salty, spicy noodles, Lola said: "Just someone looking for their lost roommate. Probably owes rent. Nothing earth-shattering."

"That's an abridged version," said Aubrey.

Vivian snorted. "Sounds better than some of your other cases."

"Leave her alone. You're just in a snit," said Veronica.

"I'm just saying," Vivian continued, "Butch's clients were all of a certain calibre, and I don't see why Lola insists on ignoring those types of people. Besides which, studio people pay well."

"Well, Lola doesn't need the money, and that's not the point." Veronica glared at Vivian. "You've always been star struck, Viv, admit it. Even after we were *retired* from the studios. Instead of a healthy bitterness, you got more and more stars in your little black eyes."

"Now that's below the belt," said Aubrey.

Vivian scowled and opened her mouth. Viola cut in: "Ladies, please. You're spoiling Lola's meal. Here, drink your tea. It'll help your digestion, dear." Lola sipped obediently. The other two women weren't as meek but they turned their argument down to simmer from boil. A tense silence filled the flat, punctured briefly by chopsticks hitting a bowl, as Lola finished her dinner. Even Viola was close to scowling. As soon as Lola placed the chopsticks on top of her empty bowl, Viola whisked them away and stalked into the kitchen. Lola was still chewing her last mouthful.

She stood and walked behind Veronica's perch on the shorter of the two sofas. She dropped off her tea mug at the mah-jongg area and went in search of cigarettes and lighter.

"Use the holder, Lola," scolded Vivian. "Your fingers will get hard and yellow." Lola obeyed, plucking an ebony holder from her purse. This was not a battle worth fighting tonight.

"All right," said Veronica. "Down to business."

The mah-jongg table sat in the northeast corner of the flat. The four women sat down randomly for the time being. When Viola brought out the mah-jongg set, Lola couldn't help smiling. The tiles were ivory and aged to a shiny parchment yellow. Her father had learned mah-jongg on this set. They both had. Hours of rules and games. Years of thumb pads rubbing, reading the characters, had faded the paint to ghosts of their original brilliance.

"Aubrey," said Lola, "stop breathing down my neck." She shuffled a few tiles from the end of her line to the centre.

"You know damned well you don't feel a thing," the Ghost replied.

"What I know is you were never this interested in mah-jongg when you were alive."

"A Ghost's got to have a hobby."

"Well, enjoy it at a distance, will you."

Vivian shook a finger at Lola. "Manners," she said primly. "No private conversations in public, if you please." She raised her gaze briefly. "And no peeking, Aubrey."

Lola heard her Ghost huff, scornful.

The game went swiftly. These four were old adversaries. Lola became increasingly despairing of a win as she watched Vivian hunt down the same tiles she needed. Finally, she was certain Vivian was about to crow with delight over a win, but it was Viola who suddenly sat up and grinned.

"*Ji maw.*" She happily showed the second tile she'd drawn.

"What?"

Lola watched, incredulous, as Viola flipped her tiles and revealed the cheapest winning hand: *gai woo*. However, a self-drawn and hidden win made up for small pickings.

"*Muen ching,*" said Veronica. "Well done, Vi."

"Squeezing every last drop out of that sorry hand," mumbled Vivian. "All right, show your tiles." She scanned Lola's hand as the younger woman returned the scrutiny. "You really were close," she murmured.

Lola sighed, reaching for her cigarettes.

Veronica counted up Viola's points and Vivian wrote down the tally. At the end of the evening, money would change hands. They were playing a nickel a point, a light game. The Aunties always played for money. When they were serious, points were a quarter apiece. Lola always sat those out. She preferred serious gambling at a parlour, not with family.

The women chatted and commiserated, turning tiles facedown and mixing once again.

"Ask them what they were arguing about," Aubrey suddenly said.

"Aubrey, be quiet."

Viola gave Lola a pointed look.

"He's just being rude, Auntie."

"Aubrey?" Her expression was incredulous.

"Yes, *Aubrey*."

"Well," said Veronica, "that doesn't mean you can be rude to him."

Vivian grinned but remained silent.

"Ask them," repeated Aubrey.

"If I could think of a polite way to tell him to stop pestering me, Auntie, I would."

"Aren't you concerned about them, Lola? Don't you want to find out if there's something you can help them resolve?"

"Aubrey, it's none of your business until someone says otherwise. Beat it."

"Lola," said Veronica.

The younger woman continued stacking tiles calmly. Veronica repeated her name, hands now still. Lola met her aunt's eyes without embarrassment.

"What's none of his business?" asked Vivian.

"Always the sharp one," commented Aubrey. He sounded amused.

"He thinks I should put my nose into your argument."

Veronica looked down at her hands and swiftly straightened tiles. There were faint pink spots at her cheeks, remnants of her displeasure.

"Fine," said Vivian, "since you're curious. We were arguing about your mother."

"I wasn't curious."

"Leave it alone." Veronica shot Vivian a warning glare.

"No," said Vivian, "I won't. That woman was the death of Butch and I am not going to forgive her for it."

"He had cancer, Vivian," said Viola.

Vivian never backed down. "She sucked the life out of him." She angrily clacked her tiles together and pushed them toward the forming square. "And now she's picked up again with that abomination."

Veronica was impatient. "Viv, please. Your flare for the dramatic has grown into a wildfire. Mayor's a Ghost. Just a Ghost."

"An *abomination,*" Vivian repeated. "A normal Ghost wouldn't be visible to everyone. A normal Ghost wouldn't be meddling in the daily affairs of a million people."

"For heavens' sake. He's still in office because we wanted it that way. *We* asked the poor man to forego reincarnation for us. And he did it. Doesn't that tell you about his character?" Veronica clacked a tile forcefully.

"You'll never convince me that entire campaign wasn't his idea in the first place. It was too perfect. The man knew he was dying. He didn't want to let go the reins of power. He chose Ghosthood over reincarnation *of his own volition.* It was simply better drama to pretend we," her face twisted, "'the fair citizens of Crescent City,' wanted him after death." She made as if to spit. "I know it. He's cunning. He thrived in the movies for over two decades," Vivian shouted. She was building a full head of steam now. "And I didn't vote for him to continue *Unto Death.* It's not right. The man should be dead and gone. Not in charge of a city of living souls. And certainly not traipsing around with an aging Crescent City starlet." She tapped out her cigarette and reached for another.

"They're just friends." Lola lit another Egyptian. "If I'm not bent out of shape, why are you?"

Vivian drew herself up haughtily. "Why *shouldn't* I be? I loved your father. We all did. You don't have the corner on that." She stood up abruptly and walked into the kitchen. Viola put down the dice she'd been ready to cast. She got up wordlessly and went to the coffee table in the living room. She returned with a newspaper and handed it to Lola. She squeezed Lola's hand before following Vivian into the kitchen.

Page Three of the *Crescent City Post.* The headline in bold: ***Ingenious* Pair at it Again?** There was a photograph of a dark-haired woman smiling up at a shadow to her left. Mayor never photographed as anything more than a person-shaped smudge. The caption was predictable, too. *"**Mayor** escorts **Grace McCall** to world premiere. Are the duo planning a reunion project?"* The article had as much weight as a cotton skirt in a stiff breeze.

Grace McCall hadn't made a film with Esperanza for years before his death. He was unlikely to give up governing the city to direct a movie, of all things. Their most famous film, *Ingenious,* was over twenty years past. There weren't a lot of things Lola liked about Grace McCall, but she admired her mother for knowing her place in the pantheon.

Veronica took the paper from Lola and folded it neatly. "It's not healthy, Lola. We all loved him. Butch wouldn't want her like this." She, too, got up. She took her mug of tea and walked to a window overlooking the street.

There were murmurs from the kitchen. Lola didn't strain to catch any words. After a moment, she went to join Veronica.

Aubrey sighed.

Veronica spoke without turning: "Were you telling the truth? It doesn't bother you?"

"Mother and Mayor?" Lola stopped to consider. She watched a lorry roar around the corner below. She shrugged. "It's her life. Her past. It doesn't matter. Dad died twelve years ago. I don't expect her to pine away for him. She didn't when he was still alive. Why should death make him mean something to her?"

Aubrey tried to say something. Lola tuned him out. He was a single note on the subject of Grace McCall. Lola was tired of the noise. He'd been her mother's best friend since childhood. She was sure that was the cruel reasoning behind his Haunting.

Vivian returned from the kitchen with a clickety-clack of her heeled slippers. Lola and Veronica both turned to watch her approach. Her face was set into stubborn lines.

"I guess I should be grateful someone's taking my father's side in this," murmured Lola. "He never seemed to."

Veronica gave her a sideways glance.

The four sat down and resumed play. They made it through six games before the round was completed. It took about an hour and a half. Vivian won the majority of games but she was still angry. There wasn't much anyone could do about it. None of them had Butch's touch with Vivian. She never could stay angry at him.

Eventually, farewells and hugs were exchanged. Lola stepped out into the damp night and pulled her coat up to her ears. The night was young yet and she was still restless. She decided to try some more substantial gambling and drove toward The Golden Bowl. It wasn't much in the way of glamour, but it was on the way home. A few hours were wasted there with some other regulars, but her concentration was thin and the table tepid. In the end, she made the acquaintance of a tall painter with beautiful hands. He was masquerading as a waiter. They adjourned to his apartment to peruse his etchings. By the time Lola finally went home, the hours were wee and the stars dim.

TWO

Wake up, sleepyhead."

"Beat it, Aubrey."

"Rise and shine, princess."

"I said 'Beat it,' you damned haunt."

"It's the middle of the morning and you have a job to start."

Lola rolled over with a groan and pulled the pillow away from her head. "When did you get so keen on this one?"

"I'm not, but I seem to recall you are." His tone became serious: "You took on a client, Lola. Sleeping in is hardly what I'd call professional. Get up."

"Get out then. I'm taking a shower."

Lola got up. She pulled off her bedclothes and stumbled toward the master bathroom, glad for the heavy drapes over the windows.

She stood under the hot spray, her eyes closed, head hanging. She organized the day ahead. There were going to be a lot of dank alleys and smelly rooms in the immediate future. She considered referring Arbogast to Shu, on Fourth and McAllister. Shu never minded the rough stuff.

A light knock announced Elaine's presence just outside the bedroom. Lola called her inside as she finished drying off. She wrapped her robe around herself and strode out of the bathroom.

"Good morning, Miss Lola," Elaine said. As ever, her spine was a marvel of natural engineering; it ran straight and true without the slightest hint of effort. Her rich chestnut hair framed a long, slender face with thin, shapely lips and intelligent grey-green eyes.

"'Morning, Elaine. I'll be doing some trawling today, I think. Did you get that stain out of those dark brown trousers last week?"

The maid nodded and slipped into the closet. She poked her head out again and watched Lola rub roughly at her dark, shoulder-length hair. While Lola frowned slightly at her own reflection in the vanity mirror, Elaine disappeared back inside the closet.

"Stop fretting. I'll put it up into a twist," Elaine said, returning with slacks. She also carried a tan blouse and a safari-cut jacket, complete with waist belt and large square flap pockets.

"You're a saint," Lola said with a grin.

"The gods know, a hairstylist you'll never be."

"If that ain't the truth, I'll be a monkey's uncle." Lola lit a cigarette.

The maid worked efficiently. "Coffee and rolls are out in the dining room." She patted at some stray hairs and tucked in some more pins. She scrutinized her handiwork with narrowed eyes. "That ought to do you, but if it starts to come down, just shake it, comb it out with your fingers and your natural waves will take care of the rest."

Lola laughed. "I'm not entering a beauty contest, angel. It's gambling joints and back alleys for me today."

Elaine smiled as she shrugged.

Lola ate in her shirtsleeves. Breakfast was a hurried affair and left her place at the table scattered with crumbs and a few drops of blueberry jam. She drained her coffee cup twice, however, without leaving any stains behind.

She grinned as she got up. Elaine shooed her away.

She returned to the bedroom while Elaine cleared the breakfast things. She exchanged the safari coat for something a little less symbolic, a lightweight brown tweed with patch elbows and a little extra room. The pockets were piped. Lola slid in a switchblade. She smoothed out the pocket until the knife sat almost flat. She slid a tiny .22 into her purse, along with her cigarettes. She fitted a larger calibre into an ankle holster and shook out her trouser leg until it draped elegantly once more. She took a few steps to reacquaint herself with the weight. She checked her watch. She'd been awake thirty-eight minutes.

Stewart, the lift boy, had ginger hair and a creamy complexion to match. His eyes were a curious blue-green. He grinned. "Got a hot one today, Miss Starke. Cleopatra in the eighth to win, at five-to-one. She's running at three this afternoon. A real pip, that's what they say, a real pip."

"A boy's gotta have a hobby, I suppose," Lola said. "Never had much interest in the ponies, myself."

"Doesn't mean you can't make some dough from 'em," he shot back amiably. "I'm tied up here all day, a double shift too. We're real shorthanded. No one can get away." His eyes widened with excitement. "But you, Miss Starke, you could place the bet for me and I'll split the winnings with you."

Lola smiled politely. "Split how? And what's the stake?"

"Ah well, here's the beauty of it, Miss Starke. You put up the hundred dollars and you'll get it back double."

"Why would I split anything if it's my money?"

"You're paying for my expertise, of course," he replied.

Lola shook her head, matching his solemnity. "Too much jack for this small-timer."

Lola stopped at the concierge for messages. As the elevator doors closed, she heard Stewart chatting up another tenant . She skimmed the slips, two from her mother, and then tossed them back down on the desk. She thanked Mr. Wang, who nodded in silent acknowledgement.

A separate elevator took Lola down to the parking levels. She didn't recognize the operator. His uniform had shiny buttons and a name tag: *Frederick*. He was middle-aged, a quiet character with a sad set to his well-lined ebony features. He tipped his hat and in a deep bass gently asked for their level.

Aubrey started talking: "I'm Aubrey O'Connell …. Nice to meet you …. You're new? How're you feeling so far? Everything all right?"

Lola kept her face neutral as Aubrey conversed with the operator's Ghost.

Frederick smiled and his face was transformed. The deep lines mapped out years of smiles like the one on his face now. He called out the parking level and tipped his hat once more. Lola thanked him and held out a small bill. Frederick nodded.

"Thank you kindly, Miss. Have a nice day now. You and Mr. Aubrey."

"Nice couple," Aubrey commented, as Lola neared her car.

"Next time, remember your manners." Lola strode to an old brown Buick with some dents and scratches.

"I didn't think you cared to be introduced," Aubrey replied. "I'll make a point of it next time. Frederick and his wife, Marcella, have been married twenty-seven years. She just passed last month. A lovely woman, too, with a smile to match his."

Lola grunted. "Another happy couple that can't stand to be parted."

After the shadowy parking area, the sunlight was whimper-inducing. Lola squinted through her dark glasses. Cars zipped, or hobbled, past as she waited for a break to turn left.

Josephson apparently liked the eastern parts of town. None of the parlours on the list came any farther west than Main. None of the other places, the ones that didn't offer gambling, were even that far toward the centre line. Lola decided to try a mah-jongg parlor first. With the sun barely risen, the chances of finding someone awake and intelligible at a junk house were slim. Drug addicts were like snakes: mornings found them drowsing under rocks, waiting until the sun produced enough heat to warm them into motion. Too early in the day and their blood was still thick with opiates.

The sky was a hammered blue, its edges thinned out to white. People walked briskly, their heads held up, their eyes bright. The metallic taste of heat was in the air. The day would only turn hotter as the hours dragged past. Better to hurry and fill the morning with movement, allow the afternoon to pass by while one huddled away from the burning light. Lola followed Tsing Drive until the numbered avenues stopped and names began once more. When Crescent City was much younger, its civic leaders named streets after themselves in unseemly numbers. Mah crossed Look, Eng paralleled Fong. It wasn't until Nathaniel Wing became mayor about one-hundred-and-fifty years ago that a system was created for ordering streets and neighbourhoods. Old Mayor Wing was a stickler for organization. He liked squares on his city map and numbers progressing according to a simple rule: avenue numbers grew as you headed northward. As for the street names, well, he was still an elected official and the populace as well as his own city councilors refused to give up the chance to have eponymous lanes, rows, drives, streets and closes. City maps were a necessity, for newcomer and veteran alike.

Lola found Silver and turned right until she hit Thackeray. Lucky Bamboo was a few blocks south, between Jade and Jasmine. It sat in what was euphemistically called a growing neighbourhood. Blocks of row houses lined avenues and streets. Dark brown, dark red, sooty yellow. Brick, brick and more brick. There were a few colourful awnings to signal a business: a grocer, a barber, a newspaper stand. There were people on the street. A woman, looking alarmingly close to labor, pushed a pram, her hair already straggling and plastered to the back of her neck. An elderly man coming the opposite way stopped to greet her, tipping his trilby. The woman smiled and stopped. A few hooligan types strutted about, their lips jutted, eyes glittering, jacket sleeves pushed up on hairy forearms. One, his hat perched at the back of his head, gave Lola a wink and a whistle as she drove past.

The Bamboo had a brightly false façade: garish red columns with gold-painted dragons entwined around their capitals. The door was thick wood, solid and heavy. Lola pulled at the ring that served as handle and was surprised at the lightness and ease of movement. Inside, the lighting was no match for natural sunlight. Lola slid to one side and waited for her sight to adjust.

A rounded opening across the foyer introduced the way to the gambling floor. The frame looked lacquered. A wooden floor, full of knotty planks and stained dark grey from countless crushed ashes, sounded solidly as Lola walked over it. A coat-and-hat check station to the right, its light off. Movement from the left side of the foyer caught her attention. A shimmering curtain concealed an alcove. That curtain was being pulled aside. A glimpse of desk and chair, elaborate floor lamp, calligraphy wall hanging. The space was the approximate size of Lola's bedroom closet.

A young girl in a satiny lime green *cheong-sahm* greeted Lola. The slit in the dress was high enough to show flashes of thigh beneath. As the girl bowed formally, her glossy jet hair swung forward, hiding her face. The dress showed slits up both legs. As the girl straightened up, she presented Lola with a lopsided smile and glassy eyes.

"Welcome to Lucky Bamboo, *siew-jeah,*" she said in English.

"How old are you?" Lola spoke Cantonese.

The girl blinked, then repeated her greeting in the same tongue, adding, "May I show you to our lucky tables?" Her gaze rested a few inches shy of Lola's left shoulder.

Lola gently took hold of a delicate chin and tipped the girl's face up. The lopsided smile never wavered. Her eyes flickered briefly and she blinked twice, slowly.

"*Siew-jeah?*"

"Never mind. I can find my way."

"Happy tiles, mistress!" The girl turned back toward the alcove. Lola walked through the round entrance, wrinkling her nose. The interior was dim and reeked of last night's cigarettes. Lola stopped and lit an Egyptian of her own, blew out a long streamer of smoke before her. A rotund man came out from a shadowed doorway in the far corner. There was no straight path for him. The tables were arranged in an arcane, meandering pattern, meant to allow *chi* to linger and spread out as it passed through the room. Lola raised her eyebrows that anyone in this dump had bothered with *feng shui.*

The man came on, following a well-tread path between tables. He wore his black hair slicked back, revealing a pronounced widow's peak. There was a small moustache, like a miniature brush, atop his upper lip. His brown suit was not quite fashionable but immaculately pressed, and his shoes shone. A tie of yellow and brown stripes didn't quite make it over the swell of his stomach. He buttoned his jacket as he approached. His round face creased into a wide smile. His teeth were yellow but straight.

"Ahhh, good day to you, mistress. We are honoured by your visit to our humble tables." He spoke in clipped Cantonese. "As you can see, we are without players to match your calibre at the moment. May I interest you in some blackjack instead?"

He motioned with a flourish, and Lola discovered another rounded doorway at the far left. A thin man waited at a single table. Four high stools stood empty as the dealer shuffled and reshuffled the deck of cards in his hands. He was chewing a cigar stub. His blond hair shone faintly in the glow of light from above. There were four other tables, all empty.

Lola turned her attention back to the round man. He surveyed her clothes with an assessing gleam in his eyes.

"I think he's just calculated the cost of your outfit, to the last penny," said Aubrey.

"Do you manage this palace?" Lola's briskness elicited surprise but the round man quickly replaced it with an oily smile.

"Sammy Lu, at your service."

Lola took out a small roll of money while Lu's eyes widened. She peeled off a five. "I'm looking for information, Mr. Lu."

He pocketed the bill smoothly and bowed his head briefly. "Yes, of course. Anything I can do to help."

"Just the truth. Understand?" Lola pulled out a photo. Lu took the proffered picture of Josephson and studied it briefly, nodded again.

His nose wrinkled in disgust. "Sunny Joe. A junkie. Always in here looking for a game, but no one wants to gamble with bad luck at their table."

"Not even to make easy money?"

Lu shook his head. "Not worth the odds."

"He doesn't gamble here? Ever?"

"Not for months, maybe a year. He was clean for a stretch. Didn't last." Lu's shrug was impersonal.

"When's the last time he was here?"

Lu looked up at the ceiling, thinking. He tapped his chin with a stubby forefinger. "Maybe last Sunday?" He squinted into the distance, the gears clearly grinding now. "Yeah, yeah. Sunday. My niece was out sick." He gestured toward the front entrance.

"She friends with him?"

"No." Lu guffawed. "Too smart for a junkie like that."

Lola cocked her head skeptically. "She's pretty small for security. Where's your real muscle?"

Lu laughed heartily. "She's a black belt. Shown a few drunks and sore losers the door in her time. Including Sunny Joe."

"I want to talk to her. How old is she?"

"Twenty." Lu grinned at Lola's reaction. "Runs in the family." He leaned in. "I'm almost sixty." His grin widened. "Don't look a day over forty." He started walking. He fired off some rapid Chinese to the girl as they came through the archway. Lola recognized the dialect, *Gum Sahn,* but it was too fast for her to follow with any certainty.

The girl blinked and grinned. "Had you fooled, huh?" Her smooth face was animated and exuberant. She still didn't look twenty, but at least she looked awake.

"Minnie's an actress," Lu explained. "She's readying for an audition." More provincial Chinese passed between uncle and niece.

The girl made a face. "I get a lot of junkies or whores, but a job's a job." She shrugged, then looked Lola directly in the eyes. "You're looking for Sunny, huh?" Her expression turned pitying. "Poor man. He was clean for so long too."

"How long?" asked Lola.

The girl shrugged, looked at her uncle. "Couple years?"

Lu shook his head. "No, three. You were just graduating." The round man nodded, satisfied at his recollection.

The girl continued, "He came in last Saturday. High as the moon."

"What did he do?"

"Looking for Uncle Sammy. Wouldn't tell me why. I was sick as a dog. Didn't much care. Told him to come in again Sunday. Don't know if he did or not." She looked back at her uncle.

Lu nodded again. "Like I said, he was in Sunday. Couldn't understand what he wanted. He was too junked up to make any sense. I had Minnie's brother, Benny, guide him to the curb."

"Did he mention any travelling plans?"

Lu shook his head. "I'm telling you. He was barely able to say his own name. I was surprised he was walking upright."

"When does your brother come in?" Lola turned to the girl.

She shrugged again. "Late shift. You can come back then."

Aubrey broke in: "Show another bill and ask Lu to 'phone. You've got a long list. This is a shortcut you can afford."

Lola gritted her teeth for an instant before smoothing out her features into casual politeness again. "Let's ring him now, shall we?" Another bill appeared in Lola's fingers. Lu smiled.

"Sure thing." The girl stepped aside to let her uncle to pass into the alcove. A telephone was mounted on the wall right beside the entry. Lola stepped halfway in and looked around. A textbook—Japanese, not Chinese—was open on the plain wooden desk. The red cushion of the matching chair was fraying at the corners. The wall hanging was a cheap reproduction of *The Mountain Pass.*

Lu made his request to the operator in a quiet voice. Lola didn't catch the exchange. Lu glanced at her sidelong. He asked for his nephew in Cantonese. A few moments passed, then Lu started speaking in *Gum Sahn* again.

Eventually, Lu passed her the phone. "Benny?" A deep voice answered in the positive. "Lola Starke. What happened after you threw Sunny Joe out on his ear?"

"Let's be clear, Miss Starke. I didn't toss him out. I walked him to the curb." Benny spoke in cultured tones.

"Fine. I'm interested in where he went after you stopped holding hands then."

"He turned left and walked down the street. He got into his car and pulled off, toward Jasmine. Then he took a right."

"Your uncle said he was barely able to stand. Weren't you concerned?"

"We're responsible for only ourselves," he answered.

"Did he mention where he was heading?"

"Listen, Miss Starke, I like Sunny, but he's a junkie. He'd steal from me in a flash if he thought he'd get away with it. I don't fraternize with thieves nor with drug addicts. Sunny was both and he was three sheets to the wind that day. I couldn't have understood him if I'd had a code book."

"Are you saying he said something that just didn't make sense?"

A long-suffering sigh. "I'm saying I didn't understand anything coming out of his mouth."

"Think on it, Benny. If something comes up, get my number from your uncle and call me. If it pans out, there'll be some bills in it for you."

Lu flapped a hand. Lola passed the telephone back to him. She didn't move out of the alcove. She waited, pulling a folded bill through her fingers like a shirt through a wringer. Lu spoke rapidly and listened carefully. After a few more seconds of unintelligible exchange, he cradled the phone and turned to Lola. She handed over her card along with the money.

"If you remember anything else about Sunny that day, call."

The girl, Minnie, spoke up. "Are you working for some insurance racket?" Lu tsked and tried to shush her, but the girl kept steady eyes on Lola.

"Nothing like that. Just a worried party with cash on hand to start a private inquiry."

"Because Sunny's harmless. He'd never hurt anybody—except maybe himself," Minnie said.

"I'm not looking to rough him up. Just to find him." Lola looked at them each in turn. "Does that change your story?" He shook his head. "Like I said, think on it."

Lu ushered Lola out, opening the door into the eye-shattering sunlight. He kept up an obsequious patter as he followed her out to the curb. Lola thanked him and walked to her car. Lu was still on the sidewalk as she slid behind the wheel. He bowed, waved briefly and hurried back inside.

Lola ventured farther east, coincidentally following Josephson's supposed trail onto Jasmine. Twenty minutes and ten blocks later,

Lola found Allan Drive. It wasn't hardly as proud as its name. Poor white families stuffed into tiny row houses built at the end of the last century. Not many had indoor plumbing. The house Lola wanted did, though. The widow Walsh made sure to charge her boarders for it.

Lola cruised down the block, searching for an opening. There were a lot of cars along the curb, but hardly anyone was out. Children would've been in school, or playing truant somewhere else in the city. A trio in shirtsleeves and tough attitudes sat out on the stoop next to the widow Walsh's establishment. They watched Lola with unsmiling faces and hard eyes. She got out and approached them. Not a one straightened up from his practiced slouch. They negotiated for the safekeeping of the beat-up Buick. When they were satisfied, and half the agreed money had changed hands, Lola offered them cigarettes from a pack of domestics.

"Do you know this one?" she asked, handing over the photograph of Josephson.

The one uppermost on the steps snickered. "Sunny owe you too?" The other two sneered.

"He owes someone," Lola replied. "Seen him recently?"

"Naw," said the first one. "Not for weeks. The word was he'd moved up in the world." He leaned back, his elbows resting on the top step.

Lola looked to the other two, but they just shook their heads and snickered. She stepped over to the widow Walsh's rooming house. It was a two-storey clapboard, the white paint long gone from decades in the harsh sun. Flecks stubbornly clung to the warped boards in places, giving the house a scrofulous shell to match its innards. The front porch was reached by five uneven steps. A sign in the front right window proclaimed that new boarders were currently welcome. Lola knocked and stepped back, checking the street and then turning back toward the windows.

A few seconds later, the widow herself showed her face. It was a remarkable one, for all its hardships. Her eyes were still large and almond-shaped, their piercing blue grown even sharper with years of suffering. Her lips still retained their trademark curve, although they were no longer as full. The widow never bothered with lipstick anymore. Cornelia Lee's career in the silent era of film was a long way from here. She had lines around her eyes and her mouth, but her cheeks looked soft and smooth. She fixed Lola with a scowl. "What do *you* want?" Lola held up the photograph once more. The widow shook her head. "Not since year's end."

"December?" Aubrey was skeptical.

"How regular was he?" Lola asked.

The widow's eyes narrowed. Her lips were tightly pursed. "Used to be few times a week." She grimaced. "Ran out of money."

Lola cocked her head toward the three toughs. "What's the rumor on Sunny?"

The widow glared. "He's not here anymore. I don't care why. His money ran out and that's the language I know." She pulled back inside and slammed the door.

Lola walked off the front porch and went around to the back of the house. Along the side pathway, a few bare ash trees scratched at her sleeves as she passed. There was rubbish strewn on the brown grass. She kicked at rotting paper and stepped over rusting tins.

The cellar door wasn't the standard set of double doors laid at a low angle to the ground. This cellar was special. Lola took the five steps down to the proper door and rapped hard on the wood. It opened to reveal a large, potbellied man. He squinted out and held out his hand, palm up. Lola passed over her fee and he stepped aside. She slid past and turned to watch him. As he closed the door behind her, she paused to let her eyes adjust to the dim interior.

"Breathe shallow, Lola, or you might never make it out." Aubrey spoke with an authority that surprised Lola, but she remained silent.

The doorman stood, his hands stuck low in his trouser pockets. He watched her with incurious eyes, said nothing. Lola nodded and started down the remaining steps into the cellar. It wasn't a high-class joint, so no art on the bare brick walls or plump-cushioned alcoves. There were benches, though, and a few *chaises-longues* in faded or patched upholstery. The ceiling was eight feet high but obscured by lack of light and a pervasive layer of smoke. Elaborate floor lamps were scattered around the large room, mostly between alcove entrances. There weren't any curtains to give privacy. It wouldn't matter anyway. The people who came here weren't in much shape to care, after a few minutes.

Lola stopped at a low table to the left. A skeletally thin blonde in a worn flowered frock held out a pipe. Lola took it and dropped some money into the outstretched hand. The blonde counted out the bills. She watched as Lola walked over to an alcove. Lola remained impassive as the blonde turned to a safe behind her and dialed the combination. She placed the money inside, sorting out the denominations into a partitioned drawer, and slammed the heavy door shut. Then she went back to her navel-gazing.

Lola looked around the room. There were a half-dozen patrons. The space could accommodate three times that number. When it did, Lola imagined the stink was tolerable only by those in oblivion. She rubbed at her nose.

"They're not here," said Aubrey. "None of these people have Ghosts."

Lola tried her shtick with the blonde. She shook her head and refused to answer questions. Lola didn't bother to leave a card. She nodded once again to the doorman on her way out. He watched her impassively, then shut the door behind her with a soft thud. The sun was still hot, the ash trees still bare, the trash still milling about the house. Lola walked to the car and paid off the toughs. They snickered and pushed off their steps, laughing roughly and jostling each other as they walked down the block.

She pulled out of the neighbourhood and continued eastward. She found nothing but a burned out shell at her next stop, the sorry remains of another basement den. It was clear the blackened hull was weeks old; weeds were knee-high within the crumbling four walls. Similar luck met her at the mah-jongg parlour closest afterward. The new owners and manager of the *Jade Phoenix* were close-mouthed and new to town. They'd fired everyone associated with the old *Golden Cock*. They took an instant dislike to Lola and a distinct lack of interest in her money. She left under their baleful glares, trusting Aubrey to warn her if they decided to jump.

Lola headed south and west then, leaving the city's slums for fresher climes. She weaved through heavy traffic and the increasingly stultifying air. The sunlight wasn't just blinding now; it was torturous. Every mirrored and shiny surface refracted its rays tenfold. She rubbed at her pounding temples and tried to stop squinting. After half an hour, she slid the Buick into a spot a block down from the office and got out. Droopy passers-by barely gave her a glance. It wasn't hard to fit in. She trudged to the corner drugstore and ordered coffee and a roast beef sandwich at the counter. The cook sat a sweating glass of water in front of her with a wink. Lola left him a little extra when she paid.

The office was stuffy and hot. Windows and the fan were the first priority. Coffee came second.

"Bit hot out for that," said Aubrey.

Lola sipped in deep satisfaction and turned her attention to the mail. Nothing urgent or even interesting. She unwrapped the sandwich and clicked on the radio. She listened and ate and thought about nothing in particular. She heard footsteps and hushed voices, moving away down the hallway, punctuated by the elevator bell. Plimpton was doing a brisk business at his surgery at the opposite end of the hall. There were always women in this town in need of a little cosmetic tweak. Crescent City had a reputation to uphold; beautiful women were the norm, not the exception. Plimpton did his costly best to perpetuate that belief.

Lola considered her corner of the floor the quiet end, and with good reason. She had a philatelist on one side and a vacant office on the other. There had been a talent agent there last month, but he seemed to have disappeared overnight. She had yet to meet the stamp collector, let alone hear him. She didn't suppose stamps made for very noisy clients.

Lunch was over quickly. Lola heaved herself back onto the streets. It was another series of grim alleyways and dim basements. The same hoods sat on indistinguishable stoops, leering and sneering. The same beaten spirits and worn dresses plodded along the sidewalks. She kept a tight hold of her gun or blade in four more junkie hidey-holes, but found no trace of Joseph Josephson. Aubrey was the only coherent Ghost in all instances, the others as far gone as their wretched Hosts. It was an inevitable side effect for Ghosts

Haunting junkies. Whatever their reasons for Haunting, they were soon forgotten, and the hunt for that next fix became paramount. If there was a lesson in that, it would be lost to them. There would be no next life in which to learn it.

Feeling filthy, Lola made for a final junk house, hidden in the belly of a shoe store. The homes became grimmer for a few blocks until they petered out completely and she was back in a commercial area. She stashed the car in the back alley, more interested in a ready retreat than afraid of larceny. The junk house had a side entrance, off the narrow lane beside the building that led from alley to sidewalk. There weren't any complicated knocks or secret handshakes, but if the doorman didn't like the look of you, you weren't getting in. Lola returned the ugly mug's beady gaze with a five-dollar note and a grim expression. He stared at Lola so long she began to wonder if he'd fallen asleep. The door finally swung open and his hand waited, palm up. She slid his graft to him. He gestured her inward and sat back down on his chair. It was a wide hallway. Lola gave him wide berth and gripped the blade in her pocket. The hall was well-lit until the single doorway at its end, where a dark green curtain hung. There would be no opiates in the air here. This was strictly a needle joint.

The set-up was familiar enough: alcoves, *chaises*, benches, tables, floor lamps and gloomy lighting. Immediately to the right sat a dark-haired man in shirtsleeves and a hat pushed up off his forehead. He looked up sharply and made to stand. Lola walked over smoothly and quickly, another bill held out to herald her intentions.

"Just looking for someone," she explained. She kept one hand in her pocket while the other took Josephson's photograph out.

He didn't even look at it before shaking his head. "I don't know no one." But he took the money from her fingers and sat back down, jabbing the air with his chin. "You got two minutes."

Aubrey was done in thirty seconds: "Not here. But talk to the one over there, by the wall." Lola looked over and saw a pile of rags. As she got near, she found a blissful face and stick-thin arms amidst the grimy clothes. Aubrey said, "I've been talking to his daughter, Amelia. She says Lucille was here two weeks ago with Sunny Joe." He paused. "Lucille said they were leaving town for something important. Something big."

"Does he know Josephson?" Lola whispered, eying the man. His eyes were closed and his lips slightly parted. As she watched, a bubble of saliva formed at the corner of his mouth.

"No," said Aubrey impatiently. "Amelia says her father's dead to the world when he's here. Wouldn't know his own mother."

"And she's not junked up like him?" Lola was skeptical.

"She's sober as a nun. In fact, she is a nun. Catholic. Was. Sorry."

"No kidding," said Lola.

"Be polite," said Aubrey.

"Skip the etiquette lesson. I need details, Aubrey." She looked around at the rest of the room's occupants. The only one paying any attention was the attendant she'd bribed. He had an unlit cigarette dangling from his mouth, but he didn't look ready to draw a gun or call in the muscle. That could change, of course.

Meanwhile, Aubrey was talking quietly and quickly to the erstwhile nun. Lola turned back to the nun's father. If he'd moved, it took a keener pair of eyes than hers to tell. She saw a pair of painfully thin ankles at the end of his jutting legs. His shoes were barely whole, their soles peeling away like wagging tongues. Lola turned away from the open sores on his legs.

She was just in time to see the attendant standing five paces away. He gestured sharply toward the door with his head. "Time's up, dolly."

"Your watch is fast."

"I ain't got a watch."

"See what I mean?"

"We don't like smart mouths."

Lola's expression turned solemn. "Life is full of disappointment, isn't it?"

The ruin of a man at her feet moaned and shivered, but didn't wake from his stupor. The attendant kept dark eyes on Lola. She shrugged and kept her eyes on him as she walked out. He followed her with a flat stare. She slid out through the green curtain. Mugsy had the door open when she got within five feet. An expression almost twitched into existence on his wide face. Lola got out before she had to see it. The door calmly clicked shut and she was back in the real world.

Lola blinked a few times and got in the car. "You'd better hope the nun had something useful to give up." She sped down the alley. A screech of tires and an angry horn greeted her sharp right onto Lester.

"You won't find out if you're dead," drawled Aubrey. After several silent minutes, he asked, "Where are we headed next?"

"Golden Phoenix."

"Wong and Second. Stop at the drug store and get some coffee."

Amelia, the former nun, was a staunch Catholic even in her Ghosthood. Somehow that conferred to her the ability to withstand her father's addiction. In her mind, and Aubrey's, God acted as her shield. Lola was happy enough to concede the point. Aubrey thought it made perfect sense. Catholics didn't believe in reincarnation, anyway, so Amelia hadn't given a lot up by turning haunt, and she was guaranteed a trip to meet her Maker when her poor wretch of a father finally achieved his drawn-out suicide. It was strange logic like this that explained why Christians were a group existing on the margins. For Lola, it increased the nun's credibility a smidge above nil.

Her story was that Josephson had begun reappearing at that junk house at least a month and a half ago. Lucille had crowed to the sober Amelia about her brother's future prospects. She had happily described gnawing away at her brother's commitment to stay clean, his trust in his best friend, his self-assurance. Josephson had planned a big score two weeks ago. Or, rather, his sister had.

"Arbogast either lied or was incredibly blind to the obvious," said Aubrey. "A month back on the needle would have been blazingly obvious."

Lola nodded slowly, lost in thoughts of junkies, Ghosts and hard-headed clients.

"So, the question is," Aubrey concluded, "do we continue to search for the junkie on his big score, likely some ill-advised drug run?"

"His call," shrugged Lola. "I'll give him what I've got. See if he has the stomach for it."

"Unlikely," said Aubrey.

"In the meantime, I'm still headed for the Phoenix."

The Golden Phoenix Mah-jongg Parlour arose in a show of gaudy squalor. Red paint flaked from ten-foot columns flanking the single front door. A sad phoenix, naked of its once-proud golden plumage, screamed silently from the right-hand column. It had only one plaster eye left and that without an iris. The three steps leading up from the sidewalk were grimy concrete weathered to grey-brown. The neon lights overhead buzzed angrily but ineffectually. None of the letters were lit. Aubrey gave warning a split second before the door flung outward and a noisome drunk barreled through in the arms of a huge bouncer. Lola breathed shallowly through her mouth for a few seconds. A frazzle-haired scarecrow met her at the inner door. He held a thin cigar with large-knuckled hands and blew smoke straight upward. It was likely the only part of him that struggled toward the heavens.

"Whatcha lookin' for, doll? We got all kinds here. All the classics. Cantonese, Shanghai, Fukien. You name it." Lola listened to his assertion with a neutral expression. A quick glance over the scarecrow's shoulder into the main room made it clear that classical mah-jongg styles were in short demand here.

"Just information."

The scarecrow squinted at her, then slid his gaze just past her, toward the outer door. Lola turned and saw two unfamiliar men standing just inside the entrance. They were staring at her. One was squat and solid. The other, tall and gaunt. Thick and Thin, personified.

Thin smirked. He wore a dusty-looking cap that didn't go with his funereal suit. Thick jerked his head at the scarecrow, who silently departed, disappearing into the gloom behind him. Aubrey was suddenly at Lola's ear; none of the Ghosts here knew Lucille.

Lola lit a cigarette, waiting for the two thugs to pass within. Neither man made to move farther into the gambling hall. When she placed the lighter in her pocket, she palmed her knife.

A growl emanated from Thick's shadowed jaw. "Somebody wants to see you."

Lola gave him the once-over and blew a stream of blue smoke at his face. "Do you know me?" she asked politely.

"Sure we know you, Miss Starke." Thick emphasized the name with a sneer. "We're here on the authority of the Assistant Deputy Commissioner of Games."

"Never heard of him." She moved slowly backward and felt along the closed blade with a finger.

Both men chuckled. "This is your lucky day." Suddenly they were on either side of her. Thick grabbed her left arm while Thin bruised her on the right. Lola popped open the knife and slashed at Thin with a free hand. She caught him on the forearm. He grabbed his wound and cursed. She twisted and slashed at Thick's face. He lurched backward but didn't release his grip. Instead, he tightened it. Lola felt her hand go numb. Thin came at her again, scowling. She struck out at him with a jabbing kick to the side of his knee. He collapsed with a howl. Aiming a hard stomp to the instep of Thick's foot, she over-balanced when he moved away with surprising speed. He chopped down at her right hand. The blade clattered away. She aimed a hard punch to his groin but he grabbed her fist before she made contact. Thin was suddenly upright. He advanced, breathing heavily through his nose.

Thick growled at his partner, "Pick up the knife." Thin slid Lola's weapon into a pocket. The larger man turned back to Lola. "Pretty work, Miss Stark." He crushed her fist in his grip. "Let's go."

THREE

The Gaming Commission was the wealthiest department in the City's government. It licensed and taxed all the legal gambling in Crescent City. There were thousands of mah-jongg parlours in the city, as well as hundreds of casinos. After the moving pictures industry, gambling was the City's biggest tourist attraction. The Gaming Commission filled a building downtown. It was eight stories of elegant lines and modernist decorative details. Graceful caryatids, stretching seven-feet tall, flanked the main doors. An intricate stonework border ran along the exterior roof. The walls were sculpted and clean, a bright white-grey that shone beatifically at every time of day. It gleamed against the blue of the sky and glowered commandingly when it was cloudy. It was the most impressive of all the government buildings, handily overshadowing City Hall's simple square structure two blocks away.

People with titles in the Gaming Commission were not to be taken lightly.

Travelling in the back of a black sedan, Lola kept her own counsel. Her kidnappers seemed inclined to do the same. They approached their destination off of Chang, which ended in a T-intersection at the Commission's very steps. Lola's expression remained blankly polite, as though she were listening to a boring anecdote at a dinner party.

"Isn't there a special entrance for kidnapped visitors?" she asked.

"Out, princess," Thick said over his shoulder.

Thin slithered out and opened the back door with another flat-eyed smile. He held his injured arm close to his body. Lola kept a wary eye on him, but he simply waited beside the open door. He remained her escort up the steps and through the centre of five sets of doors.

The lobby was as imposing as the exterior. Their footsteps echoed off of cool white-grey marble, enhanced by the vaulted ceiling twenty feet above. It was past business hours and the lobby was deserted. Everything gleamed and sparkled with the indolence of wealth. Lola caught the sound of chatter before a door banged shut in the distance. The men marched her toward the bank of gilt elevators. One had its doors open. The operator glanced at Lola's escorts, then stepped outside. He avoided looking at Lola. Thin shoved her within the panelled box. Thick pressed buttons then subsided against an elevator wall, eying his captive silently. Thin stood impolitely close to Lola. She looked at his arm, cradled against his chest. She smelled his blood and allowed herself a tiny grim smile.

The doors opened onto another deserted scene, this one a long corridor paved with the same marble as below. The corridor disappeared around a corner. Doors were spaced widely apart, marking the large offices behind them. A single long red carpet laid a path the length of the hallway. Their footsteps were swallowed by its plushness as Thick pushed Lola forward. He kept prodding until they turned the corner and reached a set of double doors that signaled the last office this way. There was no name plate.

Thick opened the door to reveal a small space. Lola walked in before either could push her again. She looked around. A single desk sat immediately across from the door. It was backed and flanked by rows of filing cabinets. The rest of the space was dominated by a sitting area: various chairs and a low table. A few cuspidors stood beside the chairs. The seats were all empty. There were no windows. A whisper of fragrant smoke lingered.

Thick brushed past her and walked to the door set diagonally from the outer door. He knocked, a quick *tap-tap-tap,* then opened before any reply from within could be heard. He held the door open and gestured for Lola to continue within. Neither he nor Thin followed. Lola walked in, and they closed the door behind her.

It was a corner office. Two walls of windows, two walls of paneled bookshelves. Burled blond wood and a large deep blue rug were accented by dark leather upholstery. There was a sitting area: a set of armchairs and one sofa clustered with a long low table made of glass and metal. A delicate porcelain ashtray sat at its centre. The seat of power was a massive mahogany desk. The windows behind it showcased sky and city architecture. The sun was still bright, but these windows faced east. Lola had a clear view of the woman who sat behind the desk. She had deep auburn hair, waved to her shoulders. A pert nose, wide sensual mouth, alabaster skin. Slender forearms were shown to advantage in the three-quarter-length sleeves of her royal blue wool-crepe dress. Gathering and yoking along the shoulders accentuated her lithe build. Her crimson red lips smiled confidently.

"Amber Jade Stoudamire." Lola was at a loss to say more.

"A.J. Copenhagen," the other woman corrected with a small smile. "Lola, how have you been?" She rose and offered her hand. Her dress settled in graceful folds.

Lola stared at her hand, then into her face.

Copenhagen laughed softly. "An introduction, if you please?" At Lola's silence, she said, "Your Ghost. Surely, you can be civil."

Lola stared.

Copenhagen clucked her tongue. "It's nothing to be ashamed of—haven't you figured that out by now?" She smiled again. "Come. Don't be a killjoy. I won't do this without you. I have utter respect for Ghosts and I insist on a proper introduction." She smiled again. Lola blinked at the open aggression in the other woman's smile.

"Lola," Aubrey said. "Tell your school chum it's a pleasure to make her acquaintance." When Lola remained silent, he got impatient. "Just do it. Please," he tacked on.

Lola ground her teeth around the introductions.

Copenhagen's smile became dazzling. "It's good to well and properly meet you, Aubrey. You were quite the subject of speculation during that last year of high school. I'm sorry Lola's attitude doesn't seem to have matured much."

"Yours seems to have sharpened," Lola said.

"It's been a long time since Rose Arbour Prep. I'm flattered you remember me." She sat back down. Lola followed suit, sinking into a butter-soft club chair and crossing her legs, suddenly the picture of ease. "I understand your confusion."

"I'm not confused. I'm curious."

Copenhagen smiled knowingly. "I don't suppose you made it to the reunion. Rah rah and all that never seemed your game."

"Any more than it's yours."

"Circumstances change a person, Lola. Wouldn't you agree, Aubrey?"

Aubrey made no reply. Copenhagen sat calmly, the same glittering smile on her face.

"How long have these circumstances been yours?" Lola asked. She waved a hand around at the office.

"Mmm, two years or so. I've been with the Gaming Commission for six." She steepled her fingers and looked over them. "I never did have the chance to express my condolences about your father."

"That was a long time ago, Amber Jade." Lola shifted slightly in her seat. The women sat in tense silence, each sizing the other up with bland expressions and cold eyes.

"It's AJ now."

"Not Mrs. Copenhagen?"

"Dear gods, no." She laughed. "I like the name, but I'm divorced. I hear we have that in common as well."

"Mine's old news."

She grinned. "How *is* Martin these days? I haven't travelled in his circles, shall we say, for years now."

"He's fine. On wife number four, I believe. A lovely southern belle, or so he tells me." Lola took out her cigarette case. "Is that enough small talk?" She lit an Egyptian, spoke through the smoke. "Or shall I ask after dear Mr. Copenhagen now?"

Copenhagen flashed a smile full of teeth. "I have a business proposition in mind."

"I have an office."

She waved her hand dismissively. "I know you make house calls. Consider this no different."

"Except for the kidnapping."

A shrug. "My assistants know my schedule. They escorted you here by the most expedient means possible."

Lola sat back. "What's on your mind then, Amber Jade?"

Another smile. "Please, call me AJ. All my friends do."

"What do your enemies call you?"

Copenhagen smiled. "No different."

She glanced at a clock on her desk. "Our delightful chat has gone on longer than I'd dared hoped. Why don't we discuss the details of your job over dinner?"

"Are you going to escort me all over town?"

She laughed. "You can drive if you like. My assistants should be back with your car by now."

Lola shrugged. "The tall one was a bit clumsy collecting me. They might be longer than you'd planned."

A raised eyebrow, but the amusement was still evident. "I'm sure they're here. I run a tight ship. I believe you know The White Crane?"

"I believe you already know the answer to that," said Lola.

"I knew you'd be flattered." Copenhagen smiled.

FOUR

The Assistant Deputy Commissioner of Gaming oversaw all the mah-jongg parlours in Crescent City. She approved licenses. She fined bylaw breakers. She amended and created bylaws. She shut down egregious violators. She taxed owners. It was a well-oiled machine. Indeed, AJ Copenhagen now had a reputation for running the best department within Gaming. High praise, especially for a *gwai* girl.

Recently, however, rumors were cropping up of illegally run tournaments. They were staged at different locations each time. Entrants were charged ludicrously low table fees, unlike at legitimate parlors, which were required by law to charge minimum fees. These fees, of course, were also set by law. The illegal tournaments were an appealing situation for underage gamblers and a sweet deal for organizers who didn't have much in the way of overhead. The tables and chairs were foldaways. It was unlikely rent was paid for the rooms. The Gaming Commission, naturally, was incensed at this snub to its authority. Lola was willing to bet that the unpaid tax revenue also had something to do with it.

"The police department are not treating the case with the urgency it needs. They've found no willing witnesses. They say it's not easy to find these secret locations. Supposedly, these tournaments happen only overnight. They keep the numbers small enough to facilitate quick set-up and tear-down." Copenhagen made a derisive noise. "The cops make it sound like a band of seditious Ghosts. I'm sure you don't need Aubrey to tell you that's utter rubbish."

Neither Lola nor Aubrey responded.

"So, here we are. I needed a fresh set of eyes, and you were recommended." Copenhagen paused, smiling. "And with Aubrey, really, I get two for the price of one."

"Whose recommendation?" Lola's voice was flat.

"Mayor, as a matter of fact. I believe he's a good friend of your mother's?" Copenhagen's casual tone contrasted with her intent stare.

"That's the rumor. So what do you expect me to do here?"

"Solve the mystery, of course. Find the organizers and help me bring them to justice."

"You tried that line on the cops–no wonder they're not doing your job. You've got to use the stick, and skip the carrot. Only way through their thick skulls."

"As opposed to you—the carrot type?" Copenhagen replied.

"Smirking doesn't become you. Didn't your mother ever teach you that?" Too late, Lola recalled that Copenhagen's mother had died when the girl was barely thirteen.

"No, I'm afraid she didn't." The smile became edged. "Speaking of mothers, I hear yours is producing a film in Europe?"

"I don't keep tabs." Lola shrugged.

"Well, it's quite the undertaking, as I understand it. Filming overseas always is. Licensing, permits, fees, casting, language differences. Really, every little detail takes ten times more effort. Producers are always run ragged on overseas projects." A pause. "Ah, but your mother has a soft spot for Europe, doesn't she?"

"As subtle as her lipstick," said Aubrey.

Lola kept silent, smoking calmly.

"A twenty-year love affair, really, isn't it?" pressed Copenhagen.

"You'd have to ask her."

"Why don't I ask Aubrey? Her best friend and confidante."

"Aubrey wouldn't presume to speak for my mother."

"No, of course not." Copenhagen smiled. "But truly, your mother is to be admired. Producing and starring is more than double duty. I'm sure her stellar acting talent will carry the film just fine, but then there's the added toll of worrying over costs and details, actor tantrums and agent demands, not to mention studio scrutiny and pressure. It's frightening to think how just one tiny detail could derail that entire train."

"You've got a point, make it."

Copenhagen gestured gracefully with her hand. "It's appalling how easily an unauthorized person can access guild records. Just imagine what would happen to your mother, say, if someone destroyed her guild license from the files. The guild would have no recourse but to fine her heavily and suspend her from work until the license was reissued. Obviously, there would be no problem with getting the reissue, but just think of the time wasted and the dollars burned up every day that your mother can't work on her own film." She shook her head. "Just terrible." She picked up the delicate tea pot and refilled Lola's matching patterned blue cup.

The noises of the busy White Crane returned in a whoosh of sound. Suddenly, the air was filled with chattering voices and clinking porcelain. Chef Liu's delectable, inimitable eight-dish extravaganza now turned leaden in Lola's stomach. She mashed her cigarette out in the ashtray, disgusted by the sight of dirty burnt ashes in the ethereal bone china dish.

A waiter appeared and removed dishes in efficient silence. Copenhagen watched Lola over the rim of her cup as she took a sip of the scalding black tea. By the time the waiter returned with a platter of sweets and fresh plateware, Lola was lighting another cigarette.

"You see, Lola," Copenhagen explained patiently, "you're a stick type after all. Also a lot easier to bully than the cops."

"And more fun?"

"And more fun," Copenhagen agreed readily. She placed an exquisite egg custard tart on Lola's plate. "After dessert, we'll take a drive over to the station house. I want to introduce you to Detectives Tsu and Luke. They'll be working with you on my case."

"You warned them yet?"

"You'll be briefed on their activities and brought up to speed on the investigation." Copenhagen bit into a *petit-four*, a miniature almond cookie. She watched Lola as she ate. "You'll be on retainer, per diem and expenses. That's your usual arrangement, is it not?"

"In your case, make it a thousand up front." Lola finished the exquisite custard and sipped the still-scalding tea. "Hazard pay."

Copenhagen smiled. "You'll earn it."

The Forty-four was a four-storey stone edifice with a cavernous lobby. Footsteps and conversation echoed coldly from the high ceiling. Uniforms milled about: coming, going, sitting, standing, talking, scowling. Suits seemed relegated to the background, glimpsed as they passed through, walking into hallways and offices. Benches along one wall held an assortment of stubbled drunks, painted girls and the occasional young tough. Opposite them sat the precinct's law-abiding citizens, clutching purses and worrying newspapers.

Copenhagen brought her thugs inside and they flanked her as the group stopped in front of the desk sergeant. His uniform's name tag said *Ping*. He sat behind a tall reception counter, a wonder of millwork and rich wood completely at odds with the tension, fear and anger filling the station lobby.

"Copenhagen to see Tsu and Luke."

The sergeant looked down his long nose at her, then at Lola. He pointed a thick finger at the latter. "She stays out here." He fixed sharp brown eyes on Thick and Thin, nodded curtly to them.

Copenhagen raised an eyebrow, turned to Lola. "Your reputation precedes you?"

Lola shrugged. Aubrey mumbled, "Oh, for the love of—."

Copenhagen slid her card across the beautiful mahogany. Ping placed a forefinger on it but didn't pick it up. He read her title without expression. He said: "You keep strange company, ma'am."

"I'm not interested in your approval, sergeant. Miss Starke is my associate, for now."

Ping gambled his career with an insolent shrug. "If you say so." He picked up the telephone at his elbow.

Copenhagen turned, raising an eyebrow, to Lola.

Lola shrugged again, her attention caught by half of an invisible conversation.

"I'm not any happier about it than you, Stan." Aubrey paused. "Let it go. It's ancient history." Pause, then a sigh. "No, it's not. And don't bring your son into it. Lola's got nothing—" The unseen anger raised the hairs on Lola's neck. "No. Tell him to back off." Another tense pause. "Empty threats," Aubrey said. Then: "If I so much as smell your sorry carcass near us, you'll regret you didn't die sooner. Now, beat it."

A little smile played along Copenhagen's mouth as she studied Lola's startled expression. Her eyes were as shrewd as her tone was insincere. "Problem, Lola?" she asked. Her gaze swung to just over Lola's right shoulder. "Something troubling Aubrey?"

Lola regained her mien of indifference.

"Well, they've got Interrogators and Catchers at every station," continued the deputy commissioner. "I've heard it can get discomforting for Ghosts. Even if they're not under scrutiny."

"He's fine," Lola replied. "Chatting with an acquaintance."

"Oh?" Copenhagen raised her eyebrows. "Seems a strange place for someone like Aubrey to have friends. I mean, your father, I could understand, but what's an actress's dresser got to do with the cops?"

Aubrey snapped, "You tell her to stay out of my business."

Lola passed on his message. Copenhagen nodded, unfazed by the hostility. "I apologize for snooping, Aubrey. It's a hazard of a curious mind." Suddenly, she shifted her line of sight. Lola turned as well. "Our escort."

A wide-shouldered man in a navy suit clambered down the steps behind and to the left of Ping. He had black hair swept back from his forehead, revealing a square face and smooth cheeks.

Copenhagen dismissed her thugs with a curt movement. They turned and left the station house with neither word nor backward glance. Sergeant Ping glared at Lola. She shrugged at his enmity. She wasn't interested in calling out his personal demons. It was unlikely he would cause her much trouble, anyway. His father was once deputy commissioner of police, before death and dementia caught him, but Ping Jr. had nothing but a gimp arm and an unstable Ghost.

Copenhagen made introductions with the detective. Detective Inspector Tsu gripped Lola's hand with exaggerated care, as though it were porcelain, and gave it a brief, limp shake. He led the women around the sergeant's perch and down a hallway that ran under the stairs. There were closed doors on both sides, but only some had lit rooms beyond them. Tsu stopped after one corner and about ten doors. This one was open, and inside was his partner. Another round of introductions. DI Luke tried to crush Lola's hand in his slender grip. He stood, tight-lipped and scowling, as Copenhagen smiled.

"I expect you to cooperate fully with my associate, detectives. She's here as my representative. She also happens to have skills pertinent to your investigation, which clearly needs to move faster." Copenhagen turned. "You've got a lot of ground to cover, Lola. I'll leave you in the detectives' capable hands." She nodded briefly and swept out of the room. The door closed firmly behind her.

The room was tight, about ten by ten, and filled with a large oak desk in the centre. Three chairs sat around its square solidity, with another two lined against the wall opposite the door. The walls were unadorned institutional grey. No windows, no mirrors, no clocks. Lola checked her watch: just past eight.

"We keeping you from something, Miss Starke?" asked Tsu politely.

"Just wondering about the commissioner's game."

"Assistant deputy," said Luke. "Her rank doesn't mean much here."

Lola took a seat. Tsu sat as well. Luke remained on his feet, prowling one corner of the room to the other, behind his partner. She waited.

Luke suddenly stopped, crossed his arms and deepened his scowl. His eyes were brown, his gaze flat.

"Why are you here again, Starke?"

"My client seems to think I can help out."

"You think so?" challenged Luke.

"No idea. Don't have enough information to know."

Tsu had a surprisingly smooth voice. "Miss Starke, you'll have to excuse us. We're just a coupla dumb mugs stuck with a tough case."

"I doubt that." Lola leaned in. "Look, I'm not here to tell you how to do your job, and I'm not here to spy. My client's forcing my hand here. She wants answers and she's impatient. This isn't my line of work, but she's got a bee in her bonnet and she can make my life miserable. Mine and yours."

"Is that a threat?" asked Luke. He stood rigidly, fists held at his side. Tsu remained sitting, relaxed and observant. He gave no indication that his partner's outburst had even occurred.

Lola's expression was bland.

"You don't need the dough. What's tying you up?" asked Tsu.

She shrugged. "I'm here to make the best of a bad situation."

He studied her in silence. Luke continued glaring. Lola waited. Aubrey might have been doing the same. He hadn't made a peep since his exchange in the lobby.

"It's *your* situation," Tsu said, "not ours."

"I doubt that's your choice to make," she said gently, getting up.

Luke blocked her exit. "I don't appreciate threats, Starke."

"Then you oughta be glad I didn't make any." She met his glare until he stepped away. Tsu also stood. They walked her back down the corridor. The same group of harried cops, bored prostitutes and worried citizens filled the room around Sgt. Ping's dais. Aubrey said not a word as the two detectives escorted Lola out the station doors and then left her to walk to her car alone. Halfway there, Lola glanced back. Luke was no longer scowling. He was talking animatedly to Tsu. The larger man was listening thoughtfully.

"That's about as much as you could've expected," said Aubrey. "They're not going to be much happier being ordered by the DS to work with you."

"It's their call. I'd've done the same. This way, they have an extra reason to give me a hard time. Soothes the ego. Won't feel so much like they need help."

Lola unlocked her door and tossed her purse on the front passenger seat. Instead of starting it up, she got the torch from the glove compartment and kneeled down on the pavement. Bracing a hand against the door, she bent down and clicked on the light, shining it on the undercarriage. She hauled open the trunk and checked around, feeling for lumps and loose lining. She gave the interior of the car the same treatment. She felt around the seat and shone the flash into every crevice along the floorboards and doors. The engine compartment was next. There were no loose wires or valves, no nicked hoses. Finally, she emptied the glove compartment and felt around inside as well.

"Satisfied?" asked Aubrey. A uniform walked past, ignoring Lola.

"Until I can take her in," Lola brushed off her trouser legs. She patted the old car affectionately.

"It drove just fine over to The White Crane."

"Her thugs had plenty of time with it while I was here."

"Seems to me she had an easier way to kill you earlier," said Aubrey. "Car bombs aren't exactly subtle."

"Listen," said Lola, "I know you pride yourself on playing devil's advocate, but you're used to playing *gai-woo*. Amber Jade Stoudamire wants *baht-fuhn* and she'll cheat to get it."

"She just hired you. Why hurt you?"

"Why not? She's never needed a reason before. Besides, her thugs owe me something for their troubles. Maybe it wouldn't have been a bomb, but faulty brakes could still get me hurt badly." She cranked the engine and slid out into traffic. Luke was still outside on the sidewalk as she drove past. He dragged on a cigarette, his eyes squinting against the smoke. He watched Lola drive away.

Station Forty-four was fifteen minutes from Lola's building. A traffic snarl at Yan and Seventeenth made it forty-five. An ambulance squatted on the northeast corner of the intersection as attendants helped an elderly man onto a stretcher. His arm flopped limply at one point, surprising the attendants, who allowed their cargo to tip precariously for a few seconds. They had to stop, place the stretcher down and move the poor man back squarely between the sides. Naturally, people had crowded on the sidewalks, stretching their necks for a glimpse of another's misery. A few motorists had exited their cars, walking as close to the scene as possible. A few uniforms were scattered around the intersection, chatting with bystanders, ordering the occasional nervy gawker to keep back. The culprit was apparently a maroon coupe, its driver bracketed by two suited detectives. She looked ready to faint. A kid driving daddy's latest gift a little too wildly. Ones like her filled the Hills around the City. They were the ones brought up with golden chopsticks. Spoiled little monsters who raced through the city with impunity, their hides covered by Mummy and Daddy's green money.

"There but for the grace of gods," Lola muttered.

"Your father did a better job than that of raising you," Aubrey scolded.

"What would you know about it?" Lola asked absently.

The ambulance hit its siren and wailed away into the distance. A couple of uniforms started directing traffic through the intersection. Lola slipped the car into gear and they began moving again. She remained silent. She checked her watch. It was coming up on ten o'clock. She drove toward home, her body tense.

Aubrey matched her silence until she pulled into the parking garage. "This isn't the time for more carousing, Lola," he said. "You've still got Josephson to find."

"I don't tell you how to be a thorn in my side—you don't tell me how to earn a living."

"The fact remains," he continued, "running two cases simultaneously is difficult at the best of times. This time, you've got two unyielding clients and some unhappy cops to juggle. It's only a matter of time before everything comes to a head and most likely explodes in your face."

"Your vote of confidence is a real relief," Lola replied. "It'd be a cryin' shame if you were to nag me every step of the way."

"Facts are not nagging, Lola, any more than snappy remarks constitute action. What are you going to do about Josephson?"

She parked the Buick, got out and stretched, eying the surrounding cars for movement. Aubrey started to speak. Lola shook her head.

"Arbogast will keep till morning. Calling him now wouldn't make him feel better. And let's face it. That's why he hired me. Handholding. Plain and simple." She strode toward the elevator.

"I'm not talking about Arbogast. I'm talking about Josephson. Sister Amelia had old news. There're plenty more places for you to look for something more recent. Josephson may even be back in town by now. Daylight doesn't suit the kind of quarry you're hunting, Lola. Take advantage of the night." Aubrey paused. "Wouldn't your father have said the same?"

"He would've trusted me," she replied. She stopped mid-stride, spun around, and headed back. Passing the trusty Buick, Lola went instead toward her other car, cloth-covered and sitting low to the ground. Impatiently, she threw away the canvas cover to reveal a bright red REO coupe.

"Dammit, Lola."

Lola smiled as she revved the engine up to a low growl and pulled out slowly. She drove deliberately and carefully east along Twenty-second until Shu, then turned northward toward the desert. Lola concentrated on the road and kept silent.

Shu Boulevard became a highway, and traffic thinned to a miserly trickle. The cold desert night swirled around Lola's bare head. She stopped just on the side of the empty highway to tie a scarf around her hair. Then she pulled back onto the pavement with a spray of gravel. She drove until her eyes wept from wind and her cheeks burned cold. Aubrey's words disappeared in a snarl of desert air and machinery, like a tail of smoke in a stiff wind.

FIVE

Lola awoke groggy and ill-tempered. She went into the bath and splashed her face ruthlessly with frigid water. Her face was still pale as she sat down at her bedroom telephone. She let out her held breath when St. John answered.

"It's barely half eight," he said, "what're you doing up, my girl?"

"Dear Uncle St. John," Lola drawled, drawing out the sound of his name: *Sinnn-jinnn.* "Sarcasm is strictly forbidden before noon."

"God girl, don't try that horrible accent this early in the day. You'll hurt yourself, you will."

"It's no more horrible than yours."

"Yeh, but I come by mine honestly," he chuckled. "Looking for your mum?"

"You know me better than that."

"Sadly, I do. What's on your mind then?"

"This's more your purview anyway. I heard a rumor there may be some mayhem down at the Guild Office. Something about lost records and missing guild licenses. Thought you ought to have a lackey swing by and check on Mother's guild credentials."

There was a long pause. "Forgive me, love, but why are you interested?"

"Call it a sudden outbreak of filial piety. Duty calls and all that rubbish," Lola replied. "Will you do it or not?"

"A reliable source?"

"A troubling rumour, let's say. Will you take care of it?"

"Already done. Grace never starts a new project until everything's in order." He paused. "What's this about?"

"You're sure?"

"Lola."

"Right. Good."

"Duty to one's parent notwithstanding, since when do you care about Grace's career dealings?"

"It's a molehill, not a mountain. I've got to go. Working a new case." Lola rang off. She blew out her breath and shook off her misgivings. St. John was the security expert, after all. He'd handle it.

Lola was wringing her hair dry when Elaine knocked at the bathroom door to fetch her to the telephone. Looking amused, Elaine took the limp towel out of Lola's hand and threw it into the hamper. With a dry one, she expertly wrapped up Lola's hair and sent her out of the room with a gentle shove.

St. John spoke in clipped tones. "Lola, what's going on? Whom did you talk to?"

"Are they missing then?"

"Everything at the Guild office about Grace is gone."

"What does that mean for her?"

"The Guild Secretary knows her too well to fine her. They're considering it a clerking error. Someone must have moved the file without proper documentation."

"And you?"

"Given my suspicious nature and superior intelligence, I'd say it's a security breach. Your call this morning tips the scale. Now, tell me what the hells you've gotten yourself into."

"You're head of Mother's security, not mine." She forged onward quickly at his sharp intake of breath. "What is she going to do?"

"Grace can't go abroad until that license is reissued. It's part of her work documentation in Europe."

"What's the delay then?"

"Most likely a week. They're being extremely cooperative, but it takes time to authenticate and verify old records." He paused. "It will help that Mayor can vouch for her."

"But it won't hold up the project start?"

"They're not slated to start for another four months. Grace is leaving in a few days. Train to the east coast and then onto the Empress Liner. Train on the other end, as well. Three months to get there and another to nose around."

"A month-long holiday?"

"Working holiday. There are some details she wants to hammer down before the director gets on location."

"I think it'd be a good idea for her to leave early. There's got to be someone she can charm at the Guild offices."

"A week *is* charmed, Lola," St. John answered. "All right, you've had your go. My turn next. Why the sudden interest in your mother's affairs?"

Lola considered before answering. She opted for truth. "Someone threatened me by threatening her."

"The records theft?"

"They overstated the results, but proved they could carry through." She sighed. "A case I don't want."

"Do what's right for you. Grace can take care of herself."

"If I knew she was out of the country, that would help."

"Sorry, love, can't force her schedule."

"You can overrule her. Make her see the urgency."

A pause. "Is there a physical threat?"

"No. Not so far," she amended.

"Just this monkey business with the Guild."

"Look, St. John, this is a powerful enemy to make. She's the Assistant Deputy Commissioner of Gaming and she doesn't throw her punches. You need to get Mother away from the City."

"Look Lola, I know you're staring this commissioner in the face here, but think about this. Grace hasn't anything tied to Gaming in Crescent City. Never has, never will. There's nothing to extort, nothing they can touch."

"They meddled with her Guild credentials."

"A minor nuisance, really. Grace probably has more clout than this assistant deputy. She's not unknown, you know."

"Don't get smarmy."

"That, love, was being smart-mouthed." He cleared his throat. "She'd be more amenable if you came along."

"Even if I wanted to, I can't."

"An impasse then." He waited a beat. "Grace is as bloody-minded as you, Lola."

"I did my part. Consider your team warned." Lola rang off again. She tore off Elaine's impromptu turban and stalked around the bedroom. Finally, she pulled open the heavy draperies and stood at the window, squinting against the morning glare.

Houses dotted the slopes of the foothills on the left, leading away to the southwest and the start of the mountains. The higher one went, the farther apart the homes became from one another, until one was left with the Beacon, the legendary home of the Wang family. It sat alone at the top, its full dimensions hidden from Lola's vantage point by thick greenery. The Wangs were the founding family of Crescent City, grown from the stock of Wang Zhi-Min some two hundred years ago, diluted by generations of *gwai* blood. The current crop looked about as Chinese as Lola did, maybe even less so. Some had blonde hair. But they carried the name and that's all that mattered.

The foothills ran roughly westward all the way to the water. Crescent City hugged a ninety-mile long curve of land, stretching back from the harbor for another hundred miles until it tapered away, eastward into desert. Lola lived ten miles from that enticing shimmer of ocean. Between her apartment building and the water's edge lay blocks upon blocks of houses and small commercial buildings. The docks were at the extreme northern end of the curved land. Private beachfront property started at the feet of the southern hills and ended about due west from Lola's spot. From there, a series of small public beaches provided a bulwark between wealthy homeowners and the start of the commercial docks. These docks sat along the northern curve of the crescent. The marina lay on the other side of the southern foothills, obscured from view by the curve of the harbour. Innumerable pleasure craft and huge tankers dotted the ocean's surface.

"Time to get moving, Lola," said Aubrey. "St. John will handle it. He's good at that. You have your own troubles to tend to."

"Leave. I'm dressing."

"Hurry, then."

Lola dressed in a grey jacket, wide-legged slacks, and a pale blue blouse. A mannish hat topped off the outfit. She slid her feet into low heels and strode out of the bedroom, stroking the switchblade in her pocket.

Elaine was just coming from the kitchen, carrying a pot of fresh coffee. The dining table had two places set. A covered platter, another with French croissants and Chinese rolls, some pots of jams and jellies, two grapefruit halves. Lola ignored them all in favor of a cup of scalding coffee.

"Lighting the fire?" asked Elaine. She lifted the cover off the platter as she sat. Steam rose from scrambled eggs and golden hashed potatoes.

"Sorry, dove. Can't stay long." Lola poured more coffee down her throat. "Why don't you call Dominic? Shame to let all this go to waste."

"At least eat a croissant and some fruit," Elaine said. She went back into the kitchen and used the telephone. "Dolly? Put me through to Maintenance. Hello, Maintenance? Yes, Miss Starke is having problems with her icebox again. Yes. Yes. Right away. Thanks."

Lola polished off the croissant and her coffee before Elaine returned. "Dee-lish, Elaine, thanks."

"You're welcome," came the reply. "Maybe next time, you'll actually taste it."

"What can I say? I'm a busy woman. People to see, places to be." The doorbell rang. "I'll let him in. Eat before it gets cold." She brushed at some stray crumbs on her way to the apartment door. She verified dark eyebrows and blond hair through the peephole before opening the door.

"'Morning, Miss Starke." Dominic's broad grin took up his entire narrow face. A thin nose gave him a pinched appearance belied by the twinkle of good humour in his pale grey eyes.

"'Morning, Dominic. Elaine started without you."

He shook his head in disapproval. "Such manners. You'd think our mother'd've taught her better." His grin broadened.

"Day and night, the two of you, huh?" Dominic ambled inside. Lola gestured. "You go on. I'm just getting ready to go." He nodded his head with another amiable grin, showing surprisingl white teeth.

Back in the bedroom, Lola tried a phone call over to Station Forty-four, but neither Luke nor Tsu were taking her call. The unnamed desk sergeant took down her name. He gave no indication it was of any importance. She packed a gat and lit a cigarette, then left the apartment.

Traffic in Crescent City on a weekday morning was crammed. Lola looked at the drivers around her and saw boredom, irritation, apprehension. There was one woman, a sleek one, who had a small smile playing about her carmine lips. She caught Lola's eye and her smile broadened into something intimate and knowing.

Aubrey spoke up. "Some familiar faces back there."

Lola shrugged, tearing her gaze back to the traffic in front of her.

"Copenhagen's helpers. Didn't seem the trusting sort, really."

Lola peered into the small rear view mirror, scanning vehicles. "The infamous black Buick again? Amateurs." It sat three cars back, one lane over to the left. She could make out Thin's misshapen cap.

"Maybe they want you to make them," Aubrey said.

"You seem terribly nonchalant about this, considering your previous panic."

"They're hardly a threat right now. It's when you can't see them that you've got to worry."

"Just a couple of strong boys to scare the little woman?"

"Something like that, I suspect. They must've picked you up from the apartment. They know where you live, that sort of thing. They want to remind you you're on Copenhagen's dime now."

"Lucky for them I'm heading down to the Forty-four anyway."

"Plenty of time to lose them later," agreed Aubrey.

A fierce smile formed on Lola's lips. A flash out the corner of my eye. The woman with the sleek black coiffure was waving, her eyes sparkling with amusement. As her dark blue Packard rolled ahead, the woman's neck scarf trailed out her open window, a shocking wing of bright orange fabric.

Thick and Thin parked in the visitors lot and leaned against their car, smoking. Lola waved from the station house steps. They stared. With a shrug, she went inside. The players were different but the scene remained unchanged, although there may have been fewer prostitutes and more drunks now. Reception this time was a red-headed giant named Bartholomew.

He grinned with hostile anticipation as Lola approached. "A little early for you isn't it, Starke? Don't you need the sun up higher to warm your blood?"

"Drinking fresh blood does the same trick, Freckles." She smacked her lips.

"Disgusting, Starke. You oughta be locked up."

"Now, is that any way to talk to a law-abiding citizen?"

"Of course not, but to you? Yes."

"Lizards have rights too, Freckles."

"This is the real world, girlie. Lizard's just another word for roadkill." He bared yellow teeth.

Lola smiled politely in reply. "I've got official business, Freckles."

His face nearly split with the enormity of his grin. "Luke is waiting for you. DS Shao called him in this morning. Bright and early. He's none too happy with you." Bartholomew's grin was full of malice.

"Tsu?"

Bartholomew shook his head. "Police business. None of your concern." He snatched up the telephone and made his call. A sudden chill had Lola whirling around. A small woman stood beside her. In heels, she barely came up to Lola's collarbone. Her dirty black hair looked faintly greasy and she stared with peculiar light grey eyes. Her nose twitched slightly. She wore a severe black suit jacket with padded shoulders. Against her right lapel, a large cameo brooch with a profile of a woman with squashed nose and thick lips.

"How do you know him?" the short woman asked.

"Whom?"

"Your haunt." Her tone was flat, matter-of-fact.

Lola weighed her options, then said, "My mother's best friend."

An eyebrow shot up. "Really. That's a new one."

"Tellin' me," Lola replied. "Everything all right?"

"Sure, sure, just making conversation. Anyone ever tell you you two look alike?"

"No one who wasn't blind," replied Aubrey.

The Catcher shrugged. "Just an opinion." She nodded and departed, a tiny girl with a cowboy swagger.

"Creep," commented Aubrey.

"Still, no point in harassing one," Lola said. "Never can tell what'll set them off."

"They harass honest Ghosts all the time," continued Aubrey. "Hunting for something to justify their bloodlust."

"Well, until you or someone else other than a Catcher figures out how they do it, I suggest you play nice," said Lola.

She swiveled back to face Bartholomew and saw Luke coming down the stairs. He tapped a file folder against his thigh as he walked. He nodded to Bartholomew, who returned a lopsided grin.

Lola greeted Luke politely.

His sneer bloomed into fullness. "Pull all the strings you want, Starke. You're still scum."

"You really know how to turn a girl's head, Luke."

He spun around and walked past the stairwell, turned right at a corridor leading beneath the steps. Lola smiled at Bartholomew's glare and followed the tall tense figure. Luke continued his march toward the detectives' den at the rear of the building. Lola caught a glimpse of the bullpen, an open room about twenty by twenty, filled with desks, chairs, and an assortment of men in suits. Bulletin boards, filing cabinets, papers. Luke whipped past it all as a roar of laughter from the assembled suits began.

Finally, he stopped and whirled around, gesturing Lola inside a room spacious as a broom closet. Three chairs of cheap metal hugged a rectangular table of similar workmanship. Lola expected a bare bulb to hang from the ceiling, but there was a proper fixture as well as a floor lamp. An ashtray rested in the middle of the table. She sat and started on a cigarette.

Luke clicked the door closed behind him. He took up a chair opposite Lola, tossed the file onto the table. "Detective Superintendent Shao has authorized your access to all information on file pertinent to the case."

"What about riding along?"

Luke ignored the question. He pulled out a pack and matches. "Move your lips if you have to, but read fast."

Lola skimmed the top page, an administrative summary sheet, then flipped through the rest of the file. It was well-organized and in chronological order, recent developments on top. Witness interviews, lists of names to be interviewed, documented raids, arrests.

She flipped back to the bottom of the file, to the start of the case: a complaint filed by Assistant Deputy Commissioner AJ Copenhagen.

"Tell me how it started."

Luke glared. "Read."

"If you talk, I'm out of here faster." She flipped through a few sheets, checking their activity reports. "Did you interview her?"

"Who?"

"Copenhagen." Lola looked up into his snarl. "Did you question her about her sources?"

He slammed his hands onto the table. Lola startled but kept her expression bland. Luke leaned forward. "Stick with tailing sneaks and cheats, Starke. This isn't part of the deal."

"That means no," said Aubrey.

After a moment, Lola shrugged and returned to the sheaf of papers. Luke settled back and lit another stick.

They'd done a thorough job. Followed up on street rumours. Interviewed high and low. Caught three morning-after sites in a month. There'd been a possible lead with the Narcotics Division, but the informant had scrambled before anything had come of it. A brief one-pager four days later described the informant's death.

"How reliable was this Hamish McIntosh you found dead?"

"More than most pipe smokers," Luke answered.

"You're sure it wasn't murder."

"Nothing's sure in this business, Starke. But we figure Mac finally ran afoul of his habit. Happens sooner or later." This last bit of wisdom was imparted with a shrug.

"Tough coincidence," Lola commented.

Luke grunted in reply, eying her narrowly.

Lola returned his look blandly.

Starting from the top, Lola flipped through the reports more slowly. Contrary to first impressions, Luke was as methodical on paper as was his partner. Leads had been tracked, but none had got very far. There was plenty to confirm the existence of illegal tournaments but no one could discover the ringleaders. Times and places were spread by word of mouth. One night, they'd even caught two teenagers, trying to run from a raid, but they were just a couple of rich kids, slumming it with the poorer elements. Their parents had charged in right quick, lawyers in tow, claiming police coercion before the door had even shut behind them. Lola could read between the lines. She imagined that Tsu and Luke really hadn't had much to use to pressure those poor dumb kids with. Underage gambling was a simple misdemeanor, nothing a few hundred dollars wouldn't settle. The lawyers made sure the kids had kept their traps shut. Lola thought it likely the parents had threatened an end to the kiddies' allowances as well. Long story short: no one was talking to the cops.

After a while, Lola sat back. Luke stubbed out his cigarette and reached out to gather the file. She lit another Egyptian. "So the kids are a bust, their families uncooperative. You can't pin anyone else down as a participant. You haven't stumbled onto a tourney in a week. Where do you go from here?"

"None of your damned business," said Luke. "You've been given the file. You've read it. That's all I was ordered to do. I don't give a damn who hired you or why. This is our case."

A sudden knock on the door, then it swung open. Tsu, with two steaming mugs. He set them down, then closed the door. Gently, Lola accepted her coffee with a smile of thanks. The other, Tsu pushed toward his partner. Lola took a sip of the pale liquid. Luke guzzled.

"Is that steam out of his ears?" asked Aubrey.

"Catcher said she caught you on the way in. Thought your Ghost looked familiar." Tsu's tone was genial.

Lola shrugged. "Aubrey was occasionally in the papers. Maybe a newsreel now and then."

"Really? What for?"

"For being an actress's best friend and assistant."

Aubrey sniffed. "And costume consultant."

Tsu looked genuinely intrigued. "Oh yeah? Which one?"

Lola dragged on her cigarette. Aubrey sighed. "As if he doesn't already know."

She answered as she exhaled. "Grace McCall."

The larger man's eyebrows shot up in amazement. "That's not just any starlet. She's the real deal." He turned to Luke. "You're a big fan, aren't you?"

Luke nodded curtly. Tsu turned back to Lola. "Well, then ... if you don't mind me asking ... why would he Haunt you?"

"You'd have to ask him," she shrugged.

Luke sneered. "You must have some serious wires crossed, Starke. No one's a shamus who doesn't have to be. You obviously don't need the dough, so you must just enjoy hanging around lowlife scum."

"My reasons aren't your business. Your case is." Lola addressed Tsu again. "What's your take on that dead informant?"

"Hamish?" A rolling shrug. "Nothing mysterious about it, Miss Starke. He overdid it. These things happen. I don't know about your line of work, but we get bad breaks all the time in the cop business. You learn to move on."

"Your next one being?"

He ran a hand through his close-cropped hair. "We've got a list of people to find. Friends of friends of acquaintances. Talk to them, see what threads we can pull up."

"And how does your DS Shao want me involved?"

"He doesn't," said Luke.

Lola kept her eyes on Tsu. The big man remained silent, weighing his options. His gaze flickered briefly to his partner, then returned to Lola. Finally, he said: "We don't need a chaperone. Frankly, you'd be in the way."

Lola nodded.

Tsu shuffled his frame inside his grey suit. "Let me put it to you bluntly. You're here because you gamble with these people. You're part of their set."

Lola was shaking her head before he'd even ended that sentence. "You're mistaken. I don't travel in these circles."

Tsu looked apologetic as he continued. "These are the rules." He straightened up, cleared his throat, and pulled out a sheet of paper from the file. He slid it over. "New interviews will be held with these witnesses. You will act as liaison between the police department and members of your society network."

Luke leaned in with a smirk. "We ask the questions. You hand out the hankies and kiss the backsides."

Lola considered the names. "You already knew who my mother is, Tsu. Why the charade?"

No apologies now. "There are a number of prominent studio people on that list."

"Get it straight, Starke," added Luke, "we want your mother's name to open doors. You're secondary."

Lola nodded, then stood. "Let me know when you've set up your appointments. I'll be in touch." She headed for the door.

Luke bolted out of his chair. "You're not going anywhere, angel."

"Why Detective Inspector, having a change of heart? I'm flattered to think my charm has worked such marvels already."

Tsu stood, restraining his partner with a hand on the shoulder. "Miss Starke, we're not making the appointments. You are."

Lola shook her head. "Sorry to bust your calendar, Tsu. I only came to satisfy my curiosity, see how far Copenhagen would push this. Tell your DS Shao whatever you like, but I'm not much of a secretary. You don't need me for any of this. We all know it." She turned once more at the doorway and smiled.

"I'll handle Copenhagen myself."

SIX

The question is, will she take no for an answer?"

Traffic was heavy. Lola managed to slip in front of a bus just as it pulled toward the curb and a stop full of waiting passengers-to-be. She ignored the horn of a tan car trying to pull into flow from its parking spot.

"No, the question is how long can I borrow time?"

"And her thugs? You can run red lights and turn wild corners all day, but it seems to me they're pretty good at this. They've stayed on us."

"That? That was just a little loosening up. I'm not trying to lose them, not yet. Just getting a feel for them."

A delivery truck lumbered into the lane and Lola braked, hard. It sped up incrementally. She waited it out in first gear, eying the gaps in the other lane as the other cars rocketed away by comparison. Thick and Thin were two cars back now, the only ones not pressing impatiently on a car horn. Grinding gears and roaring engines heralded the release of a few cars into the next lane. Lola was content to stay behind. Eventually, she even shifted into second.

"Where *are* we going?" Aubrey asked.

"*Herald* office."

"With company?"

"Without."

Lola wrangled the car into a left turn and sped down Western Avenue, heading toward the ocean. Tire squeals and car horns told her an escort was following. She threw a quick glance over her shoulder and found them coming up on the right, slowing behind a silver Wraith. A red farmer's truck pulled in behind Lola. She changed lanes in front of the Wraith and slowed to match the farmer's speed. Up ahead, traffic began to thicken as it approached one of the largest intersections in Crescent City: Western Avenue and Ocean Drive. Western widened into three lanes but Lola stayed put. The Wraith was slow to brake. It came within inches of her bumper. She saw the driver's mouth tighten slightly. He had red hair beneath his chauffeur's cap. An elderly woman sat behind him. She stared out the window at the farmer's truck. She caught his eye, in fact. The farmer slowed even more, seemingly caught by her gaze.

Lola saw an opening and tapped the gas, wrenching the wheel over to slide back over one lane. She braked in time to the farmer's horn.

A green grocer's truck was coming up on the left. The sound of it down-shifting gears briefly overrode the honking of car horns. Lola slid in front of him. Another quick glance showed the thugs trying to pull behind her. She sped up, giving the grocery driver more room to avoid hitting her bumper. Meanwhile, the thugs' black Buick managed to squeeze behind the grocery truck. Lola slowed again, letting the truck get as close as he wanted. The farmer eyed her cautiously as he pulled closer. Beyond him, in the far lane, the silver Wraith was gaining on a black sedan. The elderly woman was looking straight ahead now and her driver was as tight-lipped as before. He glanced over at Lola, slowing down slightly. In front of him, a gap widened slightly.

Ahead, cars were lined three thick, waiting for the lights on Ocean Drive to turn green. The farmer remained just slightly beside and behind Lola as he slowed. The gap in front of the Wraith increased. The lights on Ocean flicked to green. Lola had three car lengths until she met with the bottleneck of cars moving forward. She checked the farmer's eyes. He was still watching her warily. She looked at the Wraith. The redhead was shifting his gears, concentrating on the car ahead of him. His silver beauty of a car lurched slightly. Lola smiled and slammed down on the gas, aiming for the far right corner of the intersection. The farmer squealed his tires and hollered. The Wraith braked to a stall. The bottleneck cleared just in time for Lola to miss the rear bumper of a maroon sportster as she jumped forward. She slipped onto Ocean Drive, heading north, amid a fanfare of horns and curses. Thick and Thin, waiting with all the other cars to turn southbound onto Ocean, were now stuck behind the green grocer's truck as it ground its gears to a jerky start.

Ria Monteverde wore a tweed jacket padded at the shoulders, and squared at the hem. Her pleated trousers were a coordinating shade of camel. Her long black hair was tied into a demure ponytail at the nape. She pointed accusingly at Lola with a black fountain pen.

"You never came to my promotion party."

"I'm here now. Congratulations." Lola grinned.

"It was eight days ago."

Lola showed her hands placatingly. "I didn't want to steal your glory. My mere presence and all that, you know."

Ria snorted. "Ha. You never could lie to me. Admit it—you simply forgot. You don't love me at all, do you?"

Lola rolled her eyes. "I love you just fine. It's the nagging I can't stand."

"So, you ungrateful wretch," Ria continued, lowering her pen, "what do you want now?"

"Just a visit to the archives."

Ria raised her eyebrows. "What's your angle?"

"Sorry, confidential. The less you know, the better."

"That has never rung true for me. The more I know, the happier I am."

"I'm not in it for your happiness, doll. This is strictly business." Lola tapped her watch. "I'm on the clock."

"All those years at prep school, wasted," Ria grumbled. "Your manners are still atrocious."

"You of all people should understand about deadlines," Lola countered.

"Yeah, yeah." Ria got up. "Come on. Down to the dungeon."

The basement of *The Crescent City Herald* was a surprisingly bright and high-ceilinged space. The entire floor was one large library. Shelves upon shelves of old editions of the *Herald* lined the walls and stood in symmetrical rows. Framed pages from significant editions decorated one wall. Along that wall, a row of three tables with matching chairs. Reading lamps sat on each table. The elevator sat across the room from the reading area. Ria led Lola down the stairs that ended next to the elevator. Immediately within view was the librarian's desk, a large reception counter of masculine millwork and dark wood.

Someone actually got paid to index the stories and keep records of each and every piece of news that the Herald had published in the past sixty years. That someone was currently named Dinwoodie Kwong. He lit up like a firecracker in Chang Plaza when Ria walked through his door.

"Hi Woodie, got a favour to ask."

"Hello, Miss Monteverde," he answered. He stood up from his perch on a tall stool and walked around his desk. His eyes wandered briefly to Lola. Woodie looked like an overgrown kid, in an argyle sweater over a pale blue shirt with pressed slacks and shiny black shoes. His hair, however, was unruly to the point of alarm. It stood up in a medium-sized cloud. Paired with large liquid brown eyes and that shy smile, he was the picture of adorable earnestness.

Ria gave him a real dazzler, then turned to Lola with an arch expression. "Well?"

Lola motioned. "Scoot."

Ria shook her head, grinning. "Not if you want Woodie's help. He doesn't do scut work for non-employees of our great newspaper. Right, Woodie?"

He gulped and nodded, turning red to the tips of his ears.

Aubrey weighed in impatiently. "Get on with it, Lola."

After a pause, Lola gave up the name. Ria looked startled. "You don't kid around." She turned to the lovesick kid. "You heard her."

Woodie whirled around and walked over to a row of thick black ledgers sitting behind his abandoned stool. He plucked one out and took it over to his desk. Opened, it revealed itself to be an index, *CH* to *CR*. Woodie thumbed down a tiny-print list and then got out a pad of paper. He wrote with quick strokes.

"And Stoudamire, Amber Jade."

"Let me finish with this entry first," he murmured.

Ria motioned her aside. "Come clean, girlie. Nothing free in this life."

"I'm just doing some research for a case, a possible case," she added, stalling Ria's protest.

"Someone's asked you to investigate the most powerful woman, Chinese or otherwise, in the Gaming Commission and it's not my story?" She stood with hands on her hips. "Give me one good reason to keep my trap shut."

Lola jerked a thumb at her own chest.

"You?" At Lola's nod, she laughed. "You're all the more reason to dig in. You'd be almost as good for circulation as your mother!" She scanned Lola's scowling face. "C'mon, doll. Give me something."

Lola shook her head. "Can't. This is my practice we're talking about." Lola shifted her stance. "Look, I don't like holding out on you. But cut me some slack here. I don't flap lips on my clients or my cases. That's how I do business."

Ria chewed her lower lip while she considered her friend. Meanwhile, Woodie had opened up two more ledgers and was scratching away with his pen. Ria crossed her arms over her chest. "Fine, but if the story gets hot, I had better be the first call you make."

Lola put out my hand. "Deal." The women shook firmly.

Ria grinned. "So what're we looking for?"

"Not *we*."

"You were never much good at research neither," she said.

"Ancient history. I'm so far past thirteen, it's painful to think on. A career can change a girl, you know."

Ria scoffed. She turned to Woodie. "Where do we start?"

The starting was easy. It was all the work in the middle that found Lola still in the Dungeon three hours later. Woodie's scribblings had proven to be a large list of articles. The Stoudamires had been a wealth of news stories throughout the years. Everyone knew the legendary story: Elijah Bell Stoudamire arrived from the East a penniless young man with an uncanny head for capitalizing on the needs of the masses. Given that the masses in his case were the thousands arriving weekly in the throes of gold fever, he quickly found his niche: supplying tough klondikers with a steady and reliable supply of wool socks. It wasn't glamourous but it was a bona fide moneymaker of an industry. A wife and two sons later, Elijah Bell could claim paternity to a Crescent City mayor as well as a tough-minded civic prosecutor.

Amber Jade was born to the latter. Her father, Elijah James, married a Southern belle, the former Adelaide Forrest-Gentry, and their only child was born three long years afterward. It was a well-known secret that Adelaide was unable to bear any more children, due to her delicate constitution. The *Herald* had many stories about the Stoudamires, with accompanying photographs. Over the years, Amber Jade appeared in a variety of flouncy white baby gowns and pretty little girl frocks. That changed after she turned thirteen.

An accomplished horsewoman, Adelaide nevertheless was thrown from her favorite horse on a ride during Amber Jade's thirteenth birthday party. She never awoke from the blow to the head and died two weeks later. A famous picture of Amber Jade was taken at the funeral service. She wore a black dress with veiled hat. It was impossible to see her expression.

Despite the rumours at Rose Arbour Prep, Amber Jade was rarely mentioned in the papers during high school. There were articles about her father's highest-profile cases, but nothing about his family life in them. Amber Jade showed up occasionally on his arm at appropriate fundraisers but otherwise, father and daughter did not take pictures together. After graduation, however, even these disappeared. Nothing about Amber Jade Stoudamire appeared in the *Her-*

ald until her marriage to Theodore Marshall Copenhagen IV, a wealthy industrialist who'd been born a millionaire and gone on to earn his own money in oil. He'd celebrated forty years before marrying the twenty-three-year-old Amber Jade. Her gift to him for his forty-fifth birthday was a divorce.

The same year she married, Amber Jade Stoudamire became AJ Copenhagen, Assistant Deputy Commissioner of Gaming. Her husband hadn't seemed to mind. In a statement put out by his public relations office, Teddy Marshall IV was proud of his wife's abilities and commitment to law and order. He was certain that she would rapidly become an integral part of the Gaming Commission.

Similar sentiments were released to the press when the divorce became public. The couple were still dear friends; however, irreconcilable differences had led them to the decision to end the marriage. Teddy Marshall wished his ex-wife the best in her career and life.

Throughout this, the Assistant Deputy Commissioner couldn't be reached for comment.

"A smart cookie," mused Ria. "The husband took all the heat."

Lola nodded. "There's got to be more. Not even a whiff of some dish on the side?"

"For either one of them," agreed Ria.

"It wasn't about the money. She was wealthy before the marriage. It wasn't about his personality. He was so much older. I doubt she was ever in love with him."

"Doesn't strike me as the type to do things haphazardly. Whatever Amber Jade wanted, she planned and executed until it was hers. Remember when she campaigned to become Student Council President in Senior Year?" Ria looked up, a wry smile playing at her lips.

"Hard not to think we dodged a bullet at Rose Arbour. I never thought I'd be grateful to be beneath someone's notice."

"Bullets would be too messy. She'd've gone for something colourless, odourless and tasteless."

"I can't quite believe I never ran into her," continued Ria. "A mayor for uncle and a star prosecutor as daddy. I wonder why I never pursued her for the school paper."

"As I recall, you were always more interested in the athletics department than in the society page."

A slow grin spread across Ria's face, accompanied by a pale pink blush that turned her skin dusky. Lola caught movement out the corner of her eye. Woodie had just ducked his chin. A red flush ran up his neck.

Lola stood. "Time for me to blow this joint." She extended a hand to Woodie. "Thanks for the help."

Ria gave a hurried thanks herself and dogged Lola's steps upward. "Where now?"

"You, back to your desk. I'm off to hunt ex-husband."

"We've got a deal, right?"

"Don't you have an article to write or something? You've been coming and going all afternoon."

Ria skewered Lola with a dark-eyed glare.

"If you want to feel useful," Lola finally replied, "you can work the phone. Find out where she went after Rose Arbour, before she caught Copenhagen's eye."

Ria grinned. "As if I needed direction from you, of all people."

SEVEN

Lola avoided the office and grabbed a sandwich and coffee on the way uptown. The very posh offices of Copenhagen Industrial Inc. sat at the narrow tip of the downtown area. Teddy Marshall IV liked his architecture tall and imposing. That was exactly what he got from the infamous Marcel Letourneau Fong. A seven-storey monolith of bright white stone, ringed with darkened windows at every time of day, the Copenhagen Building looked like a stark and disapproving cousin to the Gaming Commission jewel in the heart of the municipal district. It too had elegant stonework and caryatids adorning its pristine exterior. It also stood out amidst its more drab neighbours. But there was something missing. Fong had very publicly denounced the capitalist spirit of the times, early in his career, only to accept, twenty years later, the commission from Teddy Marshall III for a corporate headquarters. Fong certainly wasn't about to explain his actions, but rumours circulated that he needed the money, as patrons of his inconsistent visions had thinned out considerably after the unveiling of the Museum of Modernity in Sant'Angelo, a strange twisted structure that many critics, in varying degrees of bluntness, likened to human bowels. With the Copenhagen commission, he renounced his love for the curve and the circle, the symmetry of the infinity symbol. With the Copenhagen building, he articulated his bitterness in a perfect rectangle of bland wealth. It was a sublime *blague*, an arrogant gesture of defiance, all the more ironic because Teddy Marshall III loved it. It was the perfect symbol, to him, of his very masculine sense of power. Marcel Letourneau Fong didn't attend the ceremonial unveiling, but he did release a letter to the press, stating his hopes that the Copenhagen family would find joy in their newest symbol of self-gratification.

The lobby was designed to impress and intimidate, no surprises there. Gold and glass chandeliers hung from the twenty-foot ceiling. The ten steps from the doors to the main floor of the lobby accentuated this height. Gold sconces, stylized lilies, were spaced at regular intervals along the walls. A security desk sat almost immediately to the left at the top of the stairs. A matched pair of burly young men sat with sharp eyes and pressed uniforms. When they saw her, Lola averted her gaze shyly and put an extra sway in her walk. After a few paces, she threw them another shy look over her shoulder to confirm the nature of their attentions and was rewarded with a leer. Lola continued to the bank of three elevators and waited, touching her hair self-consciously.

Aubrey sighed noisily.

Lola kept her eyes up like the others around her, watching as the dial of the middle lift slowly indicated an impending arrival. A discreet *ding* and the doors opened. A flood of people gushed outward. As the only woman, Lola entered first, giving the lift operator a small smile as he tipped his hat. She kept a pleasant expression on her face as the men filed in.

"Miss?" The operator looked at her expectantly.

"Yes? Oh," Lola exclaimed, clearly flustered. "Um, I'm so sorry, I've got an appointment with Mr. Copenhagen's assistant, uh, Mrs. … um." She wrung her hands.

"Top floor, Davey," said a man to her left. He turned back to Lola with a smile. "Mrs. Yee."

Lola sagged with relief. "Yes, that's it. Mrs. Yee. Thank you."

He looked her over boldly before speaking again. "Mind a word of advice?"

"No, of course not. Please," Lola replied.

"Lose the hat. Mrs. Yee isn't much for the mannish styles these days." He leaned in conspiratorially. "She's a real dragon, if you ask me."

Another man snickered. Lola glanced over her shoulder with wide brown eyes. The man was sneering. "Listen sister, if you're looking for a job, you ain't gonna get it wearing pants."

The first man laid a gentle hand on Lola's shoulder. "Old Don over there's just being a goon. Ignore him." He patted her shoulders. "Every girl's entitled to a confidence boost, if you ask me. And you look pretty as a picture." He smiled with very even white teeth.

Lola smiled and looked down.

The operator called out "Six" and three of the men got out, including her admirer and Old Don. The former said, "Knock 'em dead." The latter merely winked. Lola cleared her throat, straightening her blouse and jacket lapels nervously. The remaining man read his newspaper until the elevator opened up onto the tenth floor. He folded up his paper neatly and exited without a word.

Lola turned to the dark-haired elevator operator. "Listen, Davey? You must know a thing or two about Mrs. Yee. Any pointers?"

Davey eyed her sidelong, then turned to face her. "He was right about the hat. She'll hate it." He checked his watch. "You're in luck. You've got a couple minutes to fix yourself up. Mrs. Yee'll be down in the mailroom." He cranked the doors open to floor eighteen.

Unlike the other levels she'd already seen, this one was floored in gleaming dark wood. It must have cost a king's ransom, but Lola wasn't surprised. Nothing but the best for a captain of industry. The wall opposite the elevator had dark oak wainscoting that gleamed in the soft golden light from frosted wall sconces. Davey pointed Lola down the left of the corridor. "Powder room." Then he thumbed in the opposite direction, saying, "Chairman's offices."

Lola thanked him and headed to the left. As soon as the elevator doors slid closed, she changed her direction.

The thick carpet underfoot absorbed all sound of Lola's progress. In fact, there seemed very little of the usual office noises at all. She wondered if there wasn't special sound-proofing on this floor. A few doors lined the hall but not nearly enough for an entire floor. At the end of the corridor was one massive set of double doors. They were breathtaking: rich paneled mahogany that reflected the light with velvety undertones. An elaborate brass handle curved out invitingly. There was no apparent lock. Lola pushed within and caught up short at the sight of the seated security man. He gave her a once-over and stood.

Lola scanned the room, noting the empty desk on the opposite side of the anteroom. She raised her chin: "I have an appointment with Teddy Marshall. Where is Yee?"

The man reacted to her haughtiness with a tense jaw. "Your name please, miss?"

"I don't have time to be questioned by a…an underling," Lola huffed. She walked determinedly toward the vacant desk. Once there, she glanced at the appointment book, reading upside-down quickly. She slapped her gloves against her hand impatiently and turned a glare toward the security man. "Where is Mrs. Yee, I said."

"She's not here, miss. As you can see." He gritted his teeth by way of a smile.

"Are you insinuating I am *blind*? I can see she's not here. I didn't ask where she isn't. I asked where she is." Lola punctuated her apparent displeasure with a slap of the gloves. "Never mind. Teddy Marshall's expecting me." She whirled around toward the inner door.

The man was at her side immediately. He placed a strong hand on her elbow. "You can't go in there, miss."

Lola looked down at his hand incredulously. "Are you touching me?" She wriggled her arm, trying to free it from the iron grip. "Let go of me, you goon."

The outer door swung open. A grey-haired woman in burgundy stared at them. The man immediately dropped Lola's arm. Lola pulled herself up to her full height and slapped him across the cheek.

"This is completely unacceptable," Lola sputtered. She turned to the older woman. "Mrs. Yee, I presume?" At the woman's nod, she continued. "I am Mrs. Charles Butler-Smythe. I have an appointment at two o'clock with Teddy Marshall. Kindly let him know that I am here." She narrowed her eyes at the security man. "You can be sure I shall bring this up in my meeting."

Mrs. Yee bustled across to her desk. "Yes, I'm sure there's been some misunderstanding, Mrs. Butler-Smythe. Mr. Copenhagen isn't in the office at the moment. Let me see …."

Lola sputtered again: "Isn't in the office? What do you mean by that? My secretary set this meeting weeks ago. To talk about the Museum benefit next month." She pulled her head back slightly and looked down her nose at the secretary. "I'm newly appointed to the Board, you see."

The security man remained at his post, one wary eye on Lola, the other on Yee. Lola ignored him and focussed her indignation on the assistant. "What is going on here? Where is Teddy Marshall?"

The older woman raised her head from the appointment ledger and smiled apologetically at Lola. "I'm afraid, Mrs. Butler-Smythe, there's been a mix-up." She eyed Lola's hat. "Your appointment is for next week." Her finger tapped an entry in the book. "At half past two."

"Are you quite sure?"

"Yes, Mrs. Butler-Smythe, I am. You see, Mr. Copenhagen is at the Veteran's Hospital groundbreaking ceremony this afternoon." She tapped the ledger again. "And it says here quite clearly that you are scheduled for April 17."

Lola flushed hotly. "Well, I shall be having words with my secretary. Good day!" She spun on her heel and marched out. As she passed the security guard, he gave her a triumphant smirk. Lola kept her face tightly controlled until she was back in an elevator, heading down. As the old operator cranked the doors closed, she allowed herself a grin.

The site of the future Crescent City Veteran's Hospital was on the northeastern outskirts. Lola drove due east from the Copenhagen building, skirting some rougher slums to the south, and directly passing by the largest cemetery headstone and monuments maker in the City. An enormous carved statue of a tiered pagoda stood at the entrance to the outdoor show lot. After that, the car repair shops, appliance sales stores and dinky diners seemed disappointingly anticlimactic.

The line of parked cars began a block before Lola reached the right place. She skimmed onward, and eventually parked a block past everybody else. She walked pass a seemingly unending line of black cars. Some had liveried drivers. Others had drivers dressed in regular suits. All the drivers watched her as she walked by. She nodded politely, keeping an unhurried pace as she followed the fencing along the sidewalk. Lola had to round the corner before she found the nearest entrance. It was an opening in the fencing, large enough for trucks to access. She spied another black car, its nose pointing out into the street, straddling the sidewalk and blocking the entrance. Not that it mattered today, thought Lola. There was no construction happening yet. Still, she wondered if it was Teddy Marshall's car. She craned her neck, searching for a driver. As she neared, she finally caught sight of a single yellow-robed Conjurer by the passenger side back door. It was a woman just about as tall as Lola herself. The woman's hood was down and her black hair shone in the sunlight. Intense eyes in a thin face, she scanned the surrounding neighbourhood, the street, passing cars and pedestrians.

"Dammit," muttered Aubrey. "Mayor's here."

"Lot of political cache in hospitals," Lola commented. As she approached the entrance, the Conjurer stared hard at her. Lola smiled politely.

Behind the Conjurer's left shoulder was a large sign, raised into the air on wooden stilts:

Future Site of the Crescent City Veteran's Hospital

A Joint Venture by Crescent City Municipal Authority and

Copenhagen Industrial, Inc.

Engineering by J.G. Cheng and Associates

Lola could hear speaking from within the fenced area. She looked behind the Conjurer, trying to see past her.

A couple of flashbulbs were in the group, and Lola recognized one of Ria's colleagues, in rolled-up shirt-sleeves and a brown tie.

Otherwise, it was a group of sleek business suits surrounding a slightly raised platform. Mayor stood on the platform, along with his usual complement of three Conjurers, dressed in their distinctive mustard-yellow robes. One on either side of Mayor, watching the crowd. The third stood behind Mayor and faced away. On the platform with Mayor were also three men in suits.

A tall, slender man stood hatless in the centre of that group. His silver hair gleamed in the afternoon sun. To his left was a shorter man wearing a hard hat—the City's head public liaison officer, Ernesto Chin. To the right of the silver-haired man was another Chinese man. He had salt-and-pepper hair and wore a neutral expression. Lola guessed he might be J.G. Cheng.

Lola brought her attention back to the Conjurer standing guard by Mayor's car. "I'm here for Mr. Copenhagen," she said.

"Are you with his office?" asked the other woman. She was watching the space just past Lola's left ear. Lola wondered briefly if Aubrey was giving a polite smile.

Lola shook her head. "No, I'm an investigator on a private matter. Can you tell me which is his driver?"

The Conjurer watched Aubrey for a few silent moments. Finally, she said, "Mayor will be done shortly. You can wait out here." Then she pointed to the left of the entrance. Lola followed her gesture and saw a bored-looking man in dove grey livery, complete with cap, reading a newspaper as he leaned against the side of a gleaming black Packard. "That one," supplied the Conjurer.

Lola thanked her and retreated a couple paces until she was all but leaning on the right-hand gatepost. She looked over at the suits.

The photographers were getting their cameras ready as Copenhagen hefted a ceremonial shovel. Chin and Cheng were asked to step in closer to him, and the three men smiled for the flashbulb moment. Next came photographs with Mayor for the three men. Then, there were individual shots with Mayor. Lola noted with interest that the Conjurers made certain to stay out of the frame. She wondered cynically if that was part of their special training. She waited another five minutes as handshakes and big smiles were passed around. Finally, Mayor and his Conjurers stepped away from the crowd of reporters and photographers. Copenhagen, Cheng and Chin stayed behind. Lola cursed inwardly. She caught the faintest whisper of a curse from Aubrey.

"Best smile forward," he said. "Let's make it short."

Lola grimaced at his imperious tone, but she didn't have time for a comeback. Mayor had noticed her. He paused slightly, said something to his pack of guards, then smiled at Lola as he approached.

"Lola, what a strange place to see you."

"Mayor," she acknowledged. "I'm on a job." She glanced at the Conjurers surrounding him. They stared, just as intently as the first Conjurer had. Lola cleared her throat. "Your guards jake with Aubrey?"

Mayor nodded. "As ever." He greeted Aubrey with another polite smile.

Lola squinted, just a little, trying to make out Mayor's features. It was difficult against the bright sunshine. His outline wavered. Lola recalled that Matteo Esperanza had thick brown hair, always cut neatly with a side part. The transition to Ghosthood, however, had leached it of colour. Now, Mayor's hair was just a faint shade of blonde. He was still tall and trim, though; broad-shouldered and slender-hipped. He wore a sharply tailored suit, the only suit that Mayor was ever seen in. Lola guessed that Ghosts created whatever wardrobe they wished for themselves. She'd never asked Aubrey, and she had no intention of doing so now.

Mayor's deep black eyes watched Lola. His mouth was just slightly quirked upward. "I hope your job isn't to do with this hospital, Lola. We've just barely broken ground." He spoke lightly.

"Not at all." Lola kept her tone polite. "Just here to find Mr. Copenhagen."

Mayor raised his eyebrows. "Teddy Marshall?" He chuckled under his breath. "Why do I suddenly have the urge to warn him?"

Lola flicked her eyes at the Conjurers. They watched the surroundings and Aubrey with equal fervour. She replied, "I'm sure I don't know." She kept her expression neutral. "Please, don't let me keep you."

Mayor left her words hanging in the silence for a moment. Then he smiled. "Always a pleasure, Lola. Give my regards to Grace." He paused. "Although, there's a good chance I may see her before you do, I suppose," he murmured. He nodded to Lola's right. "Aubrey."

Lola watched as he slipped into the waiting car and sped away.

Aubrey said, "Why did you tell him?"

"What? Why I'm here?" asked Lola, watching the suits disperse.

"It's never a good idea to give anything away to him."

"Truth was easiest. Whatever I may think of him, I have to admit he's never interfered directly with me."

"That you know of," said Aubrey.

"You can't bait me." Lola shrugged. "I don't know what's between you, and I don't care. If you want to nurse a grudge against Mayor, you'll have to get in line."

Lola tracked Copenhagen as he walked through the entrance and turned left. She called out.

"Mr. Copenhagen?"

He smiled blandly, readying a handshake.

"Mr. Copenhagen, I'm Lola Starke, an old friend of Amber Jade's. Can we talk for a minute?"

Copenhagen's smile tightened and his hand dropped to his side. He glanced back toward the platform. The photographers chatted amiably as they smoked. Cheng and Chin had one reporter each, standing five feet apart and jotting notes furiously as the men spoke,. Copenhagen returned his attention to Lola with obvious reluctance. He dropped the pretense of the smile.

"Your name means nothing to me." He continued walking, picking up his pace. Lola easily lengthened her stride to keep up.

"I went to Rose Arbour Preparatory School with your wife. She's recently hired me for a job. I'm a private investigator." Lola held out her state license and ID.

"Ex-wife. What does any of that have to do with me?" Copenhagen reached his car, held up his hand. The driver stepped away.

"To be honest, Mr. Copenhagen, I have ethical questions about taking the case, and I'm looking into Amber Jade's background."

"No one calls her that anymore." He nodded to his chauffeur, who stepped in and opened the door. Copenhagen looked at Lola directly. "I'm not in the habit of gossiping about my ex-wife. We parted on amicable terms." He slipped into his car. His driver closed the door and went around to get behind the wheel. The shiny black car pulled away and sped down the street. Lola watched it turn the corner. A small smile played on her lips as she walked to her own car.

"Bit of a starched shirt," said Aubrey.

"I'm not done with ex-husbands yet," Lola said.

EIGHT

Lola got a perverse pleasure driving up Hill Way in her scuffed old Buick. She passed innumerable gated palaces, invisible behind white-washed walls. Here, along Hill Way, all the black iron gates ended in miniature pikes at their sculpted tops. Lush greenery exploded from behind high walls, obscuring the enormous homes within. Lola's destination appeared much like the others. A brick-topped wall of blindingly white adobe led her to its entry gate. The Chinese character for *serenity,* wrought in calligraphic black iron, adorned the gate's centre.

Lola stopped in front of the gate and idled. A short square of a man opened a door in the wall, to the left of the gate, and walked briskly over to Lola. As he neared, he tipped his cap to her, revealing gleaming black hair.

She smiled. "Da Silva, I thought you'd have moved on to better things by now."

"You and everyone but my agent." He returned her smile with a toothy grin. "How've you been keeping?"

"Not spoiling yet. Is he up?"

"Oh yeh," grinned Da Silva widely. "Mrs. Lee has him on a regimen. Up every morning by nine." The guard guffawed.

Lola raised her eyebrows. "Wonders never cease."

"Telling me. Anyhow, go right on up. This time of day, he's likely by the pool. Mrs. Lee likes him to swim." Another mischievous grin.

Lola voiced her thanks and waited while he pushed open the doors. They swung open noiselessly, perfectly poised on their hinges. Da Silva waved her through, then closed the gate. Lola saw him walking back to the gatehouse, apparently talking to himself.

Aubrey sounded amused. "Deanna is as chatty as ever. I barely got a word in."

"She's well?" asked Lola, navigating down the long drive. A line of palms lined both sides, but it was still wide enough that no shade was thrown on the car.

"As can be expected for someone so young." A chuckle. "She thinks his lucky break's just around the corner. She can feel it."

Lola shrugged. "I hope she's right. Only gets tougher once you jump over thirty. Da Silva's a decent Joe." She waited for a derisive remark in reply, but Aubrey remained silent. Lola parked the Buick on the curve, just at the corner of the five-car garage.

Martin Lee III wasn't a pretentious man. His was a modest house that sat halfway up the Hills, facing the expansive ocean. It had only ten bedrooms and six baths, barely acceptable for a supposed real estate baron. North Hills was an exclusive area; one had to keep up appearances. The fact that Martin had a tennis court and outdoor pool barely met the minimum standards for the area. Lola thought it was perfect. She'd always loved this house.

Lola had barely gained the top step to the front door when it opened. A trim man with ebony skin smiled at her with genuine affection.

"Lionel," she exclaimed. She swept into his outstretched arms and was greeted with a crushing hug.

"Lola, you don't know how glad I am to see you." He released her just far enough to take a good look, keeping his hands on her arms.

"You say that to all the girls," she said.

"But I only mean it with you." He smiled back. "I'd waste another ten minutes telling you how stunning you look and all that, but Martin would impale me if he found out I'd kept you to myself so long."

"What are you doing here?" Lola asked as Lionel linked arms and led her into the grand entryway. A vaulted, twenty-foot ceiling played host to parquet flooring and a double stairway that hugged the walls. An enormous floral arrangement sat atop a round marble table in the centre of the space. Lionel walked Lola around the table, through a large door.

"Just trying to get Martin to sign some papers." Lionel eyed Lola. "Have you met Chandra yet?"

Lola nodded. "At a Science Foundation fundraiser. Last month. Lovely girl."

"But strong-willed. And smart. Martin seems to have a taste for women like that." A grin played along the tall man's lips.

Lola grinned. "The only ones worth marrying, Lionel."

"Worth keeping." He stressed the last word. "But hard to keep."

"Is he having any luck with this one?"

Lionel shrugged. "Time will tell. It's been four months. Honeymoon's still going strong."

"I'm happy for him, then." She placed a hand on his arm. "And you? Still keeping yourself to yourself?"

Lionel nodded emphatically. "Too young to get married."

"Too busy, you mean."

"That too. It's either me or Martin. Someone's gotta run the business." Another shrug. "And we both know who's got the better head for it."

"'Real estate empires don't run themselves.'"

"Spoken like Martin Lee the Second himself," laughed Lionel. He squeezed Lola's arm. "You know, he still asks after his 'favourite daughter-in-law.'"

Lola laughed. "It's a shame my former mother-in-law didn't feel the same way."

"Yes, well," replied Lionel. "If she had, my father might still be married to her and I'd never have been born."

"That's me," said Lola, "rabble-rouser and annoyance to traditional Chinese ladies."

"From your lips to the gods' ears," said Lionel with a smile.

They'd come through a parquet-floored, wainscoted hallway with framed photographs lining the walls. Doors led off toward the library, the kitchen wing, guest rooms, the salon. The end of the hall connected with another corridor, at right angles. Lionel and Lola turned left and continued toward an open doorway, its glass-paned doors standing at attention to either side. Lola heard the rhythmic splashes of someone swimming.

Lionel gave her arm another squeeze, then released her and walked on, toward a cluster of tables and chairs. Lola shaded her eyes with a hand as she neared the pool. Someone was indeed swimming, in steady strokes to the far end of the water. Lionel picked up a pair of sunglasses and slid them on as he sat down. He motioned Lola, who'd stopped, to come on forward.

The swimmer surfaced and exited the shimmering water. Lola turned to face him, her smile widening with genuine pleasure. Martin faced away from her, towelling off with vigour. Sunlight glinted off stray beads of water on his taut body, bronzed from hours in the sun. Water beaded on his jet black hair. She crossed her arms, waited with a grin. Her ex-husband was rubbing roughly at his hair as he began walking toward her, but he wasn't looking up. Rather, he was busy drying an ear and had his face turned away.

"Lionel," he called out.

"Yes, Martin?" replied his brother.

"What time did Chandra say she was—?" Martin's upward gaze was met with a dazzling smile from Lola. He threw his towel onto the deck surface. "Lola! What the devil are you doing here?" He snatched her up into an embrace and planted a solid kiss on her lips before letting her go. His eyes narrowed as he turned his gaze to Lionel. "All right, spill. Why's the muscle here? Are you trying to get me to do something I won't like?"

Lionel sighed. "Sadly, I hadn't thought of that. No, Lola's here on her own business. Which, I must point out, she hasn't let on to at this moment."

Lola brushed a stray hair behind Martin's ear. "You need to visit your barber, Martin. Or does your wife prefer it like this?"

"I am in most things malleable to a fault when it comes to my wife's wishes. However, one must allow oneself some small recourse of rebellion, Lola. Wouldn't you agree?"

Lola countered his mischief with a stern expression. "Now, now, Lionel has informed me confidently that you and the lovely Chandra are still mooning over one another. I shan't let you make me think different." She hugged him again. "It's so good to see you."

"Then you should see more of me, my sweet."

"Seeing you more often shall suffice, I think," replied Lola.

"And Aubrey, how are you?" asked Martin.

"Tell him I'm dying of boredom and would you please get on with it, Lola."

Lola grinned. "Can't complain, thank you for asking."

Martin pulled Lola with him to the chairs and sat her down before taking his own seat. A rotund middle-aged maid came out with a tray of tall iced beverages. Martin thanked her expansively and she returned to the shadowy interior of the house without a word. Everyone took a grateful swallow of the icy tea.

"Look here, Martin," began Lionel, "I just need you to sign off on this contract. It's for our new director of marketing."

"Have I met him?" Martin asked.

"Her," corrected Lionel, "and yes you have. Delia Quon."

Martin made a face. "That one? She hated me."

"All the more reason to hire her," replied Lionel. "Now sign and I'll get out of your hair and you can catch up with your beautiful former wife until your beautiful current wife comes home."

"Oh what a tangled web I weave," said Martin gleefully. He took Lionel's pen and attached his name to the document with a flourish. "There. Your duty is now fulfilled. Go hence with my blessings, dear brother."

"Idiot. I'll be at the office until six tonight. Chandra will collect you at seven and we're meeting at The Supper Club. Got it?" Martin nodded solemnly. Lionel kissed Lola on the cheek. "You would complicate things much too much, so I shan't invite you, dear girl." Lola laughed at his conceit. Lionel gave Martin one final stern glare and turned away, walking briskly to the house.

"It's easy to forget you're older," laughed Lola.

"I try all the time." Martin set his glass down forcefully. "Now, I know you're still madly in love with me, so in order to save you face, why don't we pretend you've come for some other reason than to glance upon my handsome face with longing and ardour?"

"I need information."

"Ah yes," Martin steepled his fingers.

Lola suppressed another laugh. "Do try to be serious, Martin. I need to know everything you can tell me about AJ Copenhagen."

He gave an exaggerated shiver. "Well that's a sure fire way to give a man a shrivel." The grin returned quickly as he registered Lola's reaction. "It's a short tale, but none the less sweet.

"I was at their wedding. Barely remember it. I was with Noelle, wife number three. She made sure I didn't disgrace myself more than usual. I don't even know if Teddy Marshall noticed me. I may have kissed the bride, though. Forward five years and we met again at a fundraiser for Teddy Marshall's latest philanthropic gesture, some children's charity. We were at the Museum of Modern Art for an auction, that's right. She was a knock-out, the belle of the ball. That glorious red hair. Those calculating emerald eyes. She was the picture of the devoted younger wife, in a tastefully alluring number, hanging on his arm, making eyes at him. I was hooked. Noelle was onto husband number three and I was single once more. Late into the event, she cornered me in that niche for Antiquities, you know the one, Lola, by that statue of the Han boy. I admit, I was surprised, but she was quite ... convincing. I'm not proud of it, but I went to her home the following night. Teddy Marshall found us together. The next week, they were officially separated and then divorced by the end of the year."

"Was he violent? Angry?"

"Not in the slightest. It was most...unmanly, if you ask me. He was perfectly composed. Grave."

"He didn't threaten you?"

"Nothing like that. He asked me to leave immediately, so he could speak with his wife. He turned on his heel and left. We dressed. She was done first and left the room. Didn't say a word, didn't even look at me."

"Was she embarrassed? Remorseful?"

"She wasn't surprised, I'll tell you that. I'd venture I was the only one who was." Martin looked thoughtful. "I think she'd been expecting Teddy Marshall all along. They were both so calm." A grin Ghosted along his lips. "And she," he shrugged. "Not passionate enough. And at the same time ...." Lola waited him out. Finally, he said, "Damned if she didn't look sad as well." His grin burst out again. "Well, if a viper can look sad, that is."

"It's like prying a pearl from an oyster without any of the satisfaction," harrumphed Aubrey in the car. "Slimy and smelly." When Lola didn't respond, he said, "Other than confirming that your ex-husband is a despicable cad, that story doesn't help us."

"Even stray puzzle pieces fit somewhere."

"Oh, now you're speaking in riddles. Please," said Aubrey.

Lola was content to let him stew in silence. She found a drugstore ten minutes away and pulled over. The telephone was occupied so she bought herself a cup of coffee and waited. Eventually, a large woman wearing an eye-searing floral print dress emerged from the booth. Lola made it to the telephone just in front of a pock-faced boy in a soda jerk uniform. She waited until he backed off before picking up the receiver and speaking to the operator. There were the usual clicks and static before she was connected.

"City Desk, Monteverde."

"What've you got?"

"A headache and a raging thirst. Meet me at Arty's in thirty."

"Make it an hour. I'm down the way from North Hills. I've got to stop into the office."

"You're buying," said Ria and rang off.

Lola went back to the counter and asked for a glass of water. The kid in the soda jerk uniform shot her a dark look and slid into the telephone box. Lola just barely kept from laughing and drained her glass. She exchanged nods with the counter man and left. The street was moderately busy and she spotted no one familiar as she walked back to her car.

"Good chance they'll be waiting for you," said Aubrey. Lola pulled the Buick into traffic and sped through the intersection just as the light turned amber.

"I can lose them again," she shrugged.

"Waste more time."

"I'll put it on her bill."

Lola drove alertly through late afternoon traffic and arrived at her street in under twenty minutes. She found a spot behind a grimy farm truck, two blocks and a corner from her building. She sat for a few minutes after the car settled down and watched the street. Then she got out and slowly made her way on foot. She crossed at the corner and approached from the other side of the street.

"There," exclaimed Aubrey.

"Be more helpful if I could see you pointing," remarked Lola, but she made them too. The big black hearse of a car was squatting half a block west, on the same side of the street. They were parked perfectly to see the entrance to her building. She asked Aubrey to run ahead as far as he could and get a better angle. He assured her that both hooligans were inside the car. Lola grinned and increased her pace up the sidewalk. She passed them without a glance and stopped at the corner, waiting for the crossing light. It changed and she surged forward with the crowd. On the other curb, she turned left and walked back down the block toward her building. As she did so, she looked deliberately at the black car. Thick was at the wheel and as she expected, he showed no alarm, merely watched her with dark eyes. She smiled a small smile and went inside.

Up on the third, it was quiet. Lola wondered if she were the only occupant. Until she saw a shadow flicker behind the windows of her waiting room. The door was ajar. She smelled the familiar aroma of Egyptian cigarettes.

The man smoking wore a well-cut beige number with a salmon-coloured shirt and striped tie in red, brown and gold. His brown trilby, accented with a strip of gold around its base, sat on a chair while he paced, staring at the floor. His head snapped up as soon as he heard Lola in the doorway.

"Mr. Arbogast," she said.

"You are supposed to update me regularly," he replied.

Lola nodded agreeably as she crossed the small room to her inner office door. "This is the first time all day I've been here," she said. She unlocked her door and pushed it open, gesturing for her client to precede her. Arbogast nodded curtly and passed her. Lola stooped to gather the mail in the small wire basket attached to the door just below the slot. She gestured for her client to sit as she walked behind her desk. She set the mail on a low cabinet and sat down to face him. Arbogast threw his hat on the vacant chair and stubbed his cigarette in her ashtray.

"What have you found?" His green eyes focussed intently on her.

"A Ghostly nun who claims to have seen Mr. Josephson two weeks ago." Lola iterated Aubrey's interview with Sister Amelia, curious about Arbogast's reaction. His mouth tightened when she mentioned the missing man's Ghost, but he remained silent. He stayed that way for several moments after Lola was done. She said, "Seems Lucille is more of a leader than you thought."

"Who did you say this Ghost was? This nun?" Arbogast squinted through the smoke of a new cigarette.

"She had no reason to lie."

"How do you know?"

"I trust the source that spoke with her."

"Mm-hmm. And that's all you have?"

"I also spoke with Sammy Lu at Lucky Bamboo, a mah-jongg place on—"

"I know it," said Arbogast.

"They—his niece and nephew as well—saw Mr. Josephson a couple weekends ago. They recognized his condition readily enough." Lola paused, then added, "They had no reason to lie, Mr. Arbogast."

Arbogast sat unmoving, save for his eyes. They scanned Lola's expression for something, some hint or scrap of something that Lola knew wasn't there. She held her tongue. The next move was his.

The cigarette trembled in his fingers, its smoke wafting up to tinge the silence. He seemed to remember it suddenly and brought it up only to stop short and stare at it. After a moment, he took a deep drag, closing his eyes until he'd exhaled. When he looked at Lola again, his green eyes had darkened almost to black.

"Do you know a lot about Ghosts?"

"I wouldn't call myself an expert."

"I do. I forced myself to learn. Since I met Sunny, it seemed important to understand, you see." He studied his cigarette once more. "Most people think it's impossible to get rid of your Ghost without dying, but that's not true. There are people—very special Spell Casters—who can Disperse Ghosts without harm to the Host. It's not common, of course. Too expensive for most people. Too heartless as well. But if you're motivated enough, it can be done."

"And was Mr. Josephson motivated?"

Arbogast shook his head. "Sunny was a twin. In the way of twins, the two children made a pact. They begged their parents to make it possible and in the way of doting parents, it was done. Lucille died when they were sixteen. I met Sunny five years later. He'd been a heroin addict for three of those years, driven to it by that horror he called his sister. Lucille was an addict before her death. Ironically, she didn't die of an overdose. She was hit by a bus. But death is no match for a Ghost with a heroin habit. And if not Death, then how was poor Sunny to contend?"

"Did she know you had a marker on her head? Did he?"

Arbogast shook his head. "Impossible. I spoke only to arrange the details and I was alone with the ... person. Sunny would never have gone along with it, of course."

"Lucille must have had contact with other Ghosts. They've got a a grapevine, just like the living. Maybe she heard a rumour, convinced her brother to rabbit. He sounds susceptible to her persuasion."

"He's been clean for three years, Miss Starke. That took courage and strength beyond your imagining. He learned to depend on himself. And mistrust his sister's motives. He wanted her gone too. But I couldn't discuss it with him without her knowing as well."

"So you took care of all the preparations. When was the Dispersal set for? What date?"

"In a few days' time. The night of the fourteenth." He looked down at his hands. "It's the waning moon."

"Is the Spell Caster someone Mr. Josephson knew—in some other capacity?"

Arbogast was shaking his head before Lola had even finished speaking. "Yes, but this person wouldn't have said a word to him."

"Who's to say this person didn't approach Sunny? Offer to nix the deal for more money?"

Arbogast wasn't budging. "You don't know this person. She would never make that kind of deal. No, Sunny's disappearance has nothing to do with the Dispersal. He knew nothing about it."

Lola waited a beat before she said, "So we're back to the drugs then."

Another adamant shake of the head. "We're back to Lucille."

"I'm not a Catcher, Mr. Arbogast."

A strained smile. "Don't worry. I didn't hire you for your Ghost-hunting abilities. I've got other people on that angle. Your job is to follow the physical trail. You find Sunny and we'll find Lucille." He stood up abruptly. "I've got other appointments. Keep me updated. Good day." Between one blink and the next, Arbogast left the room. Lola listened to his long strides and the sound of the elevator. She looked out a window.

"An ostrich if ever I saw one," said Aubrey. "Makes you wonder what he's hiding from."

Lola kept her thoughts to herself.

NINE

She found herself back at Lucky Bamboo fifteen minutes later. Arbogast's flashy two-tone hardtop was half a block up. The man himself was crossing the street, carrying a black briefcase. Lola watched him from her car, tucked neatly behind a dark blue sedan.

"Don't wait too long, Lola. You're liable to lose him entirely."

Lola watched the block in silence. She flicked a glance in her mirrors. Copenhagen's thugs and black Buick were at the previous corner, waiting for her next move. She'd allowed them to come along, biding her time for a good chance to get rid of them. Now, she pulled out and gassed the car. She was turning right before they pulled even with the mah-jongg parlour. She sped down three blocks, turned right, then right again immediately. She backed into an alley and counted to ten. Cautiously, she nosed back out and continued right for two more blocks. Another couple of rights and she was back in front of Lucky Bamboo. Arbogast's car was still parked in front. She turned left into an alley at the side of the building and stashed her car.

Coming back out on foot, she eyed the street before committing to the few steps to the entrance. She pushed inside. A lean, muscular Chinese man greeted her immediately. Lu's nephew, Benny. His voice was flawlessly polite and utterly impersonal. He gestured toward the interior of the parlour:

"May luck smile on you today."

The gaming room was mostly full this time. There were plenty of Crescent City denizens who liked a bit of gambling before their supper. Many of them were depending on it for their supper as well. Lola skulked around the tables, pretending to be choosy. Most of the patrons were Chinese, but there were enough *gwai* to help her blend in. She scanned the players, thankful for Arbogast's memorable appearance, but he wasn't among them. She did a quick turn around the card room as well. Playing a hunch then, she made for the back office Sammy Lu had exited just the previous morning.

Lola was about ten feet away when the door opened. She had just enough time to turn away and pay special attention to a hot table of four matrons. They were clacking their tiles and chiding one another at great volume. The women were clearly old hands; all four ignored Lola's closeness with ease. She glanced casually back at the door. Arbogast was shaking hands with Sammy Lu, who smiled obsequiously and then began to bow to the other man's retreating back. Lola returned her attention to the table in front of her, using her peripheral vision to follow her client's progress through the *feng shui* maze. He walked out briskly, still carrying the black briefcase. Lola glanced back at the office. The door was closed once more. She hurried to catch up with Arbogast, ignoring Benny's insincere wishes for a pleasant evening.

She tossed a glance over her shoulder as she reached the mouth of the alley. Arbogast was just approaching his car and about to check the street before walking around to the driver's side door. She ducked into the alley quickly and ran to her car. She started it up and pulled out. Lola hung back a few feet from the mouth of the alley until she saw him drive past. Waiting until a grey sedan had passed as well, she turned into the flow of traffic.

It was easy to pick out Arbogast's car: a black and tan roadster. It was even easier to follow it. He drove without regard for his fellow drivers. Horns and upraised hands followed his progress, but Arbogast made no acknowledgement of the ire he created. Lola was willing to bet she could have driven right beside him in her sorry brown sedan and he would not even have noticed. She resisted the urge. Instead, she stayed a steady two or three cars back and spent two hours making the rounds of some of the City's hundreds of mah-jongg houses.

From Lucky Bamboo, Arbogast moved on to Water Lily on Yucca Avenue. He spent a total of ten minutes inside. Then it was on to Silver Temple on West Eighteenth and Huang. Fifteen minutes later, Lola was on the road again, following Arbogast to Ivory Tiles in the Bywater Hotel on Waterfront. The story remained unchanged with each place. Arbogast appeared business-like and professional. Black briefcase in hand, he strode to the manager's office at each establishment and closed the door behind him. Invariably, the managers themselves would come out to bid him adieu, some smiling like Sammy Lu, others tight-mouthed and grim.

After Ivory Tiles, Arbogast led Lola to a club unknown to her, a place called La Grenouille. Lola checked her watch. Quarter of seven. Suppressing a sigh, she climbed out of her car. Arbogast was just sliding out of his car and nodding to the valet. Unlike her client, Lola was parked on the curb, across the street. She swept past the valets, walking beneath a lighted archway that led to the glass doors.

"Subtle," commented Aubrey.

Lola nodded absently to the smiling doorman and entered a square lobby area, complete with potted palms, a coat check alcove with girl, and large lighted doorway with red velvet curtains. At present, the curtains were pulled back by gold-tasselled cords. Lola could see directly into the main gambling room. More potted palms, these taller than their lobby cousins, were scattered around the room. A twenty-foot ceiling gave them plenty of air, although the cloud of cigarette smoke certainly cut into their share. Mirrors gleamed from multiple surfaces, highlighting the blond wood walls. In addition to the cluster of thirty or so mah-jongg tables, there were slot machines and card tables: blackjack, poker, dominoes, even baccarat. Cocktail servers in *cheong-sahm* walked among the crowd with welcoming smiles, their graceful arms carrying full trays above their coiffed heads. Some had hair gems and jade dangling from sleek buns. Shapely legs peeked out from the slits on both sides of their silken dresses. Cigarette girls were dressed in fishnets and sleeveless sheaths that ended at the knee. All the girls wore three-inch heels. Around the room, scattered like dark coins, were the pit bosses: men in tuxedo suits with gold pins in their lapels. They wore identically bland expressions.

Given the room size, La Genouille was used to twice the numbers than it housed now. Lola walked straight to the card tables, noting the various dealers. She slid past a pit boss, eying his frog-shaped gold pin as a tourist might do. He gave her a perfunctory smile and shifted his attention away. She spied Arbogast walking along a wall, toward the far end of the room. Three rows of slot machines gave her easy cover. When she came out however, she caught sight of his distinctive hat bandeau disappearing around a corner. She hurried to catch up, only to stop at the sight of a hefty Chinese man in a shiny suit. He stood at the foot of a stairwell. A sign proclaimed boldly: *Management—Employees Only.*

"Help you, miss?" he asked in a bored voice.

"Restroom?" Lola asked in breathy reply.

The man shook his head. "Wrong turn, miss. They're on the other side of the slots." He jerked a thumb behind him. "Employees only." Something over Lola's shoulder caught his eye. She turned, tightening herself in readiness.

It was another shiny suit with muscles. He nodded to the first man, who said, "Escort our guest to the restrooms."

Lola smiled in embarrassment and allowed herself to be led away. She thanked her escort self-consciously and entered the ladies room. A vast mirrored vanity faced her. She looked fleetingly at her own irritated expression, then plunged forward, toward the back of the room. Stalls with doors. An attendant in a maid's uniform, her grey hair in a bun at the nape of her neck.

"For gods' sake, hurry up," whispered Aubrey.

"Shut up and get out," she replied, entering a stall. She caught a glimpse of the attendant leaning forward in curiosity as she shut the door. After, Lola washed her hands quickly, taking the thick towel from the attendant wordlessly. She tossed a dime into the jar on her way out.

Her husky escort was gone. Slot machines rang and coins plinked. Laughter from the far corner of the room drifted over. Lola sauntered along a row of slots and shot a quick sidelong glance at the stairs as she passed by. The same set of muscle stood at attention. She turned away and hurried toward the mah-jongg tables. All the while, she scanned the room for Arbogast. When her watch said she'd wasted another ten minutes, she left the room. The coat check girl, a bottle blonde with dark eyebrows and orange-red lipstick, smiled unconvincingly as Lola approached. She watched Lola with cool grey eyes as Lola described Arbogast.

"Happen to see him leave?" Lola asked in conclusion.

"Who?" asked the girl. Her face remained smooth and impassive.

Lola remained as she was for a moment, then opened her purse and slid out a bill. She showed the five and folded it neatly, then held it out. The money disappeared into impressive décolletage even as the girl nodded.

"Yeah, I saw him. I see him every week," she added glumly. A thought seemed to strike her, and she looked Lola over carefully. "Say, you work for the Commission too?"

"No. I'm a personal acquaintance."

The girl shrugged. "Well, if you don't catch him, come back next week, same time. He's like clockwork." She cocked her head to one side. "Maybe you oughta think about another line of action, honey. He doesn't play in our league." She patted the spot she'd secreted the bill. "Let me know if I can help you out again."

Lola nodded and hurried out. She barely let the doorman open the door enough for her to pass. But she stopped as she came even with the valets. She readied bills surreptitiously as she asked them about her client. His valet spoke up readily enough when he palmed the fiver. Arbogast had left ten minutes earlier, just like usual. He'd taken a left out of the lot, also like usual. Lola walked briskly down the sidewalk, then stopped short.

They were waiting for her. Thin leaned against the driver-side door. Thick stood on the sidewalk, motioning for her to continue. Lola slowly crossed the street. She stood next to her car, facing Thick. Thin came around the back of the car and stopped behind her.

"Too bad you lost him," Thick said. Thin snickered.

"Too bad for whom?"

Thick shrugged. "Does it matter? You've been wasting your time following that sad sack around. We've been wasting our time following you." He took two steps forward. A meaty hand grasped Lola around her upper arm. "Forget him. You're supposed to be working the boss's case." He squeezed and twisted, ensuring a nasty bruise. "This oughta help remind you."

Lola suddenly jerked her knee up and caught Thick in the groin. He crumpled and Lola shoved him away. Before she could whirl around to face Thin, he had her arm twisted up behind her back. Thick gagged once then managed to pull himself upright. He was breathing heavily through his nose. He grabbed Lola's jaw tightly in his hand and pulled her face up.

"I'll remember that, angel," he rasped. "Just you do your job like Copenhagen hired you to. We'll square accounts soon enough." He squeezed hard then pushed her face to the side and let go. Lola struggled angrily against the man at her back. Thin sharply twisted her arm once more until Lola gasped with the pain. He shoved her forward, releasing her. She caught herself on her car and spun around, her good arm aiming low. She kept her fingers rigid and landed a hit in Thin's gut. As he doubled over, she connected her knee with his face. Her gun was out before Thin had fallen to the pavement, but Thick made no move to come at her.

"Pick him up and beat it, the both of you," she said.

Lola stepped back, wary and watchful, as the two men glared at her. Her gun hand was steady though and neither said a word. They lurched to their car and drove away. Lola followed them closely, in plain sight, all the way downtown. About two blocks out, however, she pulled ahead. When the two men entered the lobby, Lola was waiting for them. She turned away from the security desk and its duo of aging guards. Thick walked straight, but his face showed strain. Thin was already squinting out of his swollen left eye. Lola joined them as they marched toward the elevator banks. They rode up in silence. Lola stood at the rear of the elevator, watching the tense backs of her would-be handlers. She hung back as they exited the elevator and traversed the corridor.

When they entered the outer office, Thick strode to the inner door and knocked quickly. Thin looked at Lola, who gestured for him to stand beside the other man. She remained behind both men as they waited. A voice called out from within. Thick opened the door, but he didn't step inside. Instead, he held it open and turned to Lola. He gestured sharply for her to enter.

She shook her head. "Ladies first," she said.

Thin took a step toward her. Lola tensed, readying herself.

Thick grabbed his partner's arm and shoved him inside the inner office. Lola waited until they were both within before following.

AJ Copenhagen sat, her eyes cold, her lips compressed into a thin slash of red. "What are you doing here?"

Lola took a seat on the upholstered armchair and pulled out her cigarette case. "We need to talk."

Copenhagen eyed her thugs. They stood at attention before her desk, eyes staring straight ahead, backs rigid. She said, "Get out." The two men wheeled around and marched out. Lola watched them through a plume of blue smoke, then returned her gaze to her client.

"Take your monkeys off my back."

"An ultimatum, Lola?" The other woman was suddenly amused.

Lola held the mocking glance. "No babysitters."

Copenhagen shrugged. "I apologize for my zeal." Her smile widened. "You won't see them following you again."

Lola shook her head. "You want me to waste time losing them, fine."

Copenhagen stood, spreading her hands out in a placating gesture. "I'm simply testing your resources. Consider it a check on your references." She walked over and sat on the sofa which was perpendicular to Lola's armchair. The women sat within arm's reach of one another. Lola shifted, lifting her cigarette to her lips. Copenhagen pushed a crystal ashtray toward her. "There's no call to take it quite so personally."

"If you wanted hoop jumping, you should've hired a seal." Lola dragged on her cigarette, waiting until she exhaled to speak again. "I've warned my mother and her people. She's on to you."

Copenhagen laughed loudly. "Oh I doubt that."

"Coercing me by threatening my mother was as effective as having those two shadow me."

"I didn't make it this far in my career by throwing the dice randomly. I believe in taking out insurance." There was an edge to her sudden smile. "Once I put my mind to something, I intend for it to happen."

"Intend all you want, the cops don't need me meddling in their case. They want me playing secretary."

Copenhagen nodded. "Yes, I've heard," she said. "No matter. I hired you to do the job and you will do the job."

Lola cocked her head. "You're paying me to set up appointments for the cops?"

"I'm paying you to help the police department break up a very real threat to my authority."

"I don't want this job."

Copenhagen shrugged again.

"There's no reneging with me. My intentions are more than wishes. They are reality."

"I don't want this job."

Copenhagen sighed. "Your stubbornness is forcing me to be blunt. This is simply beyond your control." She got up and strode to her desk. Opening a drawer, she withdrew an envelope. She watched Lola she closed the drawer and returned to the sofa. She threw the envelope onto the table at Lola's knees.

Lola waited a beat before picking up the package. She spilled its contents onto the table. The handwriting, forms and signatures were all familiar. She'd filed the original over five years ago and every year since then, she'd applied for renewal. It was the one thing Aubrey never had to remind her about: her investigator's license.

"You see?" asked Copenhagen sweetly, "Insurance is always a good idea."

Lola straightened out the forms and slid them back into the envelope.

"Don't worry," continued Copenhagen, "these are safe with me. Gods know we wouldn't want anything to happen to them."

Lola stood. "I'll be in touch."

"I'm counting on it." Copenhagen's smile was full of teeth.

The elevator announced its presence on the third floor with a cheerful clang. No operator at this hour of the evening. Just Lola and a woman wearing dark glasses and a scarf. She studiously turned her face away from Lola on the ride up, and Lola obliged by pretending not to recognize the Police Chief's sister. Lola trudged wearily to her office, listening to the clack of the woman's heels head toward the surgery at the other end of the floor. Plastic surgeons kept strange hours indeed.

Lola pushed into her waiting area. Aubrey inhaled sharply just as Lola saw a shadow come out from the corner. Swiftly, she knocked away the hand reaching to grab her and swept her left leg out, felling her attacker. A slender body toppled on to the low table and sent the ashtray crashing, the sound reverberating off the small room's walls.

"What the holy—!"

Lola froze in the act of stomping her assailant's leg into bits.

"Ria?"

"Turn on that damned light already," Ria grumbled, brushing glints of broken glass off her shirt. Lola complied, her hands shaking, her heart pounding still.

"Ria, for the love of—I almost obliterated your leg!" shouted Lola. "What're you thinking, sitting in the dark like that?"

Her friend scowled at her and reached up a hand. Lola pulled her up.

"I was taking a nap, genius. Do you know how long I waited at Arty's for you?" A large yawn broke into Ria's glower. "I'm tired and now, I've got a bum shoulder. Thanks to you."

Lola blew out a breath, thinking hard. "Listen, I'm sorry about Arty's. I, uh, ran into a roadblock and couldn't get free till now. I was coming in to call you," she finished quickly.

"Like I said, you're a terrible liar," replied Ria. Eyes narrowed, she pointed at Lola. "If this is you trying to 'spare me' the tawdry details of your life, I'm not buying it. We've been through this and through this. I don't need your protection. I'm just as big a girl as you."

Lola closed the door to the hall and led her friend into the office. "I can't get into the details, Ria. Simple as that. I can't have you nosing around this one. It'll cause more trouble than either one of us can handle. Just trust me on this."

Ria stopped, hands on her hips, in the middle of the office. "Just wait a damn minute. You came to me, remember? You got me involved in this. I was waiting at Arty's with information I dug up for you. For you. And what do I get? Stood up, nearly beaten to death, then lied to. By my best friend," she shouted.

Lola walked behind her desk. A quick pull on a drawer and out came two tumblers and a bottle of Canadian rye. Two fingers went into each glass. Lola tossed hers back, closing her eyes against the sting of sudden tears and the burn down her throat. She reached confidently for the bottle before her eyes were completely open again. She took another hit.

Ria eyed her angrily as Lola refilled her tumbler. "Rough night for our heroine?"

Lola shrugged, ignoring the sarcasm. "Same old, same old."

"Uh. Huh."

Lola sighed. "So, what do you want me to say? I'm not going to spill the beans on my case"

"How about an honest-to-gods apology?" yelled Ria.

Lola threw her hands up in concession. "I'm sorry already."

Ria's eyes widened. "What is so gods-damned hard about apologizing, Lola? You messed up. It happens to everyone. Just own up and say sorry. Don't make like it's my fault you have to be responsible for your mistakes." She glared. Lola stood, silent and unyielding. Ria's mouth tightened. "Aubrey, you'd better say something to her before I do something I'll regret."

Lola tensed, waiting for Aubrey to join in the lecture, but he remained silent. The sudden clang of the elevator bell broke the quiet.

Lola released the breath she'd been holding. She groped for the chair behind her and fell into it. "Can we at least sit down?"

Lola watched Ria weigh her decision. As Ria finally limped to the client's chair and sat, arms crossed, Lola felt the knot between her shoulders slowly unravel.

Lola took a deep breath. "Look, I'm sorry I forgot you were waiting at Arty's. Something came up with the second client. I couldn't avoid it. Things got hairy and I forgot to call."

Ria looked Lola over suspiciously. "Then why didn't you just say so? Why lie to me about that? I know you don't get chatty about your cases and clients, and I don't push."

Lola looked around her office. There was nothing to settle her gaze on except blank walls, dark windows and furniture. She met Ria's eyes and shrugged. "You're right. You've got me dead to rights. I'm sorry."

Ria held her gaze for several moments. Then she blew out her breath, hard. She took up the tumbler, drank off half of it. "You sure know how to show a girl a good time," she grumbled. "Fine, I accept your shameful excuse for an apology." She pointed. "You'd better remember this the next time you want to protect me from the rough stuff, girlie. I can blister your ears with the best of them." She took a cautious sip, then replaced the glass on Lola's desk with a thump. "Let's get this over with so I can go home and nurse my bad leg." Ria threw a glare at Lola before she sat back, pulling her lapels straight.

"Our girl Stoudamire. All right. She graduates from Rose Arbour Prep, same year as us She enters the Temple of Conjury immediately. Musta been one hell of an interview. Finishes four years and then kaput. Nothing. No Conjurer's robes, no thesis. Two years later, she pops up as Mrs. Teddy Marshall IV, thank you very much."

Lola placed her glass down impatiently. "I know all this, Ria. I want the skinny on those two missing years."

"Stop your grousin'," countered Ria. "I'm tellin' it my way. It's that or no way."

Lola kept her mouth shut.

"Good call," murmured Aubrey.

"So," continued Ria, "our intrepid Conjurer-that-wasn't disappears. No records of her working anywhere in the City, no address other than the ancestral home up behind the Beacon. No memberships in any of the usual socialite-in-training societies. Not even a whisper in any of the Women's Clubs. She literally does not exist for two years."

"You check the East Coast?"

An impatient nod. "Whaddya take me for—a rookie? Of course, I checked. I checked with all my people. Everywhere. Across the country. Overseas, east and west."

Lola rubbed at her temples, closed her eyes briefly. "So she was working at it. No one in her circles disappears like that without effort."

Ria nodded. "Now you're using that pretty little head."

Lola did not react. Ria grinned and took up her glass again. She grimaced after another sip, shook her head. "You keep pouring that into your engine and your liver'll give it up before you turn thirty."

"Pantywaist."

Ria shrugged and put her tumbler down with a definite thump. "So, where are you taking all this, Lola?" Her gaze was shrewd.

"Not sure. Can't see all the tiles yet." Lola stared at a darkened window. Then she shook herself and looked directly into Ria's eyes. "Thank you."

Ria nicked an Egyptian cigarette from the desk humidor and lit up, exhaling at Lola. "You owe me a meal."

"Anything for you, doll."

Ria kept her gaze on her friend's face for a long, silent while before she finally sighed, got up, and limped out of the office.

Lola's grin faded as soon as she heard the elevator bell clang. The hours pulled down on the corners of her mouth until she was left with a frown and a headache.

"You should take your own advice. Sleep will do you good," said Aubrey.

Lola replied with silence. She got up, locked up the office tight. She removed her jacket and folded it up into a square. It played pillow for her as she stretched out on the sofa and drifted off to the sounds of the occasional car passing by on the street.

TEN

The night was warm. Lola could see a bright spot high to the east, but it wavered and disappeared as she watched. She was thankful for the clouds that cloaked the moon tonight as she returned her attention to the Gaming Commission Building. The late hour guaranteed quiet. This part of the City was strictly for daytime workers who took their nighttime amusements far from here, under the glare of neon. Medium-sized Chinese elms threw out regularly spaced pools of shade from the streetlamps. Ten minutes of waiting had netted Lola zero passing cars. There had been no foot patrols on the outer perimeter of the Gaming Commission Building either. Aubrey assured her the strength of the building wards made human patrols redundant. In a strange stroke of luck, which Lola was disinclined to question, the parking lot across from the building's southeast corner had no wards at all, just a sturdy padlock that opened easily. Even the chain link gate pulled back silently, its wheels well-greased. Lola thanked whatever gods were watching for the City's fleet of government vehicles. Her sturdy old Buick looked clean enough in the night to pass for just another City car. She slumped a little farther in her seat. She knew there had to be a police car along sooner or later. She was betting on a twenty-minute rotation. Aubrey thought thirty.

Just shy of one hour later, Lola smiled in tired satisfaction. A prowl car was gliding away on Chang Boulevard It was the third pair of hollow-eyed cops so far. Lola checked her watch: three seventeen.

"Let's go," said Aubrey.

Lola counted ten beats before getting out. She closed her door quietly and crouched slightly, then stayed still. Another careful pause, another count to ten, then she resettled a dark duffle over one shoulder and ran down the length of parked cars, passed through the slim gap in the gate and over to the closest corner of the Gaming Commission Building. A line of elms ran down the length of the sidewalk. The one closest dipped down toward the concrete. Lola kept close to its trunk, searching with her eyes slit against the ambient light. Streetlights were sparsely strewn around the building. Conjurers preferred dark spaces around their work.

She knew there was an employee entrance on the north side of the building. It led to the employee parking lot, across an alley. It was arguably the cleanest alley in the entire city. The Spells set out by the Conjurers repelled the usual regiment of alley rats and feral felines. Lola judged it the likeliest place for her purposes. She stayed close to the line of elms as she jogged down the sidewalk toward the back of the building. At the corner, she surveyed the street and the alley. As rumoured, it was indeed hard to tell which was cleaner. She kept her ears and eyes alert as she walked straight down the alley, keeping to the right side, close to the employee parking lot fence.

"These wards are strong but they're not seamless," murmured Aubrey. "All I need is the smallest sliver of space between wards. I can pry it open enough for us to slip inside. The door is up to you."

Lola waited next to a chain link fence ringing the employee lot. It wasn't what she'd call cover, but it was a convenient handhold if she needed to lean over suddenly, pretending drunken illness. Why she would even be there at this time of night would be harder to explain, but she knew there was one dancing club four blocks over. It was a stretch but she knew she could sell it. She'd have to. For now, she waited, eyes alternately checking the alley and her watch.

At three twenty-eight, Aubrey called out success. "I'm six feet to the left of the door. Come forward until your nose touches the wall. That's it. Don't move."

"Now what?" Lola whispered.

"Hush." A slow minute passed. "I'm resetting the Wards to include our presence."

Lola gritted her teeth. She couldn't feel any difference. She didn't hear any differently. Most troubling of all, she couldn't see anything with her nose up against the wall. She wondered for the millionth time if she should even be trusting the Ghost of an actress's dresser to deal with Warding. As far she knew, Aubrey had never come within a European mile of learning about Spells. She couldn't be absolutely sure he hadn't, though, and he was the only way she'd be getting inside this building tonight. Aubrey, naturally, refused to elaborate beyond saying "Trust me." The more she thought about it, the worse she felt until she was ready to call the entire thing off. Finally, Aubrey ordered her to start working to pick the lock. They slipped inside after a few seconds and Lola closed the door with a firm hand. The lighting was dim. Aubrey breathed an audible sigh of relief.

"That's it?" asked Lola. "You're sure you secured the Wards?"

"Yes. I said you could count on me."

Lola shrugged, loosening her shoulders and rolling her neck. She scanned the corridor.

"Nothing," said Aubrey.

"Or the stairs?" asked Lola, looking toward the steps to her right. She moved swiftly toward them, listening intently.

"Nor the elevator," replied Aubrey. "Perhaps they concentrated everything on the outer walls."

"They must Ward individual offices."

Aubrey agreed. "No time for dawdling. There's got to be foot patrol inside."

Lola was betting that security used the elevators for their rounds. She turned to the stairwell and started upward. She told Aubrey to stay alert for Wards and trapping Spells. She would listen for footsteps.

Eight floors and three near misses later, Lola stepped into a darkened corridor. She pushed the door closed behind her softly and stood motionless, listening. No echoing footfalls from within the stairwell. Lola walked quickly down the hall, came to a corner, and paused. She kneeled before slowly peeking around. When no one came barrelling down the corridor, shouting at her, she stood and stepped forward in one continuous motion. Then she ran lightly onward until she faced a gilt door without a nameplate.

Eying the long corridor, Lola urged Aubrey to hurry.

"Quiet," he replied.

Lola ran back down to the turn in the hallway. Still no sign of security. She made her way to the bank of elevators. Pressing her ear against the cold metal of the doors, she heard a distinct whirring. She had no way to tell the direction.

"The elevator's moving," she said. "I need in."

"I'm done," replied Aubrey. "The entry Ward's open. Close the door and stay still. I have to patch it up."

The space within was darker than the hallway. When her eyes had adjusted, Lola stepped toward the inner office. In the distance, the elevator bell sounded. "Aubrey," she whispered urgently.

"Shush," the Ghost replied. "I need to be thorough. If I'm not and he has a Ghost, it'll spot the patch job immediately."

Lola bit down on her lip. She thought she heard the creak of shoe leather approaching. It was accompanied by low whistling, something jazzy and upbeat. Lola realized with a small smile that steps and whistle were in time. Apparently, this was one security guard who didn't mind the night shift. They waited until the guard passed and the elevator bell sounded once more. Three forty-eight. Lola told Aubrey to check the rooms, while she silently counted to twenty and listened for noise in the hall.

Finally satisfied, she turned her attention to the inner room. Its door stood open. Lola startled at the voice at her shoulder.

"I don't see any Wards in the room itself. Not even on this inner door."

Lola nodded and looked around the room once more.

Although the office was large, there wasn't much in the way of furniture. Just the massive desk and its attendant chair, the two visitors seats, a lone round table for four, and the sofa arrangement. Much of the room's centre was clear of obstacles. Lola went to the desk and sat gingerly. The windows behind the desk were covered by blinds.

For all of her outward elegance, the Assistant Deputy Commissioner kept a very messy work area. A blotter sat crookedly on the desk, surrounded by a few short stacks of paper. A black telephone stood to the left. Next to it were a pen and inkwell, as well as a canister filled with pencils bristling upward like quills. Lola took her pocket torch out from the duffel and clicked it on. She rifled through the paperwork. Memoranda and letters, invoices and accounting reports. It was a dull job indeed, if these were the sole testaments.

Lola replaced the stacks carefully and sat back, considering the drawers. Blank letterhead, business cards, unused notebooks and ruled pads filled the top right drawer. The one beneath it was empty. The left set of drawers was a false front of three for a single compartment. Inside was a sizable stash of candies, cigarettes, breath mints and European chocolates. Lola unwrapped a Scottish toffee and popped it into her mouth. She pocketed the wrapper.

Placing her light carefully on the top of the desk, she returned her attention to the lower empty drawer on the right. She flicked open her pocket knife and slid the edge along the sides of the drawer bottom. The knife caught on a spring-loaded latch. The bottom panel popped up just enough for Lola to place two fingers underneath. Lola reached for her light, but her eye was caught by a strange abstraction on AJ's blotter. It was illuminated in the short beam of the flash. Circles within circles. Squares and rectangles as frames. Wings even. Lola squinted to pick out more details. There was something there that had caught her attention. She just needed to see it. There. Underneath the squiggles and lines and curves, she made out a word. It was a name. A name she knew.

She sat back for a moment, considering.

"The files, Lola. Get into the files," said Aubrey.

Lola quickly flicked her light into the secret compartment. It was as empty as the rest of the drawer. She swiveled in the chair to face the filing cabinet. It was low, only four drawers high. She tried them all. Locked.

"You sure they're clean?" Lola whispered.

"Yes. I told you I didn't see any Wards in here," he replied.

Lola worked her picks for a few seconds. The drawers all opened smoothly and silently.

The hairs on Lola's neck prickled. "What now?" she asked, rubbing her neck. She glanced back at the darkened doorway to the office.

"Sorry, I felt a sudden chill."

"I thought you didn't feel changes in temperature," she said.

"I don't. I'm not sure—"

Lola didn't wait for any more. She scanned the open drawers. To her surprise, everything was neatly labeled and organized. Files on gambling establishments. Licenses and license requests. Files of wealthy Crescent City citizens. Her mother was there, as were a number of other popular film stars and studio owners. There was nothing on the name she'd recognized earlier, but she did find a file on herself, a thick one. Lola pulled it out and flipped through it. She saw an old photograph, the only one she and Martin had released to the papers. It was from their honeymoon,

Aubrey spoke urgently into her ear. "Go, Lola, now. I think … a broken Ward—"

"You're supposed to warn me *before* that happens," Lola muttered. She hefted her file and closed the cabinet drawers. It locked audibly. She pulled the shoulder duffel off. In went the file. She pulled it back over her head and strung it across her chest. She strode rapidly to the door, head turned over her shoulder to scan the dark room a final time.

"Lola!" Aubrey called out.

She felt a faint movement of air by her ear. Lola turned her head. Too late. Pain exploded behind her eyes. She tasted blood and crumpled to the floor.

ELEVEN

Aubrey called her back from the depths, his voice urgent and worried.

"Lola. Lola, wake up"

"Why are you whispering?" she groaned.

"Can you sit up?"

Lola didn't know she'd tried until she awoke again. Her head was hammering out a jig. Her eyeballs felt gritty and swollen. She raised a wobbly hand to the back of her head. There was a knot the size of a small rock. She gingerly felt around inside her mouth. She remembered blood and felt a slight gash on the side of her swollen tongue. At least her teeth were intact.

She sat up slowly, stopping whenever the pounding threatened to overwhelm her. Clenching her teeth against a wave of nausea, Lola looked around the room. The lighting was low, as though set for an intimate gathering. She was on a *chaise-longue*, upholstered in turquoise floral. An enormous arrangement of flowers in a Chinese vase towered above her from its perch on a marble table behind the chaise. The walls were paneled in bookshelves. A set of solid double doors stood closed in the centre of one wall. Opposite them were glass-paned French doors.

Aubrey encouraged her to get up. "The room's Warded. I can't even see outside the walls."

Lola stood with infinite care. It didn't kill her, although she wished it had by the time she was upright. The cut on her tongue throbbed in time to her headache. She stumbled over to the double doors facing her, grabbing furniture for support. The ornate handle eluded her twice before she could squint enough to determine its true location. She rattled it: locked. She slapped a hand weakly against the heavy oak, then turned to lean her back against it. The room threatened to spin away from her. She concentrated on breathing deeply, her hands curled into white-knuckled fists.

A beam of moonlight lanced through the French doors. Lola shuffled toward it. She leaned her forehead against the cool glass, closing her eyes for a moment against the renewed nausea. When she felt strong enough, she looked out on a well-manicured garden in the European wildflower tradition. Magnolia trees stood with their pearly white blossoms glowing in the moonlight. The dark expanse beyond the flowers sloped away into the night. Lola glimpsed a tall hedge in the distance, black in the silver light.

A sharp gasp from Aubrey overrode her better judgment and Lola whirled her head up. Bright spots filled her field of vision. She could see someone coming through the oak doors, but the face was obscured.

"Lola," said the Assistant Deputy Commissioner of Gaming courteously. "I hope you're feeling better. Can I get you a drink?"

Lola abandoned any pretense of pride. She reached out blindly. The back of her hand connected with a hard table edge. The sharp sting momentarily overcame the spinning pain in her head. The dancing spots in her eyes receded as well. She carefully walked back to the *chaise*.

"Don't you sleep?" she asked wearily.

"As a matter of fact, rarely. I don't seem to need it like I used to." Copenhagen was fully dressed, as though for the office. She even held a slim file in her manicured hands. Her expression matched her amused tone.

"Must get dull after a while," Lola said.

"Oh I don't know about that. Sometimes I get visitors at unexpected hours. Helps to pass the time." She threw the file on to a side table and disappeared behind the massive vase with its floral head. There was some clinking of crystal.

"I'll take mine neat." Lola carefully touched her head, wincing.

Copenhagen reappeared with amber salvation in a cut crystal tumbler. She handed the fragrant whiskey to Lola. "You should be more careful when you break into people's offices. You could have been seriously hurt. My assistants can be heavy-handed." She cocked her head. "Although I must admit to some disappointment in Aubrey's skills. That particular cabinet Ward was hardly the most subtle in my arsenal." She sat down in an ornate armchair, relaxed and elegant. "Don't misunderstand me, Aubrey, that was quite a feat, breaking through the building Wards." She looked around. "Our hired Conjurers are powerful and expensive. Until tonight, we thought they were worth the cost." Copenhagen returned her gaze to Lola. "Not suddenly shy, is he?"

Lola shrugged, then winced at the sudden movement. "He keeps his own counsel. I can't force him to talk."

Copenhagen smiled in amusement. "As you wish." Her smile gained an edge. "I'm surprised at you, Lola. The great private investigator, unwilling to solve the mystery closest to herself."

Lola stared at Copenhagen.

"Ah yes, back to our business together then." Copenhagen pointed to the file. "If you wanted to see that, you could have asked. It would have saved you the trouble, not to mention the concussion."

Lola recalled the tumbler in her hand. She breathed in the heady fumes, then tossed it down her throat. As the whiskey burned a trail to her stomach, Lola watched the other woman with narrowed eyes.

Copenhagen smiled. "Go ahead. Read it. I've got nothing to hide. It's my job to know who gambles in Crescent City and where they do it. You're in the upper echelon, Lola. There's no need for false modesty."

Lola reached out her hand. The other woman rose to oblige, handing Lola the file.

The photograph was the same: Lola and Martin in elegant evening attire, surrounded by the lights of a sultry night on the coast of Southeastern Europe. Lola noted, with a faint trace of wistfulness, how young they both looked. The rest of the file contained a dozen sheets now, all neatly typed. Lola flipped to the back. The photographer's stamp was dark against the whiteness. Clearly, Lola thought, Martin needed to vet his photographers more closely. She wondered how much the woman got paid to print and sell clients' personal photographs to third parties. Sighing inwardly, Lola put the photograph aside and noted the date on the file. "It starts on my twenty-first birthday."

"An infamous day in your gambling history, no? Ten thousand dollars in one round of mah-jongg. Poof, just like that?" Copenhagen chuckled. "I inherited some of the information from my predecessor. There's nothing in there you don't already know." She showed her teeth in a grin. "It's not as though you live below the radar."

Lola flipped the file closed and tossed it down next to her on the *chaise*. "How about another?" she asked, holding up her tumbler.

Copenhagen obliged silently. She stayed standing, however, as Lola drank the second whiskey in one swallow.

"You wouldn't happen to have my cigarettes handy?" Lola asked.

"But of course," replied the other woman, "you can collect them on your way out. I've called a car for you."

"Just like that?"

Copenhagen nodded. "It's been a long day, hasn't it? I'm sure you're ready for bed. You really should rest that concussion."

Lola made no move to rise. She studied the crystal glass in her hands, turning it one way and then the other. Its facets sparkled and rearranged themselves. She put it down.

Copenhagen turned her attention to the room at large. "Aubrey? Surely you know, Aubrey, that breaking and entering is grounds for revoking her license."

Lola noted Aubrey's silence. She said, "Hard to prove I was ever there, unless you want to advertise your thugs' handiwork."

"You know as well as I, Lola," replied the other woman, "this City doesn't run on truth."

"I don't scare that easily." It was Lola's turn to grin. It hurt but she could ignore the pain.

"I'm not trying to scare you, Lola. I'm simply being honest." Copenhagen walked to the oak doors. "I see no need to involve the police. Let's chalk tonight up to youthful exuberance, shall we?" She drew open the doors and stepped to one side. Standing two abreast in the doorway, Thick and Thin sneered at Lola. Copenhagen gestured, "Shall my assistants help you out?"

Lola thought of the doodle she'd seen on Copenhagen's blotter. She thought of throwing out Arbogast's name to see a reaction. Instead, she gritted her teeth and stood on her own. She stalked out of the room. As she passed, Copenhagen laid a pale hand on her arm. "If I were you, I'd remind Aubrey that there are severe penalties for

Ghosts breaking government Wards, Lola." She squeezed, hard. "The stakes are higher than you comprehend. Don't try to cross me again. You shall fail and I shall be less forgiving."

Lola stood stonily, waiting until the woman released her. She walked stiffly down the corridor and into a large circular foyer. A double stairway climbed the walls, but there was no time to gawk. Thick and Thin marched Lola straight out the front doors and down the flagstone walk. By the time she reached the taxi at the curb, her jaw was aching from tension. Thin held open the cab door with a smirk. Lola climbed inside. A meaty hand held out her shoulder duffel. She stared at it, then grabbed it gracelessly, throwing it on the seat beside her. A final snicker and the door slammed shut. Lola snarled an address to the cabbie. The silent man drove her downtown where she retrieved her car.

Back in her apartment, she heaved the duffel at the foyer closet and stalked into her rooms. Through the undrawn drapes, she could see the first sliver of sunrise lighting the ocean surface. Most of the City was still in shadow, hidden from the rays by the foothills behind her. In the bathroom, she spilled out a couple of aspirin and filled a glass with cold tap water. She kept her eyes closed as she drank down the medicine.

In her bedroom, she sat down, unclenching her jaw with some effort, to make a call.

St. John answered on the second ring.

"You're up early," Lola said.

"You're up late," he replied.

"I just want to make sure Mother did as I suggested."

"We're leaving for Europe in two days."

"Today would be better."

"Not according to Grace it isn't. She's made promises."

Lola grunted.

The silence was thick on the other end. Finally, St. John asked: "Do you want to leave her a message from you?" At Lola's silence, he said: "I'll let her know you called."

"Just take care of her, St. John."

"Get some rest, Lola. You sound like you need it."

"My guardian angel."

Lola rang off and dragged herself to the bed. She managed to kick off her shoes and climb beneath the covers. She thought she heard Aubrey but it was too much effort to listen. Instead, she welcomed the comfort of blackness as it wrapped itself around her battered body.

TWELVE

Lola bolted upright, then clutched her head. Turning bleary eyes to the clock, she realized she'd been asleep fewer than six hours. The telephone was ringing. She wrapped the top sheet around herself and stumbled to answer.

"Lola! Lola, thank the gods, I've been trying you for over an hour."

Lola's stomach plummeted. "No need for dramatics, Mother. Didn't Elaine tell you I was sleeping?"

"Darling, you sound terrible." Lola heard a long inhalation. She imagined the lit cigarette in its black lacquered holder. "Well, that makes you the pot to my kettle. I daresay you're the melodramatic one, leaving cryptic messages about threats and danger."

"Mother, why are you calling?"

"How is Aubrey, dear?"

"He's dead and Haunting me. Your guess is as good as mine, Mother."

"No need to be rude, Lola. I'm worried about you. St. John said you'd called a number of times. I don't see how any of *your* work would impinge upon me, but now it does somehow. Care to elaborate?"

"Mother, you know I can't get into details. It would—"

"Don't patronize me. I know perfectly well about confidentiality and professionalism. I didn't ask, by the way. I just wanted to speak to you myself." Lola could hear the cigarette tip, burning to ashes.

"Well, now you have. Satisfied?"

"Hardly, dear. But I don't suppose that's your job. No, what I want from you, my obstinate child, is an explanation. What is going on?"

"Mother," Lola said, "I can't explain any more than I have—"

"But you've said nothing!"

Lola continued without pause: "I told St. John the best thing is for you to leave for Europe today."

"Simply impossible, darling. It's impossible for me to cancel, even if I wanted to."

"And, of course, you don't want to."

"Please," she sighed, "It's complicated. This is a long-standing commitment. I have no choice in the matter."

"That's rich." Lola laughed humourlessly. "It appears, once again, Mother, that we are at an impasse. Shall we agree to disagree, just to keep things familiar?"

"Please darling. Don't be a hard case." Lola sat, silent. Her mother went on. "I know I can't appeal to your regard for *me*, so I am appealing to your regard for poor St. John. If you don't tell him, he'll have a devil of a time doing his job."

"I suspect that's been his job description ever since he started."

"Oh you are incorrigible. And selfish."

"Now who's the pot?"

"Dammit, Lola. You may delight in tormenting me with rudeness and disrespect, but the fact remains. We're family. I deserve more from you than this, this relentless cruelty."

"Mother, I haven't given you half what you deserve."

A heavy silence, then quietly: "Your father raised you better than this."

"You have no idea how he raised me. You have no idea," Lola repeated, her jaw clenched. She realized her hands were fisted. She carefully relaxed them and took a steadying breath. Her head was pounding. It beat at her reserves until she slumped in the chair.

As if sensing the change, her mother spoke. "This is getting us nowhere we haven't already been. Too many times, in fact," she trailed off for a moment, then, "Let's let sleeping dogs lie, shall we?"

"It's worked in the past," Lola replied. "Goodbye, Mother."

"The world isn't the dark place you make it out, Lola. You don't have to go it alone, darling."

"Your days as a naif are long past, Mother. Goodbye."

Lola rested her head in her stiff hands.

Aubrey spoke into the silence. "She's right, you know."

"Leave me alone, curse you."

"Your father—"

"Shut your mouth." Lola flung the cover sheet away. "Keep your damned mouth shut, haunt. You disgust me, you and the old whore. Neither of you even deserves to say his name."

"That's a damn fine way to make your father proud, Lola. I'm sorely disappointed in you."

"So long as you do it somewhere else, I don't give a good godsdamn what you are."

Lola stalked into her bath and slammed the door. Thirty minutes later, she stalked into the kitchen and poured herself a cup of steaming coffee. Elaine was already seated at the dining table, reading the *Herald*'s morning edition. She gestured toward the covered plate as Lola sat down, breathing shallowly.

"Eggs and toast. And a package came for you, early." She narrowed her eyes over the top of her paper.

"Package?" Lola sipped and immediately cursed as the coffee scalded her tongue. She put the mug down, muttering.

"Mr. Wang said it was a messenger, a Chinese boy with freckles." Elaine continued to stare. "Are you all right?"

Lola sat for a moment, willing the nausea to subside. She picked up a fork, uncovered her plate and started to eat, slowly. "Where is it?"

"I left it on your secretary. It can wait until you've eaten," Elaine admonished, as Lola's eyes wandered toward the maple desk.

Lola braced herself and got up. Spots danced in her vision as she made suspect progress toward the far corner of the apartment. "I've got a busy day. Might as well look at it as look at the news while I'm eating."

"Dear gods, Lola, let me," scolded Elaine. Her hands reached out to steady Lola, who was swaying where she stood.

"You really ought to stop sneaking up on me, Elaine."

The other woman clucked her tongue: "*Sawh ga lei.* Don't be a meathead."

"I like it better when you call me 'Miss Lola.'" Lola grinned.

"Here." Elaine steered Lola to a sofa patterned with dark stripes. Lola squinted in the glare from the windows. Elaine pointed a finger at her. "Don't get up." She drew the draperies.

"Pass me that package, would you? Feels a shame not to have something for my troubles."

Elaine retrieved a large yellow envelope and a silver letter opener from the maple bureau. She held out both to Lola then sat at the far end of the sofa.

"There's no return address, but I can tell you right now it's from the Gaming Commission. Same feeling as their Wards."

Lola noted Aubrey's tone of interest.

She hesitated with the letter opener. "Is it from Copenhagen?"

Aubrey took a moment before answering. "I can't tell. Perhaps. There *is* more than just the one—scent." A pause. "I can't pinpoint them all."

"Can you tie any of it to your memory of her office? Her mansion?" Lola spoke while staring at the envelope.

Elaine was clearly interested as she watched Lola talk to the invisible Ghost. Lola shooed her away, but Elaine merely grimaced at her.

Aubrey replied after another short pause. "There. Yes. It's her."

"Perhaps something more to rub in my face," murmured Lola, slitting the envelope along one end. She tipped out the contents. A leather-bound ledger and a smaller envelope tumbled out into her lap. She reached for the sealed envelope, wondering if it contained an explanation. Instead, another sheaf of papers and a now tediously familiar photograph of the newly wed Mr. and Mrs. Martin Lee III.

"That photo seems to get around," said Aubrey.

"Handsome couple like that, why not," replied Lola absently. She riffled through the papers.

"Ah, the mysterious missing pages from your file," deduced Aubrey. "Why has she changed her mind?"

Lola was onto the ledger now. It was an accounts book. Neat blue script inked out names, dates and amounts. Lola flipped quickly to the end, then returned to the first page.

Elaine stood. "I have the feeling I'm better off not knowing."

"Now you say that?" Lola retorted.

Elaine raised an eyebrow. "Oh, are you feeling exasperated with me?" She stood.

"Have a care you don't run yourself ragged today, boss-lady." She brought over coffee and began clearing the breakfast table.

Lola's attention flared back to the ledger in her hands. She read each page carefully, trying to calculate and collate in her mind. Aubrey remained silent. She presumed he was reading and thinking on his own. The clatter of dishes and the sound of running taps formed their accompaniment.

Finally, Lola looked up, her eyes distant. After a moment, she stood and went to the windows. She impatiently pulled aside the drapes and stared through narrowed eyes at the sprawling view below her.

"What's she playing at? Why take the pages out only to send them to me? And with this ledger?" muttered Lola.

"Perhaps she's being manipulated against her will?" said Aubrey. "She's sending these pages to prove good faith? After all, that ledger's pretty damning. She wants you to trust her so you'll know it's real."

"Does she?" Lola shook her head. "I don't buy it. She's playing some hand I can't even begin to see," Lola murmured. She turned around and stared at the neat little black accounts book. "I know it's real. I saw him, didn't I? I saw him..." Lola trailed off.

"What are you thinking?" asked Aubrey.

Lola was silent a beat longer. "I think we owe Mr. Arbogast that update.

THIRTEEN

She stopped in the lobby to speak to Mr. Wang. The grey-haired man unfolded himself from behind the reception desk, patting his *China Times* smooth on the desk. He offered a small, polite smile from his lofty height. Having learned from long experience, Lola halted just far enough away to avoid having to crane her head back to look into Mr. Wang's face as they spoke.

"Just wondering about the messenger this morning, Mr. Wang."

"Yes? A child in his twenties. He stopped long enough to collect my signature and tip his hat."

"Nothing about the sender?"

Mr. Wang shook his head sadly. "The boy was minimally civil." He stepped back to his desk and picked up a card. He handed it to Lola with a tiny bow of his head. "Perhaps this might help you."

Pattison Messengers Limited.
Cordial service. Competitive Rates.
Hastings 4397

"No address. Hastings ... don't know it," she murmured.

"No." Mr. Wang smoothed a sleeve of his navy silk *miehn-lahp*. The subtle pattern of Chinese symbols flashed quickly, then disappeared against its dark background. "The boy's name tag said *Lyle*."

Lola thanked the tall, gaunt man and asked to use the office telephone. Mr. Wang nodded and led her to the administrative office just to the right of the lobby. A door, patterned to match the wall, stood at the far end of the elevators. Mr. Wang used a key to unlock it. He stood aside to allow Lola to pass by. It wasn't much larger than the alcove at Lucky Bamboo, she thought, although the furnishings were of higher quality.

Mr. Wang said, "Simply close the door firmly when you exit. It shall lock with an audible sound." He bowed slightly again and left.

Lola dialed the messenger's office and asked to speak with Lyle. A young-sounding girl replied in a dull voice that he was on a delivery. She asked for particulars on Lola's package and its destination; she would see if she could slot it in on Lyle's schedule. Lola explained her purpose in calling. The girl's voice cooled but she obliged. After a few moments of dead air, she returned to the telephone to inform Lola that there had been no pick-up for the package. Someone had dropped it off at the office for delivery, a rarity, true, but not interesting enough for the girl to give a description. Lola pressed the angles, but the girl had nothing to give. She sat for a minute after ringing off.

"Seems a lot of trouble to hide her tracks when I sniffed her out so easily," said Aubrey.

Lola considered a moment longer, then stood up abruptly and readjusted her hat. She left the office as instructed by Mr. Wang and caught a lift down to the parking area. In the elevator, Aubrey chatted with Frederick's wife. Lola remained silent save for the required polite responses to Frederick's inquiries after her health. It seemed that intense thinking was enough to push away both nausea and headache. Lola was feeling better by the time Aubrey bid the other Ghost good day.

"It's not a good idea to go downtown," said Aubrey.

"For once, I agree," replied Lola. "We're going south."

Lola arrived at Grove Avenue and turned eastward. It was a busy thoroughfare, connecting much of the eastern outskirts with the central core of Crescent City. Lola was content to stay steadily in her lane. When they reached Orchard Boulevard fifteen minutes later, she made good on her announcement and continued south.

"Where did you say Arbogast lives?"

"I didn't," said Lola. After a minute or so, she relented. "The old Southern orange groves." Aubrey gave a slight grunt, then subsided. Lola was glad of the silence to collect her thoughts.

She saw the ledger once more in her mind, its neat script unable to hide the darkness of its contents. The names of over two dozen mah-jongg parlours. The money each parlour paid to avoid "bad luck." Collection dates. Late payments. Curt descriptions of how the extortionists dealt with them: "Sent Chong". Expensive joints, tourist traps, middling establishments, even dives. They were all there in the ledger: La Grenouille, Ivory Tiles, Lucky Bamboo, Water Lily, and Silver Temple. She didn't think it was coincidence she'd followed Arbogast to the very five places that had been on page one of the ledger. Bodewell Arbogast was a bagman for this extortion ring and AJ Copenhagen wanted Lola to know it. The mystery was in why.

Southern Fruit Company Limited was the third largest citrus fruit grower on the coast a hundred years prior. It had made enough to keep the Southern family moderately wealthy and to buy up over a thousand acres of adequate land on the plains east of the City. No hint of an ocean breeze touched the fruit orchards on Southern land, but the company logo of citrus tree and sea wave would argue otherwise.

Unlike many of its contemporaries, the company had built decent homes for its workers. Landscaped parks dotted the communities that grew up around the homes. Ordered streets, shiny new schools and suitably welcoming temples let Southern's employees know that they were valued. It was an attitude far ahead of its time and thus, destined for failure. A late freeze and then tree rot led eventually to the family-owned operation's demise. Bankruptcy allowed the creditors to sidle in and sell the thousand acres to a rival. That rival in turn sold the land, instead of using it, to a developer. Two years after the original bankruptcy papers were officially filed, many of Southern's former employees were able to own the homes they'd been living in. Southern had been so good to them, the steep prices were no deterrent. The groves of orange, lemon and grapefruit trees had never recovered. They were torn out and the land redesigned to accommodate more families and more housing. Twenty-five years later, the valley was carpeted by row upon row of terracotta-tiled houses. Serene seated Buddhas heralded the many temples dotting the area. The lone Christian church among the old homes testified to the Southern family's progressive ways. The large white cross still stood proudly atop the church's bell tower. The tall bell towers of the two original schools provided visual accompaniment.

The smell of lemons filled the air. Plump little yellow fruit adorned the branches of trees lining the main roadway into Arbogast's community, Southern Plains. Lola drove past the lemon trees. Her destination was far from the entrance gates. It was a medium-sized Craftsman bungalow with a front lawn the size of a postage stamp, complete with scalloped edges. The walk was bordered with bright pansies. Beds of tulips sat below windows. To the right, a Japanese maple hung its gnarled branches of delicate red leaves. Steps led up to the porch, which continued around the left of the house.

Lola killed the engine and got out. The day was bright and warm. She looked up and down the street. Tidy houses, almost identical to the one in front of her, lined the quiet lane. It was almost noon. Odds were children might begin appearing once the lunch bell rang, eager to get in, eat and get back out into the warm spring day.

As soon as she stepped onto the porch, Lola had a hunch she was facing an empty house. She raised the antique knocker and listened to its heavy thud echo within. No answering footfall. She glanced back at the street before slowly following the curve of the porch. The boards creaked slightly. Windows were shuttered and the rear door was locked. The back yard was no larger than the front. A detached garage house took up a third of the property space. Colourful flowers and an apple tree dominated the rest of the yard. Lola stepped down onto a pebbled walk and completed a circuit around the house.

Back in front, she climbed the steps and sat down in a wicker chair, facing the street. An intricately finished, wrought-iron mailbox stood just right of the front steps. Lola reached within and extracted a stack of envelopes. Personal correspondence, an electric company bill, something from the Gaming Commission. She returned everything but this last.

"Not in broad daylight, on the man's porch, for gods' sake, Lola."

Lola ignored Aubrey's anxiety. She took note of the stamped address for sender. "This isn't the downtown address." Lola felt the contents with sensitive fingers. "Just a single sheet, I think." She eyed the quiet street with interest, then pocketed the letter. Aubrey gave no indication of his apoplexy, but Lola grinned, imagining it. She pushed off the chair and was down the steps in a flash.

The building did not compare to its sister downtown. It sat square and unremarkable, a two-storey brick office building. There were no plaques pronouncing its affiliation to the beauty downtown. There were steps leading up from the sidewalk. The secondary offices of the Gaming Commission occupied a quiet corner of a moderately busy commercial area. On the same block, Lola noted a bookseller, a florist, a diner, a drugstore. It wasn't much different from her own office block. She eyed the building again.

"I recognize the Warding," confirmed Aubrey.

"So they use the same Conjurers," countered Lola, shrugging.

"I doubt the City Conjurers hire themselves out on evenings and weekends," replied Aubrey. "This is clearly another City office building."

Lola grunted.

The building was just as nondescript inside as out. A rectangular lobby with a bank of two elevators. An open stairway to the left. A security guard sitting behind a small desk, his shoe leathers creaking as he shifted his weight. He looked at Lola with dark eyes as she crossed in front and approached the directory board to the right of the elevators. She read, *Accounts I, Accounts II, Accounts III,* and so on. The entire building was dedicated to number crunching. Lola turned back to the guard.

"Bodewell Arbogast, which floor?"

His thick lips barely moved: "Have an appointment?"

Lola eyed him up and down. "You don't look like his secretary."

"I'm a man of many talents," he deadpanned, standing. Lola braced herself. The guard stepped around her, but close enough that she might have taken a step back. He grinned and motioned for her to follow, calling over his shoulder: "I'm taking a visitor up, Charlie." Lola noticed an irregularly shaped alcove tucked away behind the desk. It had appeared as a corner to be walked around. The top half of a split-door stood open. A man suddenly appeared in the open space. He glanced at Lola, then nodded curtly, stepping out from the guard station to man the desk.

Lola was led up the stairs, suddenly crowded with men in suits holding briefcases, to the second floor.

"Let me guess: Accounts," said Lola.

"You're smarter than you look, angel."

"That's quite a line from a bunny like you."

"I collect 'em." He walked down a hall lined on both sides with doors. Every one had a large pane of opaque glass in it, but no lettering. Lola's heels clicked in counterpoint to the guard's creaking shoes. He stopped midway down and opened a door with a sarcastic flourish. Lola preceded him within. A single desk sat across from the entrance. Chairs backed against two walls, all empty. A few potted plants dotted the corners, accompanied by cigar stands. Another door led deeper into the warren, closed for the moment against intruders like Lola.

A marcel-waved Chinese girl with deep pink lipstick and a perky nose looked up from her typewriter. A squawk box sat at her right, angled rakishly on her blotter. She gave Lola a speculative narrowing of the eyes before nodding at the guard. Lola heard his steps squelching away down the hall.

"Bodewell Arbogast?"

"Your appointment?" the girl answered in a high voice. She poised a pen above a schedule book, waiting with a skeptical air.

"Is this his stoop?"

The girl smiled with that perfect blend of civility and contempt perfected by the best civil servants. "May I ask your name, miss? So I can search for your appointment?" The pen remained poised.

The squawk box did its thing. The girl reached over and flipped a switch, answering. Lola couldn't make out anything intelligible over the intercom. The girl, however, answered in the affirmative and flipped the switch off. The pen dropped from its unnatural perch and the girl sat back. She took out a cigarette case and did her routine with it. Lola stared at the other door, waiting.

"She's gone," the girl said, indicating the inner office. "The boss lady."

"*Your* boss-lady?" asked Lola. The girl nodded, exhaled a grey cloud. "Back hall?" At another nod, Lola looked impressed. "Why this *is* a regular warren, isn't it." Lola grabbed a chair from the wall and pulled it over.

The girl watched her impassively. "I know you. I've seen you at The Supper Club."

Lola introduced herself, handing over her card. The girl nodded in acknowledgement and replied: "Pfeiffer." At Lola's raised eyebrows, she said, "Just 'Pfeiffer' will do." A long exhalation of smoke. "So you're looking for Bodewell. Business or pleasure?"

"'Fraid I can't say."

Pfeiffer looked amused. "I get that a lot here."

"This *is* a Gambling Commission office?"

"The whole damn building. Didn't you read the directory?"

"Mr. Arbogast is an accountant here?"

Pfeiffer said nothing for a moment, then asked, "You said 'business'?"

Lola raised an eyebrow.

Pfeiffer shrugged. "Worth a try." Another long drag on the cigarette. "I suppose he is, when all's said and done."

"Is he here now?"

"Depends." But Pfeiffer shook her head when Lola made to count out a couple of bills. "The Spring Gala's next month. The Supper Club," she explained at Lola's expression. "I want four tickets."

"So now I'm your social planner. What kind of frail do you take me for?"

"That kind of smart won't get you your answers." Pfeiffer drew in a large lungful of sweet smoke, then exhaled in a long tendril.

Lola laughed out loud. "Gimme your card and I'll have them sent."

Their transaction completed, Pfeiffer stubbed out her cigarette with deliberate thoroughness and lit another with an ivory-inlaid lighter she pulled from a drawer.

"Your man isn't like the other bean counters. He runs errands."

"For the Assistant Deputy Commissioner." Lola made it a statement.

Pfeiffer nodded, "And the Deputy. They split him." A grin. "He comes and goes all day long."

"And now?"

"Up in his cubbyhole. On four."

"You his secretary too?"

Pfeiffer shook her gleaming head. "Naw. I just keep my ears and eyes open. Reggie's my cousin. He sends me the troublemakers."

It took Lola a moment, but she pieced it together. "You mean the bunny with squeaky shoes."

Pfeiffer laughed as she nodded. "Sometimes, the troublemakers are interested in an exchange of goods or services. Reggie and I can take care of pretty much anything that comes up."

"Who's that then?" Lola tipped her head toward the inner office.

"Ms. Jayne Tsing. She makes sure no one gets their orders mixed up." Lola didn't respond. Pfeiffer explained: "Communications Manager."

"Who calls?"

"Downtown." As if that explained everything.

Lola nodded. "How do I get up to his office?"

"Take the stairs. Elevators are manned by a couple of gossipy hens named Sid and Bud." At Lola's expression, the girl continued, "Really. I don't make it up. I just report it. They tattle downtown twice a day, clockwork. Arbogast's cage is second on your left. Knock twice and enter. Like this." She rapped one-two on her desk. "It'll get you through the Wards."

"Much obliged, Just Pfeiffer."

"Be seeing ya."

As Lola rounded the third-floor landing, Aubrey finally spoke.

"A few offices on Pfeiffer's floor were Warded, but nothing frighteningly difficult. Nothing like the main building. If Arbogast's Wards are the same as Copenhagen's, we'll know there's a connection. Her office Wards and the ones at her mansion were different than the standard City Conjurers' trick."

Lola met with four people on the stairway but no one thought enough of her to impede her progress. They were all of a sort: male, suited, and in a hurry. Every one of them carried a large portfolio stuffed with files and none of them so much as smiled at her. Aubrey did say hello to the two Ghosts that trailed their human Hosts, but Lola heard nothing but politeness in the greetings.

The fourth floor hallway was much like that on the second floor. Lola stopped in front of the second office on the left. She rapped twice and went in.

Bodewell Arbogast stood up from his desk, pushing his chair forcefully into the wall behind him. Lola smiled.

"Am I interrupting?"

Arbogast recovered his balance admirably well and indicated a chair in front of his desk. "No, of course not. Please, sit down." He fidgeted with his waistcoat while Lola did so. "How did you, uh …?"

Lola gave him a measured look.

Arbogast's expression brightened suddenly. "Have you found him?"

Lola replied by tossing the accounts ledger on to the desktop. "Your boss sent this to me."

"Mr. Leung? How would he—?" Arbogast's question died in his throat. He looked up at Lola. She raised her eyebrows.

"Your other boss. Anonymously, of course. I thought perhaps you could clear a few things up, cut down on all the hoops and jumping."

The tall man groped for his chair and collapsed in a heap. "I don't understand," he said.

"I guess that's my cue to bring you up to speed on my detection thus far." Lola leaned forward sharply. "Say, you gotta a bottle back their somewhere? Take a swig, will you? You look like you need it."

Arbogast fumbled with a drawer and pulled out a bottle of gin. He reached back inside for glasses and came up with a gun.

FOURTEEN

Lola sat back. "What's the idea? You're gonna shoot me in your *office?*" She shook her head slowly. "They'll pin it on you before you even decide where to stash my body. Forget it, Arbogast. Killing's not your game. You don't have it in you. Not that there's anything wrong with that. But clearly, Copenhagen has real muscle for that. You're just her bagman."

The gun wavered then dropped onto the desk with a thud.

"All the same," advised Aubrey, "best pocket the piece."

Lola reached out and snatched it off the desk. "Her errand boy, actually. Isn't that your job? So what does that make Josephson to her? My bet is something quite a bit less respectable and a helluva lot more expendable."

Arbogast had his head in his hands. He started to tremble all over.

Lola pressed on. "What'd he do? Make off with some of the jack?"

The despondent man shook his head. He looked up with a ravaged face, tear-stained and grey. Lola suppressed her distaste. "You have no idea what's going on, Miss Starke. For all your so-called detecting skills. This little book of numbers is my doom. You're talking to a dead man."

Lola's expression hardened. "Cut the show, Arbogast. Pull yourself together. Don't roll over because she says 'trick.'"

"Let me guess. You've got just the plan to make her pay?"

Lola noted his sneer with interest.

"Save your venom. If you want my help, I need some answers."

Arbogast pulled out a cloth from a pocket, swabbed his face clean of tears and pulled out a hip flask. He didn't offer Lola anything. His eyes, cloudy just moments before, were now bright and sharp. He glared at Lola. "You think you're going to change the outcome of this? Sorry to be the bearer of bad news. You're nobody to her, to any of us. It's much bigger than you can even *begin* to comprehend."

Lola got up, leaned forward over the desk, and slapped Arbogast across the left cheek. "Cut the show, I said, and save the hysterics. Grab some more courage from that flask of yours. It's time to sing, damn you."

Arbogast held the side of his face. His eyes glittered. "If you have nothing to tell me about Sunny, then we have nothing more to discuss."

"Don't be a log, Arbogast. Josephson's disappearance has everything to do with this operation. Keeping me in the dark won't help him."

"You have no idea."

Lola's eyes widened. "Stop saying that, damn you."

"Ahh. Am I getting through to you now?" His shoulders slumped. "It's hopeless. I should never have—"

"Gotten Josephson involved with Copenhagen? His disappearance is tied up in this. You know it, you stubborn fool."

"Your persistence is misplaced." He gathered the ledger and held it out. "This is nothing but a poor joke. I'm sorry."

Lola glared at the tall man. She laughed harshly. "Keep it, why don't you."

"I'm hardly interested." His hand was as steady as his flat gaze.

Lola cursed, took the small book reluctantly.

"Good day, Miss Starke. I hope you won't take this ... distraction to heart. I know Sunny is out there somewhere." He nodded toward the door. "I'll be in touch."

Lola stood her ground. "You hired me, Mr. Arbogast, to find someone. Let me do my job." She waved the ledger in the air. "I don't give a damn about your crooked schemes. I'm no rat. Hells, I'm not even a concerned citizen."

Arbogast placed one hand on the telephone receiver.

"Having me thrown out won't keep your low profile," warned Lola. "Tell me the story and we can both get on with our jobs."

Arbogast retrieved his hand and looked at his watch. He gave Lola the steely eye. "In thirty minutes, I want you gone."

"Done. Now offer me a drink, for gods' sake."

Word had spread quickly through the gambling association: pay up or burn down. Three roaring fires—Spring Temple, Lucky's Grotto and Piano Garden—had convinced everyone to pay. Word even now, three years later, was that none of those three owners still lived in Crescent City, if they lived at all. So, a routine was established. Weekly payments were picked up by Arbogast. Missed payments accrued interest at a hideous rate. Rate increases were assessed according to profits stated on government tax filings. Payments were tailored to each establishment, and enough was always left for legal taxes to be paid.

"Who better to balance the two?" concluded Arbogast.

"The Commission gets their cut, in taxes, and never gets antsy."

Arbogast nodded.

"How'd you get involved?"

A shrug. "Wrong place, wrong time. I *am* a real accountant, Miss Starke. That's why I keep the books on this."

"Which she keeps in her personal safe."

"I don't know where she keeps them. I keep tabs in my head while I'm out. Every day, at the end of the day, I record the day's tally, in her presence at her office. She watches me count the money. I've never seen where she places the ledgers or the cash."

"How many?"

"Ledgers? Less than a dozen."

"Is her handwriting anywhere on them?"

He shook his head. "I'm it. The perfect scapegoat."

Lola nodded. "What about Josephson? Why did you get him in on this?"

Arbogast looked faintly amused, but it passed quickly. "He was the arsonist."

"So he brought you in?"

The thin man nodded. Absently, he poured some gin into a glass, grimaced as it raced down his throat. "We met at a social function. A week later, the Assistant Deputy Commissioner offered me a job here." He gestured vaguely around him.

"That's pretty far afield from extortion."

"Sunny and I developed a close relationship, quickly." He shrugged. "He needed a place to live. I had an entire house. He moved in. Shortly after, I, well, I came into some trouble with the bank, about the house payments. Sunny said he knew a way for me to make some money on the side."

"You didn't think anything of the timing?"

"Why would I? These things happen to people all the time."

"You said he'd been clean for three years," prompted Lola.

Arbogast nodded curtly. "He was off the heroin before we met. I'm not the kind of person that would welcome a junkie into my house, Miss Starke."

"So you knew from the start that your 'side job' was illegal?"

Another shrug. "I ran errands for the Assistant Deputy Commissioner for three months. It didn't seem strange to have muscle. Some of those places weren't much better than holes and just as filled with snakes. Then one day, Manny Silva at Eternal Springs got brave and my escorts put him in line." His gaze clouded over. "One of them made sure I was watching. Later, I tried to get out, but she had me dead to rights."

"And your handwriting's been on record ever since."

He didn't even bother to nod. He swirled the gin in its cheap glass and drank it in one smooth movement. The glass made no sound as he set it down. Then he pulled out a long cigarette and lit up.

Lola pushed on. "This new job we talked about—"

"The rumour from the nun?" asked Arbogast, his mouth twisted in disdain.

"Sunny said nothing about it?"

He shook his head. "That's why I don't think this had anything to do with it. He wouldn't have hidden anything from me. I'm already in neck-deep."

"The last arson was...?"

"Years ago."

"So how did he make his jack?"

Arbogast made a noise of disgust. "She had him snoop for extras. Things she could use to 'increase the yield.' Sunny had a knack." He looked across at Lola. "In another life, he would've been good at your job."

"He might already be *in* his next life, Mr. Arbogast," she said quietly.

That darkened Arbogast's face. "I would know, wouldn't I, if you were actually any good at your job?"

"My reputation speaks for me. Cheap talk won't tarnish it."

"Nevertheless, you have done precious little on my case. Where is Sunny now, Miss Starke? You can't even hazard a guess."

"That's not so. I have hazarded the same guess to you a number of times. You simply refuse to hear it. As for this," she proffered the ledger, "tell me why your boss is trying to scare you. What does she need from you?"

"Scare me?" he asked, leaning away from Lola. "What makes you think this is about me?" He gestured to the accounts ledger.

"She's too smart to think I wouldn't sniff her out. Her thugs followed me the day I tailed you to those five joints on page one. You said it yourself. You're the perfect scapegoat. I've got enough in there to start all sorts of trouble for you with the cops." Lola shifted, narrowed her eyes. "So start thinking. What does she want from you?"

Arbogast's flushed angrily. "You're no better than her, then. You're extorting me for information, that's all."

"Information that will save you, man," retorted Lola. "She's using me as the messenger here, but the message is for you. What does she want?"

This time, the shrug was forced. "Ask her. I do my job diligently and quietly. She has nothing to complain about."

"Do you know for a fact she's got nothing to do with your man's invisible act?"

"No, of course not," he answered, "but that means nothing."

"Or everything. The point is, you don't know." Lola cocked her head to the right as she assessed her client. "Did you tell her you came to me?"

"No, this is personal business."

"I have the feeling AJ Copenhagen doesn't differentiate," said Lola.

Arbogast shrugged. He shot his cuffs and skimmed a hand over his hair. "Still."

"Did you know she hired me the same day I started on your case?"

"To find Sunny?" His voice was painful with hope.

"No."

Arbogast stiffened. "I'm sure I have no idea why."

Lola nodded curtly. "That's one thing we can agree on."

He stood. "Your time is up, Miss Starke."

"An ominous pronouncement," commented Aubrey.

"What'll you do now?" asked Lola.

"I have my collections this afternoon. Afterward, as usual, I go to the Assistant Deputy Commissioner's office." Arbogast raised his chin and stared defiantly at Lola.

Lola regarded him silently for a moment before replying. "Put a brave face on, Mr. Arbogast. You'll need it."

FIFTEEN

An hour upstate from Crescent City, Lola drove on to the campus of Sylvia Choi Westbrook College for Women. It was the sole reason for the existence of the small city of Northport, which wasn't a port at all. It lay fifty miles from the ocean, at the foot of some very small mountains called the Vendenberg Foothills. Lola searched and easily discovered the visitors' parking lot. It sat right outside of the main administrative building, a modest three-storey brick affair. She had expected ivy-covered walls, but got massive magnolia trees instead. This early in the spring, they were just beginning to bloom.

Lola stretched demurely as she exited her car. What her beautiful little roadster had in speed, it lacked in cushioning. She checked her watch and looked around her. If there had been more ivy, this could have stood for any monied private school in the country. As it was, although the climate was temperate enough, the college board of directors was definitely not the usual club tie types. They were all alumni who believed in pinon trees, cherry blossoms and astronomical fees. After all, it took money to produce accomplished and brilliant women who were expected to become leaders in their fields. Or very impressive wives for powerful men.

Ten minutes after stepping out of her roadster, Lola was seated in the office of the Dean of Admissions, Deborah J. Fitzsimmons. The dean was a plump lady in impeccably stylish business attire: navy suit with subtly striped silk blouse. A pair of gold-framed glasses hung around her neck from a sparkling chain. They swayed as she moved to serve tea from the silver service.

Lola politely took her cup and saucer.

Dean Fitzsimmons settled herself more comfortably in the armchair and smiled. "I'm so excited to be a part of the next Grace McCall movie," she exclaimed.

Lola smiled in reply. "Well, I appreciate you seeing me with such little notice." She sipped her tea, then set it down and pulled out a tablet of lined paper and a pen. "As I explained on the telephone, I'm a researcher for Miss McCall's next film. Unfortunately, I'm not at liberty to divulge the title."

"Oh of course, I understand," tittered Dean Fitzsimmons. "I found the records you asked about." She pointed to a thick file on the table between them.

"Capital," exclaimed Lola. "I assume you'll need to see these?" She held forth two sheets of paper.

The dean placed her glasses on her nose and took the documents. Lola watched the woman's eyes reading over each and every paragraph of the top sheet before settling it down, turned over, onto her lap. She then took up the final page and read it just as carefully. When she came to the signature line at the bottom, she held the paper up to the light and peered intently. Satisfied, she sat back, collating the two sheets neatly, and placed both papers on top of the file.

"It's not exactly the same as our standard form," began Fitzsimmons.

"But the gist is clear?" finished Lola.

The plump woman thought for a moment, then nodded. "Yes, I mean, confidentiality of school records is a school policy, not a legal matter." She smiled again. "And Mrs. Copenhagen has given written permission at any rate."

"Superb," continued Lola smoothly. "I'd just like to take a look over these and make my notes. But before that, I'd like to ask you some questions, if I may, dean?"

"Yes, of course." The older woman beamed.

"Were you by any chance here when Ms. Stoudamire was attending?"

Fitzsimmons nodded. "She was quite the bright young lady. I actually interviewed her before she began."

"Do you happen to recall her areas of study?"

"Oh, I'm sorry. I wouldn't know that. But I do recall she made a strong impression with two of our faculty members. Dr. Sarah Yip and Dr. Felicity Yuen."

"Are they still on staff here?"

A nod. "Dr. Yuen is. She's the Chair of Spectral Studies. Dr. Yip left us once she wed. Her husband's job required a move to Northern China." A thoughtful pause. "Her name is now Mrs. Smith, I believe."

"Do you happen to have Dr. Yuen's schedule handy? I'd love the chance to speak with her while I'm here."

"Yes, just a moment." Fitzsimmons got up and went to the door. She cracked it open and spoke to her secretary. "Candy, would you get me Dr. Yeun's schedule for today, please?" The sound of papers being flapped, then: "Thanks, dear." Fitzsimmons read as she returned to her guest. "Yes, here we are .... It appears that Dr. Yeun is teaching until one o'clock. Then she has office hours until half past three." She looked up at Lola. "Would you like Candy to make a spot for you?"

Lola smiled brightly. "Yes, please. That would be ever so helpful."

"Now," bustled the dean, "I'm afraid I've got to run to a meeting. I apologize I wasn't able to reschedule it, given the short notice of your visit."

"Oh, of course, I'm so sorry about that," Lola replied dutifully, "I'm terribly grateful for your assistance as it is."

"I insist that you use my office, Miss Stanwick," continued Fitzsimmons. She pointed out the large round worktable as well as the low table in front of the armchair Lola currently occupied. "They're at your disposal. I shall return in, oh, I should say about an hour?"

Lola thanked her host with gushing gratitude and got down to business. Precisely one hour and ten minutes later, the dean returned to find Lola sitting in the same armchair, enjoying a final sip of tea. She rose when the older woman approached.

"Thank you so much, Dean Fitzsimmons, for your generosity. Candy's made my appointment with Dr. Yuen in fifteen minutes. She was wonderful, Candy was. Made up another pot of tea for me. I'll just pop in with Dr. Yuen and then be on my way." She handed the dean a card. "Please feel free to contact me if you have anything to add."

Fitzsimmons's face lit up with pleasure. "Wonderful," she enthused. A shyness came into her demeanour. She coughed lightly. "When do you think this might all come to fruition, so to speak?"

Lola pulled a moue of disappointment. "I wish I could tell you. It's just that it's all very much on the QT, as it were. Speaking of which," she pulled out another sheet of paper for the dean. "Please, if you would, our confidentiality agreement. This simply ensures that we keep as tight a lid on our project as we can. You understand."

The older woman signed, smiling widely.

Lola returned the document to her slender briefcase. The two shook hands pleasantly, and Lola was given brief directions to the Spectral Studies Department. It was a five-minute walk through the heart of the small campus. Lola passed young women of all shapes and sizes. They ran the expected gambit from serious to flighty, preoccupied to devil-may-care. And yet, every one of them had a similar ease about them; each knew that she was among peers. Not a one gave Lola anything more than a cursory glance.

"Seems you may be more your mother's daughter than you think," commented Aubrey. Lola remained silent.

Dr. Felicity Yuen turned out to be a willowy woman with luminous gray hair. She wore an ivory blouse and navy slacks and had a taste for menthol cigarettes. She lit one as Lola introduced herself and explained her presence. Yuen nodded and gestured for Lola to sit.

"I haven't spoken with AJ since she left," said the other woman. "Although I'm not surprised she's a high-ranking official. She's extremely bright. And driven."

"Did you expect her to stay within your field?"

Yuen nodded, her silvered hair gleaming in a stray shaft of sunlight. "She was without doubt the most brilliant student I've ever had in Spectral Studies. Her thesis—have you read it? I'll get you a copy before you leave. Her thesis work was stunning. Insightful and creative."

"You were her supervisor?"

"Yes. Dr. Yip—I suppose I should say Mrs. Smith now—was unable to accept another student, so I got lucky." Yuen smiled. "Sarah was quite disappointed, I remember."

"Do you keep in touch with Dr. Yip?"

"Hmm, yes. She writes lovely, funny letters about being a foreigner in Northern China, despite looking just like everyone else there." Yuen waved at the smoke from her cigarette. "Sarah and I were genuinely thrilled when AJ was accepted to the Temple."

"That was after her two years here?"

"Mmm. AJ completed her accelerated program in one less year than anyone else in the history of Westbrook College, Miss Stanwick." Yuen raised a sleek eyebrow. "That's thousands of girls, you understand. She was something truly special, was our AJ. Gifted with Spells as well as intellectually ambitious. I always thought she would set the Temple alight."

"Do you know when she completed there?"

"Well, she didn't actually. She sent me a letter, personally, to explain that she'd had a change of heart." Yuen finished her cigarette with a shrug. "I always wondered if her father had something to do with it."

"He didn't approve?"

Yuen considered the question. "I think he had more political leanings in mind for his only child. Clearly, that is now the path she's on."

"Did she ever explain her choice to you, personally?"

Yuen shook her head. "We never spoke in person again, actually. Different circles, you know. AJ made her choice and no longer had a reason to stay involved or interested in Spectral Studies. Some students are like that," she explained. "One doesn't take these things to heart, Miss Stanwick."

"Is the Temple of Conjury the only training available to gifted Spectral students, Dr. Yuen?"

The professor nodded.

Lola sat forward, slightly closing the distance between herself and Yuen. "I'm wondering if there aren't other ways for someone of Miss Stoudamire's talents to have gained more training. Perhaps she travelled abroad? Aren't there Masters who are not affiliated with the Temple? Would they not be able to teach a talented student as well as the Temple?"

Yuen frowned slightly. "Of course, there are, Miss Stanwick. Not everyone appreciates the regimented life at the Temple, although one must admit, it certainly produces the finest quality Conjurers." She shook her head. "No, I don't believe AJ took issue with her schooling at the Temple. She was herself always a very disciplined person. Aside from that, she had already completed Year Four when she stopped her studies. By then, I'm quite certain she was long past any adjustment difficulties." Yuen looked at Lola speculatively. "Are you suggesting AJ continued her studies without sanction from the Temple?"

Lola sat back abruptly with a small laugh. "I wouldn't know, Dr. Yuen. I'm just getting background for the script, but wouldn't that make a great story?"

Yuen laughed, clearly disarmed. "I suppose it would. You'd be the better judge of that, Miss Stanwick."

As soon as Lola got in sight of a drugstore back in the City, she pulled over and made a telephone call. Betta listened silently to the entirety of Lola's request. She made no promises of success, but she told Lola to call her the next morning. Lola rang off and relinquished the booth to an elderly man in dark orange tweed. She ordered a sandwich and a coffee, sat at the counter to eat. When she was done, she asked for a glass of water and drank half of it. She left a dollar tip and drove on.

She entered her office to the sound of the telephone ringing.

Pfeiffer sounded impatient: "I've been trying you for ages."

"You sound like my mother," replied Lola. "What's the bee in your bonnet?"

"Your man Arbogast. He caused a commotion with the Conjurers."

Lola checked the clock on her desk: five-forty-eight. "Conjurers? At what time?"

"Quarter of five. They were right on time, like always."

"To set the building ward?"

"Mm-hmm. Everyone knows you don't get back in if they're here. Whatever you forgot, it's forgot 'til morning. But Bodewell ran right past one of them and almost made it inside the building. The other one came out the door then and caught him up. They had what one would characterize as a heated discussion."

"Did he make it inside?"

"Nothing doing. Conjurers aren't known for flexibility, if you hadn't noticed."

"And then?"

Lola could practically hear the shrug over the line. "Bodewell beat it and peeled out of the lot in that racy coupe of his."

Lola thanked her for the tip and they rang off. She sat for a moment, then sprang back up, grabbed her hat and purse, and was out the door.

SIXTEEN

The colourful flower beds and poetic maple stood as before. Lola walked up the front steps and rang, but it was mostly for show. She once again instinctively knew that the house was empty. She looked back out toward the street, then walked slowly along the porch. The windows were still shuttered. The floorboards still creaked.

"You've got an audience," said Aubrey.

Lola shot a glance to her left and caught a flicker of curtains settling back into place.

Aubrey continued: "Getting inside will take time."

"What can you do in five minutes?"

"Tell you what a bad idea this is. Over and over."

"Never mind. Let's go talk to the nosy neighbour."

The house to the left was a warm buttery yellow. The greenery lining the walk was well tended. A simple front porch held a chair and a smoking stand with a pipe dish. A hanging pot of clematis adorned the far corner from the steps. A rush mat proclaimed this "Home Sweet Home." A wall scroll in calligraphy conferred wishes for "Safe Entry and Successful Journeys." There was no bell. Lola knocked politely.

"That Japanese maple looks the twin of Arbogast's, same height, exact same colouring," said Aubrey. "And I didn't notice any other lawns sporting pricey little beauties like these. Could be more than just simple nosiness."

"That's what I'm betting on," murmured Lola.

A cough from the other side of the door preceded some measured Cantonese: "Just a minute."

The door was painted white, to match the shutters and trim. It opened in less than a minute to reveal a tall, slender man wearing a camel-coloured cardigan over a plain white shirt. His shirt bulged out slightly at waist level. From his careworn features and slight stoop, Lola guessed he was somewhere this side of fifty. His hair brushed the tips of his ears and the original black was overrun with grey. He smiled with yellow teeth. Lola caught a whiff of mellow tobacco. "Yes?"

She smiled tentatively in response. "Uh, hello. Do you know if Bode—I mean, uh, Mr. Arbogast is in? We had a, um, appointment tonight." She checked her watch. "He wasn't there."

"And you came here to …?"

"I, well, I, um, I don't think that's any of your business."

The older man looked her square in the eyes. "You don't seem his type," he said.

Lola spluttered indignantly, then huffed, "Never mind. I'll just wait on his porch." She whirled around.

"Just hang on there, miss," he called out. He was amused now. "You're going to have a tough time with his Wards, if you try to break in."

"Beg your pardon?" Lola blinked owlishly.

"His house," the man gestured with a pipe, "it's Warded tighter than City Hall. It's not worth it." He smiled benignly. "If you tell me who you are and why you're really here, I might be able to help. Bodewell and I, we watch out for one another's homes, you see. Though, truth to tell, it rarely amounts to much more than misdelivered packages and such. And something tells me you're not the delivery girl." He watched Lola with an amused expression.

Lola's eyes fell to the pipe as she considered it. It had a straight stem and unembellished bowl. She said, "My father smoked a Canadian like that. Smoked it every night without fail." She looked up into the man's eyes, noticing the shrewdness she'd missed before. "Might be a sign in this."

He offered his hand: "Jed Wing."

"Lola Starke. I'm working for Mr. Arbogast on a personal matter. I'm a private investigator." She handed over a card. "Apologies for the shiftiness. Force of habit."

The older man carefully read her card. "Bodewell mentioned he'd hired a private dick." Wing stopped abruptly. "Sorry, don't mean any disrespect."

Lola waved it off. "Have you seen Mr. Arbogast today? We've been in touch regularly up to this point," she lied, "but I haven't been able to track him down today."

"He was home, about an hour ago, but I didn't see him leave. Not unusual, though. I was making my dinner, not keeping tabs on my neighbours." He smiled.

"Does he park in his garage when he comes in, usually? Would you have noticed him leaving out the back?"

Wing shook his head. "Maybe if I'd been eating at the dining table, but I never do that when I'm alone. I was in front of the radio." He gestured with a thumb behind him. Lola peered over his shoulder and saw it in the corner of the room, next to a large green armchair.

Lola squared her shoulders. "Mr. Wing, I'll be level with you. I need to get inside your neighbour's house. Something's troubling Mr. Arbogast and he needs help," she finished. "Can you help me?"

The man hesitated. He looked past Lola's shoulder at a passing car. He watched it until it pulled up in front of a house halfway down the block. Lola glanced at it as well. Wing coughed lightly.

"As a matter of fact, I can." He pinned her with a stern look. "But I'm not leaving you alone in there. I'm going in with you."

He waited for her short nod, then retreated, walking over to a neat secretary under a window. He retrieved a key ring from a tiny drawer. Wing closed his front door firmly and left his pipe in the bowl on his porch. He led Lola back around his own house. They walked along the side of the house and passed through his back gate. Soon, they'd crossed over to Arbogast's property and were peering into his garage window. No car.

Lola asked, "Does Mr. Josephson have his own car?"

Wing shook his head, his expression sad, but he said nothing. He continued into the yard, latching the gate behind Lola, who followed him to the back door.

"What about the Wards?" asked Lola.

Wing waved his key. "This will disarm them. They won't reset but I'll explain it to Bodewell when I see him."

Lola nodded. She watched as Wing used his keys. Then they entered Arbogast's kitchen.

Papers littered the countertops and floor. Chairs had been pulled out from the table in the nook. The table itself was turned on its side and stuck partway out of its nook. All the cabinet doors were ajar. Even the oven door was open.

Wing's horrified glance swept the room.

"I take it Mr. Arbogast is usually very tidy?" Lola asked.

Wing nodded, still openmouthed. He gathered himself with a visible effort. "We need to call the police."

Lola said, "Hold on there, Mr. Wing. It's not as bad as it looks. I'd like to take a look around before we decide on anything."

"But something's happened to Bodewell. You said it yourself. This is clear proof of it," the older man countered.

"No, I said he was troubled." Lola exited the kitchen and walked down a hallway, entering the living room. It was as jumbled and messy as the kitchen. "I'm worried, that's the truth, but let's not jump to the wrong conclusions. We don't know that Mr. Arbogast didn't do this himself. It's obvious someone was searching for something here. It's clear they weren't concerned with neatness, but that doesn't mean it wasn't your neighbour. Nothing's broken here. I understand it must be a shock." Lola watched Wing closely. "The alternative is that someone broke through the wards in the light of day and ransacked the house. They also then left, re-establishing the wards, without you noticing. Didn't you just try to tell me these wards were substantial?"

Wing considered Lola's words carefully. Finally, he said, "You're not going anywhere without me."

"Fair enough."

None of the furniture or decorative items in the living room was actually damaged, but everything was out of place. Photographs were over turned. A *chaise-longue* and coordinating armchairs were pulled across the room, dragging the rug with them. Cushions lay on the floor.

The same disarray was in the formal dining area, which also had a modest fireplace. Lola checked the grate but saw no evidence of recent ashes. The table was pushed against the wall. The six chairs were overturned, their legs pointing to the stairs.

Wing picked up a framed photograph.

"I think this was Sunny's favorite."

Lola walked over. A boy and a girl sat with their arms around one another. They had the same slim nose, broad forehead, and clear pale gaze. The girl's lips formed a full rosebud. The boy had a wider mouth. Even without knowing they were twins, one knew they were close. Neither child was smiling. They wore clothes from twenty years ago. Behind them, the lighter shading indicated daylight. Lola saw trees and part of a picket fence, painted white, judging from the brilliant sheen even in the grey shades of the photograph.

"The twins," said Lola. "What do you know of them?"

Arbogast's neighbour carefully replaced the photograph, right side up, on the otherwise messy sideboard. He hesitated, clearly considering whether or not to start tidying up all the pictures in their upended frames. Instead, he sighed and turned to Lola.

"I know she's been Haunting him for a long, long time."

"Mr. Arbogast said she was the problem, not the heroin."

Wing shrugged. "Frankly, Miss Starke, Bodewell was jealous of Lucille. He always had a blind spot when it came to Sunny's faults. She was convenient to blame."

"Do you think she would have encouraged Sunny to leave without telling Mr. Arbogast?"

"I don't know," he said. His expression sad, he looked at Lola directly. "Do you think Sunny's coming back?" Lola didn't reply. His shoulders slumped.

Lola went to the staircase and headed up. She noted an access door, square and recessed into the ceiling at the top of the stairs, most likely for the attic. The second floor held two bedrooms and a bath. The master bedroom had its own private bathroom as well.

"This is Mr. Arbogast's room?" asked Lola, pointing to the master suite on the left. Wing gave her a considering look as he nodded. A large bed with two night stands. A very modern bureau. Every last drawer was pulled out. Clothes covered the floor. The bed sheets were torn off, one end still tucked in under the mattress, pillows thrown against a wall. Lola picked her way over to one of the nightstands. Another frame tipped over. This one turned out to be Arbogast and Josephson together. They were smiling, confident, raising champagne flutes to the camera. Behind them, the ocean under a breathtakingly clear sky. Lola imagined the sun blazing overhead, causing the men in the photograph to squint happily as someone clicked the shutter. Lola straightened up suddenly. She looked at the bed, at the other nightstand. She walked over to the closet, large enough to be its own small room. Arbogast was a clotheshorse, no doubt about it, but he didn't purchase clothes in different sizes. She looked over, meeting Wing's gaze.

"Now you get it," he said, nodding.

Lola remained tight-lipped as she sifted through the contents of both nightstands. Nothing caught her eye except a well-worn journal. It was leather bound, its pages brittle and yellowing. A fringed page holder nestled within. The pages were blank.

Aubrey's voice seemed loud in Lola's ear, after his long silence. "It's hers—Lucille."

"Invisible ink?" murmured Lola. She indicated the journal to Wing. "I'm taking this. I'll return it to Mr. Arbogast when I see him."

"Fine by me. If I see him first, I'll let him know." He still seemed bewildered as he scanned the room. "Should we clean up?"

Lola shook her head. "I need to be blunt with you, Mr. Wing. The stick boys won't help us find Mr. Arbogast because he's not been missing long enough to bother them. Cops don't think it's worth troubling them until it's gone two days. However, I think you should call them tomorrow if he still hasn't returned. Say it's a break-in. That'll get their attention faster. You've got my card. Ring me after you call the cops. Of course, if he *does* come back tonight, please ring me right away."

Together, they went through the rest of the house. The same mess greeted them in every room, except the attic and the cellar. Lola walked those spaces carefully, wary for dusty footprints leading to walls or possibly hidden compartments. She found neither, up nor down. Wing followed Lola into every room, his hands jammed into his pockets and his mouth compressed into a line.

The theory Lola had so blithely mouthed to Wing was weak, but it could still have been true. Perhaps Arbogast had searched for something he thought Josephson had hidden. She didn't want to lay odds on the probability of truth in it, but if it helped to get the old man on board, she wasn't going to point out its faults.

"Maybe Sunny came back? Looking for something to pawn?" Wing said. They were back in the kitchen.

Lola looked up from checking inside the oven. "You knew he was back on the needle?"

"It was obvious, if you had the eyes to see," the older man sighed. He gestured around. "But no, that wouldn't make any sense. There's the silver tea service right there. He'd probably have taken it."

"There are certainly enough things still here to rule out a burglary—the gold cuff links upstairs, that diamond tie bar, the crystal. Even the cops will see that." Lola searched the neighbour's lined face. "Just tell them the truth when they talk to you. You've got nothing to worry about."

"I suppose there's no point in not talking about Sunny's...history. That was the truth. He was addicted to heroin. That can change a man."

Lola replied absently. "Even if he had come back for something to sell, he wouldn't have torn the house apart. He'd've known where everything was." She stood up, stretching her lower back a little. "I doubt you'll be responsible for making the cops think less of him."

Wing stiffened. His voice was cool. "It's time. This isn't our house. We don't belong here."

Lola gave him a brief stare, then obeyed without comment. Wing ushered her out and closed the door firmly, locking it once more with his key. He made Lola walk before him, back around to the front. On the sidewalk, next to her car, she held out her hand.

"Thank you, Mr. Wing. I appreciate your help. Please, ring me if you see Mr. Arbogast tonight." She paused, then: "I truly am concerned for him. And for Mr. Josephson."

The older man shook hands without speaking. He remained on the pavement, watching Lola walk around to get in the car. She had the door open by the time he finally spoke.

"If you're right about that journal, if it really does belong to Lucille, I think Sunny would've taken it with him," said Wing. "He wouldn't have left it—not if he thought he was never coming back."

Lola offered a sad smile of her own: "That's what I'm afraid of."

SEVENTEEN

Early the next morning, just after four o'clock, a keen-eyed beat cop patrolling the harbour along Waterfront Drive spied a floater. He and his partner fished the body from where it had caught up along the pier pilings. They called it in, and two detectives from Central Homicide were dispatched. In a surprising stroke of luck, the deceased's wallet was still intact, with driver's license and the poor man's name. A call to dispatch passed along details and the name. The murder cops put in charge did some quick detecting and a home address was obtained. They found an empty house in a moderate middle-class neighbourhood. However, a neighbour was roused and he provided them with a set of keys and some useful information. He also gave them Lola's card.

Lola got the story when she was collected by two patrol types and driven in silence downtown. Lola had been in bed all of ninety minutes before they'd come knocking. She fell asleep in the back of the cop car and didn't come to until her name was called out gruffly. She opened gummy eyes to the sight of an open door and an impatient cop. Lola smiled politely and headed into the lion's den.

Inspectors Bednarski and Marks awaited her with grim mouths and flat gazes. They were of equal height, but differed considerably in width. Bednarksi had dark brown hair, cut in a military style, accentuating his square head. His cheeks were shadowed with stubble. Lola guessed it was because it should have been the end of his shift. His shoulders strained the beige suit jacket paired with a pale blue shirt and grey tie with blue pin dots. His eyes were light green. They watched Lola opaquely for all their paleness.

Marks, in contrast, wore an expertly tailored suit in navy, matched with crisp white shirt and dark blue-and-grey striped tie. He was lean in leg and waist, clean-shaven and looked freshly pressed. Lola noted a thin line of a scar running from the left corner of his mouth down to the centre of his chin. Its shiny texture caught the light of the overhead light when he moved a certain way. He watched Lola intently with his dark eyes. She wondered what was behind his glare.

If she was surprised at the pairing of two *gwai* cops, she didn't show it. She asked for some coffee to help her stay awake. Marks grunted and obliged. While he did, Lola sat quietly and watched Bednarski pace the small interrogation room. When he was reunited with his partner once more, Bednarski spoke.

"Tell us about your relationship with the deceased," he suggested in a gravelly voice.

"We didn't have one," replied Lola. "I've never met him."

"Tell us about your relationship with Bodewell Arbogast."

"He came to my office a few days ago—"

"When?" interrupted Marks.

Lola paused. "Two days ago. We spoke of a business matter."

"Did he hire you?"

"Have you asked him?"

"Don't be coy, Miss Starke. It just makes everything more difficult." Marks spoke without inflection.

Lola looked at him closely. "I'm not trying any tricks here, Detective Inspector. I can't speak of what passed between Mr. Arbogast and myself. Professional ethics."

Bednarski waved away the words. "You're no lawyer. There's no legal protection."

Lola shrugged.

The big man leaned in with an air of camaraderie. "Listen, I know it's hard, especially for women like you. No one takes you seriously. Am I right?"

Lola glanced up at Marks. The cop gave her nothing. She returned to the big man. She shrugged.

He said, "We can smooth things out for you."

"Why am I here again?"

"Obviously," replied Marks, "you can't identify the body. We need the lover for that."

"No family?"

"You tell us," said Bednarski.

"His sister Lucille was his Ghost. They were twins. But I suppose she's just as gone as he is." Lola shrugged. "Jed Wing probably knows more than I do."

Bednarski nodded absently. "We've spoken with him. We know Arbogast hired you to find his lover." He sat back. The wooden chair creaked. "Tell us what you know about Josephson."

Marks pushed away from the wall he'd been leaning against. He pulled out a chair, turned it around and straddled it. He threw a notebook onto the tabletop and unscrewed the cap of his fountain pen.

Lola thought for a moment. Then she started talking. It wasn't long before she stopped.

Marks said, "Doesn't sound like a lot of progress. You must be double-clocking."

Lola retained her casual air. "Yes."

"What about that?"

"Tsu and Luke, in Vice. They can fill you in."

Marks's expression tightened for a moment, then relaxed like ripples disappearing from a pond. He left the room. Bednarski waited with Lola in silence. Five minutes passed and then a quick one-two on the door. The big man lugged himself out of the room without an explanation. Lola didn't bother to strain her ears. Tsu and Luke were going to vouch for her, whether they liked it or not.

Marks and Bednarski returned, giving their best blank face. Marks started in immediately, "Your connections won't keep you from the inside of a cell."

"No, but the fact that I've done nothing illegal will."

Bednarski watched Lola with clinical interest. "Let's go over it again. Why did you follow your own client?"

Lola answered patiently. "I thought he was holding out on me. Information that was pertinent to his case."

"Why would you think that?"

Lola shrugged. "Call it intuition."

"Where did you follow him to?"

"La Grenouille, Lucky Bamboo, Silver Temple, Water Lily and Ivory Tiles."

Marks jumped in, "In that order?"

Lola shook her head. "Does it matter?"

Marks countered, "You tell me. What happened?"

"Nothing. I was following my client without his knowledge. We didn't speak. I didn't find anything that afternoon to help find Josephson."

"What was Arbogast doing at those places?" asked Bednarski.

"You'll have to ask him."

"Where can we find him?"

Lola shrugged.

"So you followed your client around all afternoon and came up with zilch. Then what?" challenged Marks, "Gave up? Moved on?"

"I had an appointment with another client. I put Mr. Arbogast's case aside for the evening."

"You gave up the prime time for finding a junkie gambler and went to shine on your next client?" Marks crossed his arms.

"I had an appointment with another client," repeated Lola.

"Were you working that other case? Or just taking what you'd call a 'well-deserved break'?"

"It's not relevant."

"Sure of that? How do you know?" countered Marks. "Maybe Josephson coulda been found that very night, before he got dead, while you were busy elsewhere."

"Are you trying to say something? You think I murdered him?"

"We didn't say it was murder. Why assume that?" Bednarski seemed genuinely curious.

Lola stared at him. "You're Murder Squad."

The big man shrugged. "Floaters in the harbour fall under the category of suspicious death. We don't know yet if it was murder." He eyed Lola silently, then: "You aren't surprised Josephson turned up dead?"

"No. He's a junkie." She paused, considered her next words. "I said as much to my client when he pitched the case."

Marks interjected. "Did you check the hospitals? Temple shelters? Church shelters? The morgue? All logical places if you figured him for dead or close to."

Lola shrugged. "Save the lecture, Detective Inspector."

A hard-knuckled double rap to the door shot through the room. Lola started. The other two didn't so much as twitch. The door opened and a short, squat man with black hair stepped in. He looked perfectly pressed and ready for a news conference.

"Superintendent Locke," said Lola politely.

"Lola," the man answered. His mouth twisted, as though he'd just tasted something unpleasant. "Gentlemen," he addressed the inspectors. They nodded and stood up.

"We'll contact you if we need more," Bednarski said mildly to Lola. He held up her card in surprisingly long fingers. Marks simply nodded, his face utterly bland now. The men waited as Lola let their superior officer escort her out.

"I'll take you home." Locke said. "We have some things to discuss."

Lola smiled politely and kept her face pleasantly blank as they exited the corridors. They came to the Superintendent's car at the front curb and climbed inside. The driver, a beefy young officer with manicured hands, kept those hands firmly on the steering wheel. He inclined his head a fraction of an inch when Locke told him the address.

Lola smoothed out her slacks and settled into the cool seat. "Well? Satisfied?"

"Do I think you were truthful? No," answered Locke. "But I've heard enough for the time being." He eyed Lola with disapproval. "Your mother was worried about you."

"How long did you wait before telling her where I was?"

"We spoke about thirty minutes ago." He glanced at his watch.

Lola laughed, harshly. "Don't suppose you told her I'd already been there four hours."

"It wasn't necessary." He picked an invisible bit of lint off his dark trousers. "Your license doesn't make you bullet-proof, Lola. Leave the investigation to my men. They know their business and they have the authority to get answers. I won't interfere if you're arrested for obstruction."

"At least you didn't say 'when'," commented Lola.

"Your father always knew how to stay on his side of the line. I suggest you take a page from his notebook."

Lola stiffened, but refused to take the bait.

Locke continued. "I don't want to hear your name involved in this again."

"Tell your men to stop making me involved. I came to answer questions about why I was following the trail of a dead man. I didn't have anything to do with him being dead."

Locke grunted, looked out at the passing scenery.

Lola changed tack. "I'm curious why you're involved at all. Not much political leverage to be gained from another dead junkie."

Aubrey hissed a warning. Lola kept her expression bland.

"I'm involved because your mother is my friend," replied Locke. "Don't mistake my presence for approval, Lola. There are very definite limits to my friendship with Grace." He turned away.

Lola pressed. "Was it an overdose then?"

Locke said nothing.

"I'll simply find another source—you know I will." She shrugged.

Locke eyed her shrewdly, came to a decision. "Stay away from my investigators."

"My pleasure," Lola replied.

Locke opened a file he took from a black briefcase. He flipped through some pages. "Josephson died from an internal overdose. He had balloons of heroin in his stomach. They burst. A high risk venture for mule and dealer alike."

"Smuggling? From where?" asked Lola.

"Down south. Vice says this case is rare, though. It's usually the illegals who play mule. It takes a certain amount of desperation," Locke concluded.

"Then someone tossed him into the drink," said Lola.

"Perhaps he fell. Perhaps he was in a boat and they tossed the dead weight." Locke glared. "It's not your concern anymore. This is our job now. If you want to help, tell us how to reach the lover."

"Sorry, can't help you there." At Locke's narrowed eyes, she repeated the truth, "I don't know."

"Don't make me regret believing you," growled the Detective Superintendent of Crescent City Homicide. He leaned forward suddenly. "How much longer, Steven?"

"Fifteen minutes, give or take, sir" came the soft reply.

Locke sat back. "Good. I've got some papers to go over."

Lola rode in silence until they stopped in front of her building. Locke held her arm for an instant before she disembarked.

"Your case is over. You've found Josephson. Solving his death isn't part of the job description. Find your client. Be the smart girl your father raised—convince Arbogast to come down to Central. And when he does, make sure you come with him."

EIGHTEEN

Lola entered her apartment to find her mother pacing in front of her windows, her cigarette a smouldering metaphor.

"Dammit, Lola." Anger highlighted the lines around Grace McCall's smoke-blue eyes. Her black hair was a beautiful sleek bob. A pale blue jacket with flared hems and a pencil skirt to the knees highlighted her slender figure.

"I hope you're not alone," sighed Lola. She tossed her crumpled jacket onto the sofa and collapsed down onto the cushions.

Grace wrenched the cigarette out of her mouth and pointed with it accusingly. "Whatever the hells you've got yourself into, get out of it. Now."

Lola laughed, a bitter sound even to her own ears. "You can say that again." She rubbed at her temples. "If you've come to rake me over the coals, save it. Locke's boys did the dirty work for you."

Grace sat down immediately. She stubbed out her cigarette and took Lola's hand. Lola shook it off. Grace's expression was complex. "Lola. Darling. Can't we stop bickering? I'm worried for you."

"You can stop anytime. Causes wrinkles, don't you know."

Aubrey hissed at Lola. "Stop it."

"Time for you to go," Lola said to her mother. She searched out a cigarette and spoke coldly. "Get on a steamer for Europe. Your favorite getaway. You can forget all your cares there. Isn't that right, Mother?"

Tears glistened in the older woman's eyes. "That was cruel." Her voice was steady, quiet. Lola looked away from her mother's shaky fingers as Grace pulled out another cigarette from its case.

"Life is cruel, Mother. You taught me that when I was four."

Grace grimaced then set her jaw. "I'm sorry I left you. I'm sorry. Do you hear that? Do you know I mean it? I never wanted to hurt you. Gods be damned, Lola, it was never about you." She grabbed Lola's hand again. "Twenty years, you've been punishing me. Can you even hear what I'm saying now? It was never about you," Grace repeated.

Lola roughly flexed her hand, throwing off Grace's hold. She turned her gaze out the windows. Water sparkled in the distance.

Grace looked away from Lola. She took a long, trembling breath and held it. When she finally let it out, she looked at her unlit cigarette as if for the first time. She lit it and stood up. "I'm not changing my plans," she announced. Her face was shuttered. "I have an engagement I can neither cancel nor reschedule. I'm leaving for Europe the day after tomorrow. You know how to reach me, if you wish."

Lola kept narrowed eyes on her mother, then played a hunch: "Let me guess—our illustrious Mayor."

Grace remained silent.

"Is that your 'engagement'? Is he why you won't take my advice?"

Grace sighed. "This isn't a competition. It never was. Mayor needs my help at a special ceremony, a private, very personal event. Please, try to understand. I made a solemn promise to him when he first … changed," she said. "It's not something I can renege on. Nor would I."

"Unlike your marriage vows," Lola said. She compressed her lips, but it was too late to take back the words.

Grace's face crumpled with weariness. "I never stopped thinking of you, loving you with all my heart. Your father and I, we simply weren't meant to be together." She paused. "He understood that. He let me go," she finished gently.

"He didn't." Lola shook her head fiercely. "I saw it. He loved you the rest of his life. But you were gone and it broke his heart and none of it mattered to you." Lola raised her chin and looked down at Grace. "You were gone and it was the best career move you ever made."

Grace stood, open-mouthed for a second. Then she scowled. "Don't you dare imply I'm a whore, Lola Evangeline Starke. You of all people."

Lola rubbed at her face. "I think it's time to call it a show, Mother."

She leaned back, then pushed up from the sofa abruptly. Lola refused to meet her mother's eyes. She stepped to the windows and stared blindly at the distant ocean. Her heartbeat was too fast, her cheeks too hot. She fiercely fought the urge to continue airing her injuries.

Silence grew until it gathered weight. Finally, Grace gathered her purse and hat. The kitchen door opened. Elaine came through, followed by a man with broad shoulders. He wore a beautifully cut blue wool suit, with pearly grey tie and checked shirt. He was placing a blue trilby on his head of thick brown hair. He threw Lola a hard glare as he strode to her front door ahead of Grace. Lola remained mute. She stood, rooted to the spot, until her mother and St. John were gone. Then she turned and stalked to her bedroom, swiping furiously at her eyes.

She could feel Elaine's stare on her back.

Aubrey waited until she was at the doorway. He spoke in subdued tones. "You forget that Butch forgave her."

"You don't know anything about it," Lola said. She stopped, took a deep breath, slowly released her clenched fists.

"You don't corner the market on this story. Grace has a side to tell, too," he said with surprising gentleness.

"Fine. I hope it keeps you warm at night. It doesn't do a damn thing for me." Lola kicked off her shoes and watched with satisfaction as they slammed into the wall and fell onto the floor. "I need a bath. Go feel sorry for her somewhere else, haunt."

"She's not the one I feel sorry for," came the faint reply.

Betta sounded distracted but cheerful enough: "Lola, hello."

Lola cradled the telephone so she could reach her pen and a pad. "What's the story with the Temple? Whom am I meeting with today?"

Betta chuckled softly. "You really do expect miracles."

"You're the only miracle worker I know, Betta."

"Gee thanks, but flattery won't get you anywhere. Not with this bunch anyway."

"No go?"

"Technically, that's true. However, all's not lost." Betta's smile was evident in her tone. "The Temple records are sealed to all outsiders but I made some calls to other alumni, and I do have some information for you."

"Shoot, O Worker of Miracles." The cheerfulness rang false even to Lola's ears but she pushed on with it nonetheless.

There was a beat of silence.

"Well," answered Betta slowly, "like you told me, your friend was accepted at the Temple but didn't complete her training. She spent four of the five years at the top of her class, then abruptly withdrew her candidacy for full honours."

"What does that mean? How much training did she receive?"

"Wait. Let me finish. Your friend was apprenticed to a very impressive Conjurer for her fourth year. That would have been the first of two years, if she'd completed the training. As it was, her mentor died before your friend's fifth year."

"Her mentor? I just spoke with her yesterday. Dr. Felicity Yuen."

Betta explained, "Dr. Yuen was her thesis advisor at the College, nothing more. Your friend's Temple mentor was a well-known Conjurer."

"Was it murder?" Lola asked.

"No, nothing like that," replied Betta. "He was old, well over ninety. No one was surprised."

Lola sat, thinking. Betta waited patiently.

"How much would she know, with only four years training?" Lola finally asked.

"Enough to sense Ghosts, perhaps see them even. The most gifted ones attain that ability more quickly."

"And Warding? Spells?"

"Some, yes. Not intricate ones. The fifth year involves a binding of sorts with the Ether. Without that binding, the training is mostly memorizing theory and technique. Practical applications require a binding. Without it, true Conjury is impossible."

"And this binding is only possible with the Temple's consent?"

"Not just consent, Lola. It can only happen on Temple grounds."

"Which are powerfully Warded."

"Of course. The Temple is very strict about its secrets."

Lola considered for a moment. "Can I trust your source?"

"Absolutely. He's a retired instructor with the Temple. He remembers your friend vividly. Called her the most brilliant natural talent in generations."

"Your source gave you all that willingly?" pressed Lola.

"Yes," Betta answered. "We're friends."

"What about binding away from the Temple then? Overseas somewhere?"

"Sure," Betta answered slowly, "that's possible. Unlikely, though. The Temple of Conjury here is the most highly regarded Spectral Institution in the world. Why would your friend leave for a minor school? She clearly had the talent, and my friend tells me she also had a true passion for it. Binding through the Temple would simply be more powerful than elsewhere." Betta paused, then continued uncomfortably, "The gossip from back then was that your friend also had familial obligations to fulfill. My friend felt very sad for her. Losing one's Temple mentor is terrible. Add to that an unsympathetic family and who knows how a young girl will react?"

Lola thanked Betta and rang off. She sat for some moments, lazily fanning herself as she gently swiveled in her chair. She considered this new information from different angles. Finally, she stood and left her office, making sure to lock the door behind her. Once on the street, she walked to the corner drugstore and bought herself lunch. Thirty-five minutes later, she returned to her aerie with a newspaper under her arm and her head full of swirling thoughts.

She opened the door into her waiting room and stopped, surprised to find it occupied.

Bodewell Arbogast stood, hat in hand, face calm. He inclined his head slightly. "Miss Starke." Today's outfit was dove grey. A white armband sat high on his left arm.

"You've heard then," she said.

Arbogast nodded solemnly.

"I'm sorry, Mr. Arbogast. Truly I am."

She led him within her inner office. He waited until she sat before he did as well.

"Murder is a sad business," he said, lighting a cigarette.

"What did you hear?"

He shook his head. "Tell me what the police wanted with you."

"For starters, they wanted to know where you were. They figured the hired help was a good start."

"Miss Starke, you seem angry with me."

"Mr. Arbogast, you seem surprisingly at ease."

He barked out a laugh. "You're not a very good judge of people, Miss Starke. I know Sunny was murdered and I know who did it. I'm as good as dead."

"You're not alone in this, man," Lola said, exasperated. "There are people who can help you."

"Like the ones who helped Sunny? I think not." He stood. "I'm here to settle my bill. Obviously, my case is closed."

"Doesn't feel that way to me."

"Oh but it is. We know where Sunny is now, don't we? I'm handling the rest on my own." He pulled out a billfold from an inside breast pocket and extracted a cheque, folded neatly in half. He placed it precisely on Lola's desk.

Lola's gaze never left Arbogast's face. "Keep your money."

"Buy yourself a few drinks and forget about this case, Miss Starke. That's the best advice I can give you."

"I'm interested in the truth," said Lola.

Arbogast laughed that harsh bark of his again.

"The cops say he died while smuggling heroin in his stomach," Lola pressed.

"Cute story. Sunny was too smart for some cooked-up idea like that. He would never have swallowed those balloons."

"A nice shot of heroin might have helped him change his mind."

"Exactly. And since he was clean, it seems glaringly clear that he was forced."

Lola forced herself to relax her suddenly tight jaw. "What are you going to do now?"

"Justice, Miss Starke, is an elusive concept for our fair city's police force. I, however, am unencumbered by politics and incompetence. There are people in this City who think the laws don't apply to them. The saddest truth is that they're absolutely right. Immunity is a commodity that the police sell to anyone with enough money. Don't try to tell me different," he said.

"I can still help," Lola said.

Arbogast shook his head. He crushed out his cigarette in the alabaster bowl atop the desk. "It was a gamble coming to you." He shrugged. "I knew that."

"Then you owe it to Josephson to come clean. Another death won't bring him back."

The man laughed. "Is that what you think?"

"This can't end well."

"Perhaps not, but it *will* end, Miss Starke." He carefully put on his hat and touched the brim. "Good day."

Lola listened to him exit her offices and walk down the hall. She grabbed a hat and whipped out the door. She almost ran over a startled man in spectacles, but grabbed him by the shoulders just in time to sidestep him. She then threw him a hurried "excuse me" and made for the stairwell. Lola hoofed it down three flights and opened the door to the main lobby just as the elevator bell rang. Through the narrow slit, she watched Arbogast exit briskly out the main doors and turn left on the sidewalk. Lola followed him out the lobby but turned right once outside, heading for her car.

NINETEEN

Arbogast took a right at Delmetri then left onto Ada. Lola suddenly realized where he was headed.

Aubrey echoed her silent disbelief: "He's going to work?"

Lola found an empty spot across from the building, just behind a delivery truck for an automobile parts shop. She watched Arbogast stroll inside the Gaming building. A glance at her watch. She'd give him ten minutes, then hop in to chat with Pfeiffer.

Eight minutes later, however, Arbogast returned to his car. He swung a black briefcase at his side. The tan Olds was in flight once more, a preening bird among lumbering oxen. Lola weaved between and behind the City's ignorant masses—smoke-belching behemoths and purring town cars alike—keeping one eye steady on Arbogast's little beauty.

Eventually, he entered East Town from its western borders. Lola's sloppy old sedan stuck out like a black eye on a beauty queen. The cars here sparkled with wealth. There were more chauffeurs per capita in the City than anywhere else in the world. The west part of East Town was where their employers lived. On the outer edge, before the gates and tall walls began, sat the Fat Fat Mah-Jongg Emporium. It wasn't a pretty name in English, but Lola had learned from her aunties long ago that it was an auspicious name, as was its location.

Across from it stood the largest Buddhist monastery in any non-Buddhist country in the world. Many gamblers stopped in at the public temple and prayed, offering alms before they crossed the street and read their fates on little ivory tiles.

Lola idled half a block away from the monastery entrance. She pulled out a map and pretended to study it. Not more than ten minutes later, Arbogast exited Fat Fat. He walked briskly to his car.

"He doesn't look nearly anxious enough," said Aubrey.

Silently, Lola agreed. Amateurs bent on revenge ought to be nervous, not self-assured. At the very least, he should have been looking for a tail. Lola sighed as she pulled a U-turn, lining up behind a silver sedan.

Arbogast headed straight downtown from there. Lola followed him as far as the employee parking lot and slid into a spot one row away from his. It was just past four-thirty. Lola figured another half hour before the lot began to empty in earnest. As it was, people started hightailing it out before twenty-five minutes were up. Lola was just starting to move her car when Arbogast came back to his Olds. She quickly pulled out of her spot and moved her old Buick behind his tan baby. She got out and walked to his window.

Whatever quip she'd had died on her lips without a sound. Arbogast sat, pale and trembling like a house of cards in a gentle breeze. He gripped the steering wheel with white knuckles. His eyes were wide and glassy.

"Arbogast," Lola exclaimed. "What's happened? Are you all right?"

He started. A bead of sweat streaked down from his brow along the left side of his face and dripped onto his collar, blackening the grey fabric. "Miss Starke." It came out as a whisper. He swallowed and tried to moisten his mouth.

"What's happened?" she repeated.

Arbogast looked around his car and finally noticed her sedan in the rearview mirror. "What are you doing? I need to get out."

"Tell me what's going on. I can help you."

"You don't understand. I'm leaving the City. I don't have much time."

"You're liable to lose a filling, you're shaking so hard. You'll cause a wreck inside of half a minute. You can't drive like this."

His face fell apart and the sorriest excuse for a laugh came out of his mouth. "You haven't the faintest."

Someone was coming. Arbogast looked up in panic. Then his entire body relaxed. He started his car up. Lola watched a wasp-waisted girl teeter her way over on four-inch heels. She smiled uncertainly at Lola as she climbed into her burgundy car. It was parked nose-to-nose with Arbogast's Olds. The girl backed up expertly and drove away.

Lola put a hand to Arbogast's shoulder. He brushed it off and threw his car into gear. Lola wasn't fast enough; she got her hand banged up by the car frame as Arbogast sped forward. She rubbed her hand, cursing as she watched her former client peel out of the employee lot.

"A lady should watch her mouth," drawled a husky voice behind her. Lola whirled around. Copenhagen's thug smirked at her and tipped his hat. Just behind him, his leaner cohort smiled unpleasantly. Thick placed a meaty hand at Lola's elbow. "Time for another meeting with your client."

She shook her arm, but his grip was a vise. He dug his thumb into the tender spot on her inner arm, just beside the elbow. A dagger of pain lanced through her as he harshly massaged the sensitive nerve.

"A lady should appreciate her escorts," he said.

Lola stood her ground with gritted teeth. "I know the way."

Thick increased the pressure. "We walk like this or you don't walk at all."

No one met Lola's eye as they marched her inside the Gaming Commission Building. Aubrey buzzed with tension. Lola felt him like a pressure in the air beside her, changing sides as he moved around her in the Ether. Lola considered her options.

Copenhagen was waiting behind her massive desk when they delivered Lola into the office. Lola rubbed gingerly at her arm.

"Let's get this over with," she growled.

"No need to be rude," said Copenhagen. "I am your client, after all. You work for me."

"I work for myself."

"Come now, there's no need to sulk." The other woman regarded Lola with amusement.

Lola stared stonily, refusing to be drawn in.

Copenhagen raised an eyebrow. "Surely, you have time for a client?" she asked.

"What do you want?" Lola ground out.

"I have a serious situation, involving an employee of mine. I need you to handle it."

"This related to your illegal tournaments?" Lola asked.

Copenhagen shook her head. "No, not at all. As a matter of fact, the cops have dug up some promising leads, and I've been assured arrests are imminent."

"Just like that."

"Mmmm. Timing is everything, isn't it? Ah, but don't look so dejected, Lola. It's not as though you failed. I'm willing to admit I jumped the gun by hiring you. But your…interaction with the detectives certainly spurred them into quicker action."

"Your plan all along, of course."

Copenhagen gave a very European shrug. "Nothing personal, you understand. It got the job done. Here." She gestured to an envelope on her desk. "Easy money. A retainer for the next job is also included."

"The next job," repeated Lola, her gaze level on the other woman's face.

"As I said, I have an employee in a troubling situation." Copenhagen motioned for Lola to sit. She hesitated. Thick pushed down on her shoulder and Lola fell into the chair. "A man named Bodewell Arbogast. Know him?"

Lola remained tight-lipped.

Copenhagen sighed theatrically. "I'm afraid I haven't been entirely honest with you, Lola. You see, I know Arbogast hired you to find Sunny." She got up, paced to the windows then returned. "Sunny was a paid informant. He was spying on Arbogast. For me."

"How did you pay him? With smack?"

"Oh no. Poor Sunny was already back on the needle when I approached him. He was as twisted up in this extortion business as Arbogast, but he was desperate for more money. Sunny was the perfect weak link, and I needed to find the start of the chain. I paid him to keep tabs on his lover."

"Oh now we're being honest, are we?" said Lola. She leaned forward. "You sent me that little black ledger book. Aubrey could smell your Wards on it. You knew we'd sniff you out. I don't know what the point of sending it anonymously was, but I do know this." She leaned back slightly, bracing herself.

"*You're* behind the extortion ring. Arbogast was working for *you*. He thinks you had Sunny killed. What did he do? Threaten to expose the ring?"

Copenhagen's eyes widened. "I'm glad to see the old gears grinding, Lola, but you're sadly far from the mark." She reached into her desk. Lola tensed.

Copenhagen brought out a small black book. "Look familiar? We buy them by the hundreds. What I sent you is nothing but gibberish. I knew you'd been following Arbogast that day. So I gave you a little something to think about. I planned for you to show it to him. I hoped you'd wade right in, throw your weight around. Toss it in his face, even. And I was right." She paused, waiting, but Lola said nothing. "Still haven't figured it out?" Copenhagen's smile was all teeth. "We've been trying to catch him for months. The extortion ring is Arbogast's brainchild, not mine. I wanted you to use that ledger, to push him into doing something to tip his hand.

Copenhagen shook her head.

"We'd known about the ring for months before we finally narrowed it down to Arbogast. So we recruited Sunny. As I said, he was desperate for money. We paid him regularly and he gathered information for us. He confirmed our theories."

Lola considered the other woman's explanation. "Arbogast said he met Sunny after he was already working for you."

"Two stories, one truth. Whom do you trust more, Arbogast or me?" said Copenhagen. "A tight spot, isn't it?"

Lola narrowed her eyes. "Did you send Sunny down South?"

"No. I tried to get him arrested before he disappeared."

"Is that what pushed him into becoming a drug mule?"

Copenhagen shook her head. "Still a beat behind."

"Enlighten me."

"Lucille was the mastermind behind that operation. Narcotics affect Ghosts as much as Hosts, Lola. Ghosts can become addicts as easily as if they were still living. Imagine poor Sunny, trying to reform, fighting his body's dependence but still under siege from his own dead sister's addiction." Copenhagen shrugged. "Lucille must have sent him South. She must have made him swallow those terrible balloons."

"Why'd you try to sic the cops on him? Before he disappeared?"

"Sunny tried to extort more money from me. He threatened to tell Arbogast of our surveillance and then dismantle the entire ring. I refused. An arrest was supposed to take care of Sunny without tipping his co-conspirators."

"He must have got wind of the cops and *that* pushed him into a bad decision. You're as responsible as anyone."

"Which is to say, no one was responsible, least of all Sunny himself." Copenhagen shrugged. "At any rate, Lucille undoubtedly dictated the timing."

"Why didn't you arrest Arbogast when he was here?"

"He threatened to expose Mayor in the *Herald* as the head of this extortion ring."

"Mayor?" asked Lola skeptically. "How is he involved in any of this?"

"As far as I know, he isn't. But Arbogast swears he's doctored up papers that say otherwise."

"No one would believe that," countered Lola. "What would Arbogast possibly have against Mayor?" She shook her head."

"I'm not taking the chance that someone *will* believe it," replied Copenhagen. "Are you?" She paused. "Or perhaps, you think this a perfect opportunity to take revenge." She eyed Lola speculatively. "Is that it? You'd prefer Mayor humiliated and exposed as a lying cheat."

"I'm not doing your dirty work," said Lola. "You've got plenty of muscle to bring one simple accountant in. You should've arrested him when you had the chance."

"Use your other muscle, Lola, please, the one in your head." Copenhagen narrowed her eyes. "You need to find Arbogast, quickly. Clearly, Sunny's death has driven him mad. How else to explain this bizarre plan to frame Mayor? You need to find him," she repeated, "because you owe it to him. There's no way for him to reach Mayor that doesn't end badly for him. You owe it to him to find him and stop him. For his own good."

"I heard you the first time," said Lola, a snarl in her voice. She stared at Copenhagen as she considered her options. Copenhagen kept a neutral expression as the silence stretched out. Finally, Lola said, "This stinks and we both know it. Keep your money. I'm not on your dime. When I find him, I'm taking him into the cop shop."

Copenhagen nodded genially. "Of course. I wouldn't have it any other way." Lola glared suspiciously at her a moment longer, but Copenhagen's earnest expression didn't waver.

When Lola got back to her office, she half-expected Arbogast in the waiting room. Instead, she got four angry cops and little space to manoeuver.

"Where is he?" asked Luke.

Lola refused to squeeze past any of them. She stood in her doorway and crossed her arms, slowly. "Have a seat, why don't you, Luke." She nodded to the others. "Bednarski, Tsu, Marks."

"This ain't a social call," said Luke. He pushed off from the wall he was holding up and took a step toward Lola. "Where's the junkie's boyfriend?"

"I lost him." She faced Bednarski. "What about you? Did he ditch you too?"

The big cop nodded curtly. "Who were the two palookas handling you?"

Lola considered her answer. "A coupla monkeys working for the Assistant Deputy Commissioner of Gaming." She looked to the two Vice cops. They gave her nothing.

Marks spoke. "Why the rough stuff? Client unhappy with your work?"

Lola made an impatient noise in the back of her throat. "Copenhagen's not much for hands-on work, Marks. Why get her hands dirty when hired thugs work so much better?"

"Sounds personal," commented Bednarski.

"Have you ever met her?" asked Lola. The big man shook his head. Lola spoke slowly, "Of course, it's personal. She's a nasty piece of work." She looked at each of the men in turn. "Look, are we square here?"

"Far from it," answered Inspector Tsu. "You owe us some legwork."

"I'm not some Saturday night frail, Tsu. I don't owe you anything. You got your new leads. I didn't get in your way and now, the Assistant Deputy Commissioner's taken me off the case. I'm out of your hair. What more do you want?"

"The junkie's boyfriend," repeated Luke.

"Why you're a regular broken record, Luke. You must be a helluva hit at cocktail parties."

Luke stepped even closer. Lola could smell Chinese tobacco, overlaid with an angry tang. She met his eyes calmly even as she readied for a fight.

"Leave the smart talk for the scum you work with, Starke," Luke said in a low voice. "You're not among friends here."

"Back. Off," she replied. Luke waited a beat before stepping back. A twitch played around his lips. Lola continued. "What's your interest in Arbogast, Luke?" She gestured to the two *gwai* cops. "I know why they're looking for him, but how does he connect to your gambling ring?"

Luke stared at Lola. It was Tsu who replied.

"We hear he's a gold mine of information. Likely knows a lot about the City's mah-jongg operations."

"Who told you that?"

"Copenhagen."

Lola took a calming breath and began again, "Arbogast said he was leaving town. Copenhagen wants me to find him. She thinks he's a nut with a gripe. You think he's a murder suspect. I think he's scared to death of her. You're the cops. *You* find out why."

"What about you?" asked Bednarski. "What do you owe him?"

Lola's lips tightened into a thin slash. "Out. All of you."

The cops looked at one another, passing an inscrutable glance around, before taking their leave. Lola thought Luke might bump her on his way past, but Tsu nudged him away. Luke grimaced and walked on. Lola stood in the hall, watching them. No one spoke as the elevator ground its way up. The men entered one by one. Last was Marks. He turned, gave Lola a considering look, then disappeared into the lift. Lola heard the lift-boy's cheerful voice. She turned away.

Lola entered her office, thoughts grim, teeth grinding. She snatched the phone up and growled at the operator, knowing it was futile. No one picked up, and she imagined the telephone echoing through Arbogast's empty house.

Still standing, Lola called her mother next. Aubrey didn't even have to insist, although he did, as a matter of form.

"Lola, what is this about?" Grace sounded exhausted.

"Mother, has Mayor cancelled your engagement tonight? Are you still going to see him? Tonight?"

"No, yes and yes," Grace answered.

"He hasn't cancelled?" repeated Lola.

"Darling, he can't. It's too complicated and none of my business to explain, but the simple answer is, he can't cancel and he can't postpone it. Tonight is the only time for the—," but she didn't finish.

"Mother, you can't go," Lola broke in. "There's something going on. I can't explain. You might be in danger."

"Lola, we've been through this so many times, you know the lines as well as I do."

Lola surprised herself by saying: "Then let me accompany you."

"Absolutely not," replied her mother. "It's not my decision to make, and I know Mayor cannot allow it." She softened her tone. "Darling, I know it's difficult to understand but this has nothing to do with you."

"It does now, godsdammit," said Lola.

"Please don't make this even harder for me. It's not my choice to make. I'm sorry." Grace rang off.

Lola slammed the receiver down, then quickly picked it back up. "Juniper 387." Her lip curled up in a snarl.

"Hello?" answered an urbane voice.

"St. John," said Lola. "You've got to talk sense into her."

"I'll do no such thing, unless you come clean with me."

"Dammit," exploded Lola. "Stop harping on that, man. That's not what's important. She can't go tonight. Not to his mansion. There's a potential danger, a disgruntled employee—"

St. John laughed. "I'm sure Mayor's security can handle an unhappy worker. My team and I will be there to take care of Grace. She's our only priority. Mayor will have to deal with his flunkies on his own."

"I want to go with her," said Lola.

"You'll only muddy the waters, girl. Let us do our jobs, eh? I've been at this longer than you've been walking, Lola. I know how to protect Grace."

St. John rang off. Lola threw the receiver onto its hook, listening to it clatter uselessly.

"What are we going to do?" asked Aubrey.

Lola clenched her jaw. "What else is there?"

She took to the streets, driving aimlessly at first while she thought over the conversation with Copenhagen. She knew she was missing something. There had to be another angle. Instinct was screaming that Copenhagen was lying through her perfect pearly-whites. The problem was that her story was just as plausible as Arbogast's. It truly was a case of "he said-she said," and Lola was certain Copenhagen would have the better proof, regardless of the truth.

Cursing at her own indecision, Lola turned toward Arbogast's house once again. It was a lousy long shot, but it was what she had. She took deep breaths of the lemon-scented air as she drove down the main boulevard of Southern Plains, trying to clear her head. All too soon, she arrived at Arbogast's patch of sidewalk. Jed Wing was outside on his lawn. He watched Lola pull up, a sad cast to his haggard face. He tapped an unlit pipe against his thigh.

"You're too late," he said by way of greeting. "He's gone."

Lola fought the urge to curse long and loudly. "Did he tell you where, Mr. Wing? It's important." Wing shook his head. "Please, Mr. Wing, I'm on his side."

"You misunderstand," the older man replied. "Bodewell told me you'd likely come here. He was agitated. I thought he was overwrought by Sunny's death. I tried to get him to come inside, to my house. I didn't think his house was..."

"When did he leave?" asked Lola when Wing didn't finish his thought aloud.

"What's going on?" Wing ignored her question. "Why are you searching for Bodewell? Was Sunny murdered? That's what Bodewell thinks. I'm not sure what to think. The police, this morning, they said it was an accidental death. Why does Bodewell say Sunny was murdered?"

"Take pity on him, for gods' sake," said Aubrey. "He looks ready to keel."

"Here," said Lola. She took him by the elbow and led him up his front steps and into the chair. He stared at the pipe in his hand for a few seconds before settling it lightly in the ashtray. "I'm sure it's been a long day for you."

"Don't patronize me, Miss Starke," said the older man. "Bodewell seemed to think you truly were trying to help him." He eyed Lola coolly. "He also said there was nothing you could do for him."

"I'm doing my best. I need to locate Mr. Arbogast as quickly as possible." Lola asked about possible other homes in the mountains or perhaps up the coast. She asked about the yacht in the photograph she'd seen of Arbogast and Sunny. Wing thought it belonged to a colleague from the Gaming Commission, but he didn't have a name. Lola doggedly kept up her questions, but nothing new came up.

"If Mr. Arbogast returns, ring the police immediately," said Lola. "Ask for Detective Inspector Bednarski. They'll track him down. Cooperate with the police fully and they'll take care of Mr. Arbogast."

"You didn't answer me." Wing face was grey around the edges, but his eyes were clear and his jaw set. "Why does Bodewell think Sunny was murdered?"

Lola considered her reply. She decided on the truth. Wing shook his head sadly as she told him of the heroin-filled balloons. Lola concluded grimly, "Mr. Arbogast is looking for someone else to blame."

Wing rubbed his face, then clasped his hands together in front of him. He looked down at them as he spoke. "I don't think he left town. He had only a briefcase with him." Wing raised his gaze to meet Lola's eyes. "But I'm afraid it's too late already. He could be anywhere in the City."

"I need to get into his house, Mr. Wing, find an address book, get contacts for his friends, family, acquaintances, anyone he may have gone to for help."

"I don't believe the Wards have been reset," replied Wing, rubbing his face again. "Look near the telephone, in the kitchen. They usually kept their book nearby." His voice was thin, weary. "Neither had any family left."

Lola left Wing sitting on the porch, staring out into the street. She strode over to Arbogast's back door. It wasn't locked and she entered without issue. The table and chairs had been put upright. The oven door was firmly closed now. Papers had been gathered into piles, but they still covered the countertops. She found a dark green leather address book within seconds. Lola flipped through the pages quickly before snapping it closed. She hurried through the house and took the stairs upward. She checked the closets in the master bedroom. Not that she'd taken a full inventory the day before, but she didn't see any gaps or empty clothes hangers now.

"Wing was telling the truth," said Aubrey. "Arbogast is likely still in the City." He paused. "He may come back here."

Lola remained silent as she looked at her wristwatch and calculated. She slapped the address book against her palm a time or two. Finally, she looked down at it. Making her decision, Lola returned to the kitchen downstairs. She pulled over a chair and sat at the counter. She opened the address book to the first entries and picked up the telephone receiver.

A frustrating forty minutes later, she returned the receiver to its cradle for a final time. Closing the green address book, she pushed it away. Lola shoved away from the countertop and stepped to the back door. Once outside, she took out her cigarette case. Turning at a sound, she found Jed Wing staring at her from over the fence.

"No one's heard from him," she said. She chose a cigarette, found her lighter and put it to use. She inhaled deeply of the pungent smoke.

"Why are you still here?"

Lola shrugged. "He might've returned. Seemed quicker just to stay and make the calls." She exhaled, putting the case and lighter away in her purse.

Wing looked up. Dusk was beginning to settle over the houses and lemon trees. "No moon tonight," he said. Lola took another long drag of her Egyptian, nodding in absent-minded agreement. She ran through a mental inventory of gin joints and speakeasies. She doubted he was welcome at the parlours.

Abruptly, she went still, running the older man's words through her mind. "Isn't there something significant about the new moon in April, the dark moon?" She furrowed her brow, trying to capture the fleeting thought.

Wing shook his head slowly after a few moments. "You'd have to be more specific than that, I'm afraid."

Aubrey suddenly inhaled so sharply, the sound was like a high-pitched whistle in Lola's ears. She winced. He said, "Mayor. It's his Death Moon." Lola raised an eyebrow, trying to fit this bit of information into the bigger puzzle. Aubrey broke into her thoughts, his voice urgent. "We have to go. Now. I don't have a damned clue where Arbogast is and I don't care right now. I'm talking about Grace. She's with him tonight, on his Death Moon night. That damned Ghost has something planned, and she's a part of it. I don't trust the timing. So stop staring at the fence, for gods' sake. Let's go," he shouted.

Lola went.

TWENTY

Twenty-five minutes later, Lola drove slowly up to an ornate gate of scrolling, white-painted metal. She watched a guard step out of his little house and wait for her to stop. She obliged and rolled down her window.

"Miss." The guard tipped his hat. He glanced into the back seat. "Are you lost?"

"No," replied Lola. "I'm here to see my mother. Grace McCall. She's expected."

The guard neither confirmed nor denied it. "Your name please?" He held a clipboard and a fountain pen, its cap already unscrewed. Lola heard the nib scratching the paper as he jotted down her answer. "Please remain in your car, Miss Starke." He stepped away and re-entered the small guardhouse. Lola heard another voice murmur something that sounded like a question. The first guard replied in equally low tones. Lola guessed they'd be ringing up to the main house for instructions.

When the guard reappeared next to her window, Lola had her best polite smile in place. The guard nodded. "You have been cleared to go up, Miss Starke. However, I need to search your car before I can let you proceed."

Lola immediately set the hand brake and turned the engine off. She got out and, following his gesture, waited next to the guardhouse. The man drew out a hand torch and peered inside the car, under the car and inside the boot. Lola felt a presence just to her left and turned to find a stout woman in guard's uniform watching her. Lola nodded in greeting.

"Good evening," said Aubrey. So, this guard had a Ghost. Lola imagined Aubrey was giving his best polite smile as well. The earlier panic in his voice was now nowhere in evidence. Rather, he sounded smooth and urbane.

"Yes," he continued. "Aubrey O'Connell. Yes, I was." He gave a good-natured chuckle. "I'm flattered you remember me at all. We grew up together, in fact. Is she here yet?" A pause. "Oh. Well it would be a great favour if we could await her inside. I'm sure Mayor won't begrudge us some time in his library." He paused again. "Yes, I do. We both do. We just saw him a few days ago, as a matter of fact. What was that?" he asked genially. "To be honest, it's a private family matter between Miss McCall and her daughter. I'm just along for the ride. You know how it is." Lola had to give it to him. Aubrey struck the perfect tone as the put-upon Ghost of a flighty young woman.

Lola waited with a blankly polite expression. The male guard completed his circuit of the car. He stepped over to Lola and his coworker. "It's clean." He nodded to Lola. "I'll drive you up to the main house."

Lola nodded. The man stepped around and held open the passenger side door. Lola slid in as graciously as she could. Aubrey bade the other Ghost farewell. The gate split down the middle and a gap opened silently for them to drive through. A few minutes later and they arrived at the circular cobbled driveway that fronted a large manor house of dark brick and columns flanking the massive front door. Shutters framed every window. A huge semi-circular window above the front door showcased an enormous chandelier inside. Exterior lights, styled to resemble carriage lanterns, brightened the front of the house. Lola recalled that tours had once been given of this property. Many tourists had paid good money to see Matteo Esperanza's home, its European style and build such an anomaly on this coast. When he'd originally been elected the City's mayor, however, Esperanza's security detail had immediately cancelled all house tours.

The guard drove until the drive was just beginning to round away from the main house. He parked next to a dark Packard. The guard exited quickly. Lola waited for him to come around for her. She thanked him. He returned her car key and gestured for her to step to the house. He escorted her to the door and rang the doorbell. Lola waited patiently to be handed off.

The door opened. Lola had expected another guard, but it was the majordomo who greeted her instead. The man was easily a head shorter than Lola. He wore a severe grey coat and black trousers. He gave her a bow in the European fashion, short and clipped. Lola thought it strange seeing a Chinese man do so. Just beside her, the guard tipped his hat, murmured a "miss," turned on his heel and walked away down the driveway.

"If you'll follow me, Miss Starke," said the majordomo. Lola thought she detected a very slight lisp. "I shall lead you to the library. Miss McCall shall be down shortly."

Lola stepped inside. The foyer was rectangular, and to her surprise, warmly inviting. She noted two vases of flowers, two jade carvings of traditional Chinese lions, as well as a number of potted jade plants. A flight of stairs went up the right wall. At its foot was a door leading to what looked like a single room. Lola guessed it was the drawing room, filled with a few pieces of furniture and perhaps a small fireplace. On the left wall, a large rectangular mirror, framed in simple pewter, reflected the chandelier's brilliance. To either side of the mirror were two doors, both closed. Lola followed her guide past both of these and down the hallway that led off from the far left corner of the foyer. She eyed the stairs briefly, but the angle didn't allow her to see the second floor.

The majordomo stopped at a set of double doors made of dark wood. He opened one and moved aside for Lola to precede him inside. Once she passed through, he said, "I shall bring refreshment." He closed the door. Lola listened for the click of a lock turning, but she heard only his retreating footsteps.

Aubrey spoke quickly. "Grace is already here. They won't allow us to see her until Mayor's security clears it. And no, I don't understand what that means. However, this room is Warded against us leaving."

"So we wait in the library," said Lola. She kept her tone brisk. Starting at the nearest shelf, she walked along the wall, examining book spines.

"You're being awfully cooperative," said Aubrey. "Why *did* you agree to come here?"

Lola trailed a finger against the books as she walked. "It still bothers me that Copenhagen didn't arrest Arbogast when he was right there in her office. I don't buy that Arbogast threatened to frame Mayor at all. So why bring Mayor into this? She's got some plan running in the background—you can count on that."

"So lacking any leads on Arbogast, you figured this was as good a place as anywhere else in the City to find him?" Aubrey's skepticism rang clearly.

"No," replied Lola patiently. "Your panic at recalling Mayor's Death Moon reminded me. Arbogast isn't the centre of this. For all I know, Copenhagen sent Arbogast somewhere, and she's got me running around town for her own twisted amusement. Five gets you ten there wasn't a word of truth in anything she told me."

"But the fact remains," Aubrey said, realization dawning in his voice, "she brought Mayor into the equation."

Lola nodded. "I aim to find out why." She turned back toward the centre of the room just as the door opened.

"Darling, what are you doing here?" Lola's mother hurriedly entered the room, followed by St. John. "You must take Aubrey and leave immediately." Lola had expected her mother to be in evening wear, replete with pearls and diamonds. Instead, Grace wore a simple frock in white and blue, covered with a light wool sweater in dove grey.

St. John closed the door. "I'm with Grace on this one, girl. It's not safe for you to bringing your Ghost here."

Lola put up her hands. "He's the one who wanted to be brought. Wouldn't leave me alone until I did."

Grace embraced Lola tightly. When she moved back, she slid her hands down Lola's arms until mother and daughter were holding hands. She looked directly into Lola's eyes. "Darling, please. I wish you could stay, I do, but it's not a good idea."

St. John spoke up before Lola could reply. "And it ain't personal, neither. Tonight's a bad time for your Ghost to be here."

"Let me speak, for gods sake," said Aubrey.

Lola conveyed her Ghost's request.

St. John's expression flashed with irritation then smoothed out.

"You tell them they'd better come clean. Now. I want an explanation as to why Mayor wants Grace here on the night of his Death Moon. Once I'm satisfied with the reason, then we'll leave."

Lola relayed Aubrey's demand, watching her mother's face darken with each word. Grace's hands spasmed briefly. Lola winced inwardly as her mother's fingernails dug into her vulnerable palms. Then Grace abruptly let go.

"Oh, you overprotective, overbearing..." Lola wasn't exactly clear to whom her mother was speaking but she held her tongue. Grace sputtered for a few more phrases before she finished with, "You're driving me mad."

St. John raised an eyebrow at Lola. She noted his light grey suit had thin maroon chalk stripes. She asked him, "How many men'd you bring tonight?" He put up two fingers. Grace glared at both of them before turning to Lola.

"I'm fine. St. John has me well taken care of, as always."

"Tell her I'm waiting," said Aubrey.

Lola kept her voice neutral as she complied. She must have managed fairly well as Grace only compressed her lips into a thin line. She glanced at St. John. "The time please?"

He checked his wristwatch then nodded.

"I can't say more than this," began Grace "This is an annual ceremony on the new moon of April, and I'm a part of it. Nothing untoward has ever occurred. I have never been harmed nor has anyone else who's involved, for that matter. Does that *satisfy* you, Aubrey?"

"Why isn't Mayor here to tell us this?" asked Lola.

Grace sighed, clearly exasperated. "Because you asked to see *me*. Think what you will of him, but Mayor is still gentleman enough to give a friend privacy for a family matter." She touched her earring, smoothed her black hair. "Now, I must go and so must you. Jiang will show you out."

As if on cue, there was a knock at the door. St. John did the honours. It was the majordomo with a service cart. "Refreshments, Miss. Madame, Mayor has requested that Miss Starke remain until afterward, when he can visit with her properly." He bowed low, this time in the Chinese manner, until his upper body was perpendicular to the ground. He held the position for the traditional few seconds before returning upright.

Lola caught a few choice words from her mother, but Grace was muttering under her breath so they weren't entirely clear. St. John shrugged when Lola glanced at him. Grace bussed Lola on the cheek hurriedly and left the room. As he followed Grace out, St. John said, "See you later then, girl."

The majordomo, Jiang, pushed the cart toward an arrangement of two armchairs near the fireplace. On the medium-sized table between the chairs, he laid out a tea service complete with small buns, sweet tarts and fruit. Lola chose one of the armchairs, upholstered in dark leather, and sat. The tea smelled strong. Lola didn't recognize it but she was happy to try it. She murmured her thanks as the majordomo poured into a tall cup patterned in pale green leaves. Jiang bowed low again and departed. Lola listened again for the sound of a lock, but it didn't come.

"She didn't explain much of anything," said Aubrey.

"I'm curious he wants us to stay. Even though Mother and St. John were both at great pains to tell us it was dangerous."

"Mayor's nothing if not arrogant, Lola. As well as unpredictable. You'd do well to remember that," said Aubrey.

Lola shrugged.

She turned her attention to the tea and food. It didn't take long. Dabbing at her lips one last time, she then folded her napkin precisely and left it next to her plate. She stood, picking up her teacup, and stepped over to the windows. She took a sip of tea, turned and wandered around the library, in clear view of the windows. Five minutes or so of this and she was satisfied that the security detail watching from the exterior grounds would see her safely tucked in at the library. She made sure to take down a book from a shelf in line with one of the windows before returning to the armchair. She forced herself to read five pages of *Heretical Feng-Shui in Feudal Times.*

"Tell me about the Wards," she said in a low voice.

"They're strong," replied Aubrey, "but I've found a tiny crack. Here, near the bottom of the shelf to the right of the door."

"Will it set anything off?"

"Hasn't so far." Aubrey paused. "I've been working on it since you started eating."

"Isn't that a long time for you to crack a Ward?"

"Mayor's a well-known adept. His Spells are complicated, intelligently woven. He ties his magic to his essence. Don't ask me how. None of us normal Ghosts know."

Lola was curious. "Is that why you don't like him? He ignores the rules in the Ghost Handbook?"

Aubrey's taut voice came sharply: "Something's happening."

"Is it the Warding?" asked Lola. "Did you trip an alarm?"

Aubrey's voice was stretched thin: "We have to get out. Something feels...wrong."

"Did you break the Ward?' Lola got up. She kept her body low and duck-walked to the door, making sure the furniture was between her and the windows. She stopped at the door, listening hard. Nothing.

"Aubrey. Did you break the Ward?"

"No," he replied faintly. "I mean, yes, it's broken but I didn't do it."

"Aubrey," Lola whispered sharply. "Stay with me. What's going on?"

"There's something not right in the Ether." he replied. "Be quiet. I need to focus."

Lola ground her teeth but remained silent. She strained her ears, heard nothing. No running feet. No low murmurs as orders were given or locations ascertained. If there was something going on, it didn't involve the security detail. Nor St. John's men, she realized. Her mother should be safe.

"Are we jake?" whispered Lola.

"I can't figure it out," Aubrey said finally. "It was so slight, but I know I felt a disturbance."

"Does that mean a Spell was cast? Mayor's ceremony?"

"No coincidences, remember? It has to be connected. I've just never felt a Spell reverberate like that."

"So it could just be this mysterious ceremony," said Lola. "You can debate the whys later. I'm leaving this room now." She took a few moments to rehearse her move mentally. She would be exposed to anyone watching through the windows, but it was her best chance at leaving the room. Taking a deep breath, Lola stood, turned the door handle, swung open the door, stepped out, and closed the door behind her in one smooth motion. She immediately stepped to the side of the double-door frame and glanced down both ends of the hallway. Flattened against the wall, she kept her breathing easy and calm, and listened for approaching footsteps.

"There's a trail of sorts," began Aubrey in a halting voice. "I think I can direct us to the disturbance."

Lola nodded. "Likely our best way to the ceremony. Lead on."

"Down the hall. No, away from the foyer, toward the back."

Lola moved swiftly along the edge of the hall, avoiding the centre, as it had the highest likelihood of creaks from constant use. A few feet down, she had to creep past the kitchen doorway. A quick peek within revealed a rack of pots and pans, hanging over a large butcher's block, a wall of counter space and cupboards, and Jiang's back as he chatted with a woman who luckily had her head mostly hidden by the open icebox door. Farther on, past the kitchen door, the hall then took a sharp turn to the right. Lola cursed. The kitchen opened onto this hallway as well. This time, Lola couldn't count on the angles. She'd pass right through Jiang's periphery. Glancing down the hall she'd already traversed, Lola made sure it was still empty as she waited impatiently for Jiang and the woman—perhaps a cook—to shift.

She heard the majordomo say he was going to check on their guest.

"Hurry," said Aubrey. "The trail's stronger down this way. We won't have much time when he finds you gone."

Lola pressed her lips tightly together and watched the two servants through narrowed eyes. She judged her moment and slid past the doorway. There were three doors on the left of the hallway. All opened into a vast room, darkened now. Lola could see clear through the space to the far wall and its triple sets of French doors that presumably opened onto a rear garden and the rest of the grounds. On the right side of the hall, along with the access to the kitchen, Lola also found a set of back stairs, likely for the servants. Another very European feature, she thought. Just past those, the hallway met the corner of the building. Lola guessed it must lead back through the side of the house and that sitting room to the right of the front foyer. There may even be another large public drawing room or some sort of public entertaining space. The library she'd been in struck her as much more intimate.

She paused at the bottom of the servants' stairs and glanced around. Grateful for whatever luck had been with her thus far, she quickly crept up the first few steps.

"Wait," said Aubrey. "Go back. The trail's too faint here."

Lola obliged, wondering how much longer before her luck ran out entirely.

"Stop," commanded Aubrey. "Into the ballroom."

Lola hesitated. It was utterly black inside the room, and she wasn't about to announce her presence with a light. A clatter of footsteps came from the front of the mansion. She couldn't make out words but the urgent tone rang clearly. Lola stepped into the ballroom and scanned the murky space. "Do we go through here?" she asked.

"I don't think so. The feeling's strongest here."

"Can you see anything in the Ether in here? I'm as good as blind." Lola made her way with cautious steps, keeping close to the wall. She heard hard footsteps and heavy treading from above.

"It doesn't work like that," replied Aubrey in a distracted tone. "It's a feeling. And it's concentrated...here." He paused. "I can't make out what it is. I'll come back and lead you to it."

Lola felt pressure on her left side, so she veered left.

Judging by the angle to the doors, she knew she was walking toward the centre of the room. Feeling foolish, she groped through the air in front of her and took awkward sweeping steps. It was slow progress, made more maddening as she heard the sounds of Mayor's security coming alive through the building.

"It better be close," she whispered. "They'll be on top of us s—" Lola's foot caught on something in the dark. She lost her balance. Her hands, reaching blindly out for something to catch her fall, brushed against soft fabric. She clutched at it convulsively, wondering what sort of Spell instrument it might be, but it clearly wasn't sturdy enough to hold her up. She felt a change in air pressure, heard a faint *pop,* and realized she'd somehow broken a Spell, not just brushed against it. She cursed. Whatever she'd tripped over must have been propped up with magic and that magic had just disappeared. The fistful of fabric was suddenly a heavy weight that came with her as she crashed to the floor, landing across her torso. Unable to break her fall, Lola landed on her head. She cried out as her head bounced and smashed against the floor again. The *crack* as her skull met the hard wooden floor reverberated in the echoing space. Stunned and dazed, Lola was unaware of anything for a few seconds save a static-filled noise within her head. She came out of it intensely aware of a weight on her. She immediately jack-knifed her body, trying to push it off, feeling a sick revulsion crawl across her skin.

She panicked when the weight rolled but wouldn't budge. She didn't know which way to turn to roll it off all the way. "Get it off, get it off."

The lights overhead suddenly came on. Lola cried out again as an explosion of pain rocketed within her head.

"Hold it right there," shouted a man's voice.

"Get it off," Lola replied. She tried to open her eyes but they refused to cooperate. She tugged at her hands, caught between herself and the dead weight. The movement rocked her head painfully.

"Lola, stop," said Aubrey. "They're coming over."

Lola couldn't comply. The compulsion to get out from under the weight overrode all else. She pushed and shoved, managed to get her eyes open to slits. After an eternity, a shadow fell over her face and she felt hands on her shoulders. They held her in place as the weight was pulled off of her. Then she was pulled up to standing. She swayed a little, nausea clawing at her gut. When she opened her eyes fully, her gaze fell to the dead body that had trapped her. She felt her stomach drop.

Bodewell Arbogast laid face up, an expression of pain and fear etched into his features. His light green eyes were now dark and filming over. His coffee-with-cream skin had turned grey. His rumpled clothes and splayed limbs were difficult to look at. But she refused to turn away. It was the only thing she could give him now.

A dull roar sounded in her ears.

Lola blinked.

She pulled her gaze away from her dead client. She watched dully as St. John walked briskly toward her and grabbed her roughly by the shoulders. "What the hairy hells are you doing here?"

Lola winced audibly as the pounding in her head resumed. She had to close her eyes against the light again. She heard voices around her. Mayor's security explained what they'd seen, once the lights had come on.

"Dammit, girl." St. John's gentle tone belied the curse. "This is a right fine kettle of fish you've turned over. Hey, all right, yeah, we'll get her story soon enough. Can you snag me a chair? And a glass of water?" He stayed with Lola, a firm grip on her shoulders. "Tell me you've been downstairs this entire time."

"I've been downstairs this entire time," Lola said dutifully.

St. John made an irritated sound. "That had better be the truth, girl. You're in a mess of trouble."

"He was my client. Bodewell Arbogast. I lost him this afternoon," said Lola.

"That was alarmingly close to babbling," said St. John. "Let's get you sat down, shall we? Plenty of time to tell your story later."

Lola sat where he placed her, drank as ordered and generally gave an accurate impression of being a docile simpleton. It wasn't a ruse.

People began arriving, then: more members of Mayor's personal security, in crisp suits and tense expressions; Mayor, trailed by three Conjurers; and Grace, her expression thunderous, followed by two men Lola recognized as part of her mother's security.

"Let me talk to your mum now, girl. And for the love of all that's holy, do not move off of this chair."

Lola nodded slowly.

Ignoring her mother's furious gaze, she watched Mayor instead. He wore a sweater over a collared shirt and dark tie. Lola couldn't tell the colours well. She didn't know if it was the lighting or his state. Around him stood a huddle of mustard-yellow robes and suits. His Conjurers made sure to place themselves between their charge and Lola. They faced outward, their eyes trained to a spot just above her right shoulder. Apparently, Aubrey was staying close to her.

Mayor glanced at Lola a number of times as his people tried to explain how they had discovered Lola pinned beneath a lifeless body.

Finally, he approached, stopping a good five feet from her. He studied the body of Bodewell Arbogast. After a minute or so, Mayor swiveled to face Lola.

"Do you know him?"

Lola nodded.

Mayor stared at her for a few more seconds, his eyes flicking to Aubrey briefly. "The police are on their way. Let's wait in my study. If you would, Grace?"

Lola's mother nodded coldly and wheeled around. She stalked out of the ballroom and turned left. St. John signaled his men to follow Grace. Mayor gestured toward Lola. St. John helped Lola up and gave her his arm. She took deep breaths and walked as steadily as she was able. Mayor and his Conjurers came next, and one of his bodyguards brought up the rear. It was a silent procession. Before Lola exited the room, she glanced back. Four of Mayor's suits stood guard over Arbogast. Two of them watched Lola with cold eyes.

The study was as one would expect: a large desk, a few built-in bookshelves, a fireplace, comfortable sitting area, masculine accoutrements. Lola, Grace and Mayor were the only ones to sit. The others spread themselves around the perimeter of the room and remained standing. No one spoke. The Conjurers had eyes only for Aubrey while the guards avoided eye contact for any length of time. St. John was as vigilant as his men. He stood just behind Grace's left shoulder. Mayor attended to the telephone at his desk. Grace stared steadily at Lola, who turned and looked out the window at the dark.

Mayor returned the receiver to its hook. He motioned for Lola to approach. She chose one of the two club chairs in front of his desk.

Lola motioned toward the Conjurers. "What do they think? Is it murder?"

Mayor canted his head to the side. "You tell me."

Lola took a deep breath. "Judging from the expression on his face, I'd say so."

Mayor nodded abruptly. "The police should be here any minute. They'll know one way or another. I prefer to hold off on the questions until I speak with them." He stared at Lola until she got up and returned to her prior seat. She settled herself as calmly as she could and waited.

Eventually, the police arrived with their own glacial glares. They spoke with Mayor, just on the other side of the open study doors. There had to be a couple of detectives, but Lola didn't catch a glimpse of them. At the end of the discussion, the cops continued deeper into the house, toward Arbogast. Mayor went with them and so did his Conjurers. Through the open study doors, Lola saw a middle-aged woman with a shock of gray hair and thick-rimmed glasses, carrying a large black tackle-box, walk after the group. The coroner, thought Lola. A couple of uniforms rounded out the humourless group.

St. John remained standing behind Grace. The other three security men were scattered around the study: one stood next to the windows, another by the study doors, and the third waited opposite him.

“This has gotten entirely out of hand,” said Grace. Lola swung her gaze back to her mother. “I should never have let Butch talk me into letting you do any of this.”

Aubrey murmured, “He didn't have much say in the matter.”

Lola shrugged. “He knew me.”

Grace widened her eyes incredulously. "Murder, Lola? Dead bodies? How can you be so calm? Is it just all in a day's work now? Is this how your father raised you?"

Lola sighed. "Leave him out of it." She rubbed at her face and blinked eyes suddenly filled with grit. Or maybe she was only noticing it now. She added it to the growing list of physical complaints and shoved it out of mind.

"I have no idea what you thought," Grace continued, "coming here, but I can't help you out of this, Lola. I don't even know where to begin."

Lola rubbed her face again. She rose, walked slowly over to Mayor's desk, fished out a cigarette from an enameled box and lit it up. She grimaced with her first exhalation and returned to the sofa. Grunting slightly, she sank into the cushions and closed her eyes, absently rubbing at her temple with her free hand. The image of Arbogast, dead, rose up immediately. The rumpled clothes and splayed position disturbed her deeply for some reason. Lola felt her heart squeezed with regret. What the hells was he doing here? Why would he be in the middle of Mayor's ballroom? What had killed him? Was it Copenhagen, as he'd feared? How had she got him in here then?

The questions rose too rapidly for Lola to keep track of. They swirled in her mind in a riot. She refused to open her eyes, though, forcing herself to stare inwardly at the memory of her dead client's final expression.

Lola heard the scuff of feet at the study doors. She opened her eyes and watched as the guard immediately blocked the entrance. A few sharp words were exchanged and the man stood aside. A stubbled face surveyed the room, then zeroed in on Lola.

Inspector Bednarski seemed disappointed. "You found your client."

Lola grimaced as she tapped her cigarette ashes into an ebony ashtray. She leaned back against the sofa cushions. Grace was on the end opposite Lola, but she watched the two cops warily as they approached her daughter. Bednarski parked his bulk in a wingback armchair, while Marks stood at attention directly across from Lola. Unlike his partner, his clothes looked freshly pressed. Dark pouches underscored his eyes, however.

Mayor entered within minutes of the two murder cops. He spoke in quiet tones to his three Conjurers as he walked into the room. The Spell Casters flicked their glances regularly over to Lola, but none of them approached her.

"They're wondering about me," Aubrey said in a low voice. "I don't know why." Lola felt his tenseness as his silence stretched out. "It still feels queer in this place." Another pause. "Especially around him. I can feel it from here." Mayor now stood, conversing with his Conjurers, about ten feet away from Lola. "There's something...not right—" Aubrey abruptly stopped talking.

Mayor had finished with his Spell Casters. They formed a tight semi-circle behind him as he walked toward the seated group. Mayor gave Grace a reassuring look before settling in the armchair opposite from Bednarski. His Conjurers arranged themselves behind him. They ignored Lola, kept their eyes on Aubrey.

"Inspectors," said Mayor, "let's hear what Miss Starke has to say. Then I'll add what I know."

Lola smoked her cigarette. "As the detectives already know, Bodewell Arbogast was my client. He hired me to find his lover, Mr. Joseph Josephson. But Mr. Josephson was recently discovered dead, an accidental heroin overdose. I believe Mr. Arbogast went mad from the shock. He'd already been in denial about Mr. Josephson's drug addiction. It didn't make any sense to him, and he claimed that Mr. Josephson had been murdered. I've been searching for Mr. Arbogast since this afternoon." She paused to take a drag on her cigarette. "But that's not the reason I came here tonight." She glanced at Grace. "I was concerned about my mother."

"Why?" asked Bednarski.

Lola looked at Mayor. He returned her gaze, an expression of curiosity on his face. Lola considered her words before continuing. "I knew that she was involved in something tonight, something concerning Mayor's Death Moon. Aubrey didn't like it." She shrugged. "So we came."

Grace interjected. "Really, Detective Inspector, it's nothing but misguided intentions. Sometimes these two get it into their heads that I need their protection. We agree to disagree. I met with Lola prior to...I mean, earlier, when they first arrived here. I had all but convinced them to leave when Jiang invited them to stay." She turned her gaze to Mayor. "He said you wanted to visit with them."

Mayor nodded. "Yes, I was curious about their arrival."

"And your Ghost, he much for magic?" asked Marks suddenly.

Lola raised an eyebrow at the seemingly unrelated question. "No, he was my mother's childhood friend and her dresser. Not a lot of study time for Conjury."

"But Ghosts, all Ghosts, can handle simple Wards," said Marks.

"Doesn't make them Spell Casters, though. Isn't that correct?" she asked Mayor. "I understand you had to train for years."

Mayor smiled genially as he nodded. "I can vouch that Aubrey isn't a dangerous magic user, Detective Inspector."

"There was a Ward on the library, where we waited," said Lola. "And yes, Marks, I know about it because I tried to get out. I'm naturally curious that way. But the Warding disappeared suddenly. That's how I left the room." Lola finished her cigarette and tamped it out in the ebony ashtray. "I knew Mayor's security would find me soon enough, but Aubrey had been disturbed by something in the Ether. So I went exploring. We tracked it to the ballroom."

"And that's where you saw your dead client," said Bednarski.

Lola winced inwardly, but she kept her voice calm. "The lights weren't on then. I quite literally...stumbled across him." For a moment, she felt the weight of him on her chest again. She took a long, deep breath, willing her gorge to stay down. She cleared her throat. "My guess is he was propped up, likely magically, and I broke the Spell when I...made contact."

"No idea why he'd be here?" asked Marks. "He didn't say anything about Mayor this afternoon, before he disappeared?"

Lola was relieved to be able to answer truthfully. "No."

Bednarksi and Marks exchanged a glance.

Mayor cleared his throat politely. "I'd like to speak with Miss Starke alone now please. Inspectors, my staff is prepared to answer your questions now." Mayor stood.

Marks said, "Sir, we need to speak with Miss McCall privately now."

"I'm staying with my daughter," stated Grace.

"A few more minutes, Inspectors?" Mayor asked, as though it were an actual request.

Bednarski stood and placed a hand on his partner's shoulder. He nodded at Mayor then turned to Lola. "We're your escort downtown. Don't leave without us." Marks grunted and marched out of the room, his spine ramrod straight. The larger cop followed. Lola watched his rumpled back until he closed the door softly without a backward glance.

Mayor started pacing. "As you've noticed, my Conjurers are less than pleased with your presence. I had to vouch for your integrity." The Spell Casters remained motionless behind the chair Mayor had vacated. Their eyes, however, tracked left to right, left to right, just over Lola's line of sight. She guessed Aubrey was pacing. "There's a reason I don't normally allow other Ghosts near me. At least, Ghosts who aren't already Haunting my Conjurers. It's common knowledge that my Death Moon lands on the night of the new moon in April. What's not well-known, and by design, I might add, is that I must Ward especially on this night every year. It's a special Warding against Spells that involve other Ghosts. I won't get into the details. They're unimportant to you, I'm sure."

"St. John made sure to ask if I'd stayed down here. Were you Warding upstairs?" asked Lola.

Mayor nodded. "My Conjurers prefer to ask questions later, if you understand me. It would not have gone well for Aubrey to find you near me during the ceremony."

"You'd completed the ceremony?" asked Lola. Mayor nodded. "Nothing unusual occurred?" she pressed.

"Everything went according to ritual, as always. Didn't it, Grace?"

Lola's mother shifted. "Yes, I didn't think it was different from any other time."

"Arbogast had to have been there," said Aubrey.

"We would have sensed him," said Mayor.

"Maybe you didn't," countered Aubrey.

"You sound terribly certain," replied Mayor.

"The disturbance I sensed in the library. Its trail led me to Arbogast. When you first came into the ballroom, I sensed the same thing. You were ten feet away and I felt it. I don't believe in coincidence."

"Neither I nor my Conjurers seem to have your *sensitivity*," replied Mayor. A hint of a sneer flitted across his narrow, handsome features.

"What did Aubrey say?" Grace asked Lola.

Lola ignored her mother, keeping her attention on Mayor. "Are you certain you didn't feel anything strange happen?"

"I believe I've already answered that question, Lola," replied Mayor.

"Fine." She glanced at the Conjurers. They stood like statues, only their eyes keeping pace with Aubrey's pacing. Mayor's assertion seemed not to make any impression on them. A thought occurred to Lola then, as she considered Mayor's bodyguards. "Why are you so concerned about other Ghosts?" she asked suddenly.

The Conjurers shifted. Mayor stopped pacing. He looked from Grace to Lola. He settled on the latter. "It's not the Ghost. It's what someone with the right power can do with the Ghost." He cocked his head to the left. "Obviously, you don't have that sort of power. It's the only reason you and your Ghost are allowed to be here."

"Do you mean a Dispersal Spell, using another Ghost's essence?" asked Aubrey slowly.

Lola felt uneasy at the horror in Aubrey's voice. "I'm no Spell Caster," she said. "Neither was Arbogast, who wasn't Haunted. Josephson had a Ghost but she was an addict, like her Host. No one we spoke to ever even hinted that Lucille was able to Cast." She cocked her head at Mayor and his Conjurers. "I'd wager you have your own list of enemies, ones capable of that kind of Spell."

"Of course."

Lola considered for a moment. "Is AJ Copenhagen on that list?"

"I'm not familiar with that name," replied Mayor. He looked to his bodyguards. The Conjurers shared a glance. The shortest one, a woman, looked at Mayor and shook her head.

"She's Assistant Deputy Commissioner of Gaming," explained Lola.

"And why do you consider her a possibility?"

"I don't know if I do," replied Lola. "She—"

A knock sounded on the door. Bednarski stood, a pad of paper and a capped pen in hand. "Excuse me, sir, it's time to take Miss Starke downtown."

Mayor stared at the detective a few moments in silence. Bednarski met his scrutiny with weary calm. Finally, Mayor smiled slightly. "I'm sure Miss Starke is anxious to give her statement. I can, of course, vouch for her presence here. I'm sure you've checked with my gate security." The big man nodded. "Please report to me tomorrow morning, Detective Inspector. I expect to be updated on your progress."

"Yes, sir. Miss Starke?"

Mayor held up a hand. He turned back to Lola. "You as well, Lola. Tomorrow. I believe you have more to tell about this Assistant Deputy Commissioner. For tonight, however, I feel confident my security can do its job."

Lola stood. "I'll be in touch, Mayor."

"Darling, wait," said Grace. "We need to talk."

"It can wait, Mother. It'll have to." Lola stopped long enough to give her mother a sombre face. "Locke can't save you from their questions, you know."

"I don't need him to. I've nothing to hide and I don't have anything to do with this horrid business." Her mother's face was tight, her dark blue eyes ringed with fatigue.

"You should go home as soon as possible. I'll find you when they're done with me." Lola turned away.

"You could do worse than comfort your mother," said Aubrey quietly.

Lola pressed her lips together and walked out of the room.

When they turned her loose outside the station house, Lola wanted nothing more than a few hours' sleep. Her eyes were blurry with fatigue and her teeth felt covered in fuzz. She allowed herself to slump once she climbed into her car, but she knew it would be another hour before she would find her own bed. Lola drove, shifting in her seat restlessly, unable to settle. There were plenty of vehicles on the roads even at this time of night. It was a point of pride that the City was open for business *and* pleasure at all hours. Lola let her mind drift as she drove westward and upward.

There were few homes high up on the Northern Cliffs. Chinese thought it bad luck to build atop such a precarious perch as a wall of stone sitting atop a beach of sand. European transplants, however, were an entirely different story. Still, the homes up here didn't try to compete with those in North Hills. That would have been sheer foolishness as well as arrogance. The few builders in the City willing to construct homes on a cliff were bold, not stupid.

There was only so much one could do against erosion.

Lola drove through a simple barred gate. The driveway was modest, perhaps fifteen feet in length. It curved in front of a two-car garage and joined itself, forming a loop. Lola parked just past the garage, facing back down the driveway to the gate. She hauled herself out and stretched the kinks out of her neck. She hid a yawn behind her hand.

The house itself was typical of the homes on the Northern Cliffs: white painted adobe walls and red terracotta tiles on the roof. A main set of double doors, with the traditional Chinese circular handles of iron, faced Lola dead on. She walked past them and made for the covered path to the right of the house. She could hear the rhythmic *shush* of waves from the ocean below. Lola followed the flagstones around to the back of the house. As she walked, with the wall of the house to her left, she looked through the graceful arches to her right. An expanse of lawn, dotted with flowering pots and small trees, led to an outdoor swimming pool, covered now. A small building, just big enough for two changing stalls, sat dark.

Lola rounded the corner of the house and there it was, the ocean at night, with nothing in her way but clear sky. The moon wasn't making an appearance tonight, she knew, so she barely spared a glance at the dark waves spreading to the edge of the world. Lola had an obligation and she was dead set on fulfilling it.

She stopped short, suddenly realizing that there was a closed door in front of her. Shaking her head, she raised a hand to knock.

Grace opened the door herself. She had a deep blue silk dressing gown, its collar a profusion of pale cream ruffles, wrapped tightly around her slender body. The house behind her was quiet. Grace stepped aside and Lola entered the kitchen. A pot of coffee was still percolating on the stovetop. It filled the room with its rich aroma. Lola dragged herself up onto a stool at the counter. Grace sat lightly on the stool beside her. The women were silent as they waited for the coffee to brew. Grace poured out a mug and added a splash of whiskey. She placed it in front of Lola. After a moment, Lola took it and drank gratefully, welcoming the scalding heat. Grace's eyes were hooded, wary, as she watched her daughter. Lola imagined her own gaze was much the same.

She savoured her coffee and thought about closing her eyes. Instead, she told her mother, "I gave my statement. I'm sure they'll be checking it out."

Grace nodded. "Do they believe you? About that poor man?"

"Hard to tell. But they can't prove that I did something I didn't do." Lola sipped at the steaming coffee. "They know I'm no Spell Caster, and Arbogast was certainly killed by a Spell."

The silence stretched out for so long that Lola was almost asleep when Grace spoke. "Things are different now. Between us. With Matteo. He needs me to be there for this ceremony and I go. Not just for me, but for all of us. In the City. It's the only regular contact I have with him anymore." She sighed. "Matteo is gone. He's only Mayor, now."

"And your film premiere? Last week?"

Grace shook her dark hair. "I hadn't asked him. He called me and asked to accompany me. I don't want to see our ancient history in the papers any more than you do." She sighed, reached for a jewel-encrusted cigarette case. She picked out a long cigarette and snapped the case closed. "I suppose Penny put him up to it. She was the best manager in the business." She fitted the cigarette into a lacquered holder and used a squat, leather-cased lighter.

"What did he have you do?" asked Lola.

"You mean the ceremony?" Grace pushed the lighter around on the countertop, aimlessly making circles with it. "I stand in a certain place and shiver when it's cold, perspire when it's hot. I don't say anything, don't do a special dance. I don't even have to be conscious, for all I know. It's all very arcane and hair-raising—I mean that literally. All I do is supply my physical presence." She pulled over a cut crystal ashtray.

"Because you were there the first time, when he turned."

Grace nodded. Lola thought for a moment, then said, "Do you know what goes on?"

"It's just as he said." Grace shivered. "That's why I was so concerned that you'd brought Aubrey to the house. On the very night of the ceremony." She paused. "He didn't say it, but before this Warding, I mean, this annual one, he's at his most vulnerable."

"Because it's the month of his death," supplied Aubrey. Lola nodded absently.

"They don't explain anything of the ceremony to you?"

Grace shook her head. "And I'm not sensitive. Except for the hairs standing up, I wouldn't know when it was over. His Conjurers are even more close-mouthed than he is."

"He seemed mouthy enough to me," said Lola.

Grace's laugh seemed just as surprising to her as it did to Lola. "He's fond of you, I think."

"Does he talk to you? Confide in you?"

"No, we're barely friends anymore." Her sentence ended abruptly. A look of surprise sat awkwardly on her face.

"You got enough friendship out of him years ago." The words came out unbidden, sounding tired and worn even to Lola.

"Please, just stop." Grace wrung her hands; her knuckles were white and tendons stood out in sharp relief. She managed to avoid the burning cigarette tip even as she swiped at her tears wearily. "You don't know anything about it."

"I know what I know," said Lola.

"And that's not nearly enough for you to judge me," Grace replied. Her challenging tone belied the hollow exhaustion of her face. She was getting worn down, slowly and surely. Lola turned her face away and looked down at her mug of doctored coffee.

"Anything else you can tell me about this arcane ceremony?" she asked.

"I've said all I know." Grace took another drag of her cigarette. "You'll have to get your answers from him." She began to rub at the edge of the crystal ashtray.

Lola drained her toddy. "Good night, then, Mother. It's been a long day. Get some rest." She stood.

Grace hurriedly laid down her cigarette and holder on the edge of the ashtray. "Lola, darling, you can stay here. Your room's always ready." Grace came over to stand in front of Lola, her hands on her daughter's arms. Lola was the taller of the two. As she looked at her mother, she thought she glimpsed grey in the roots of her hair. It distracted her from the expression on her mother's face.

"I sleep better in my own bed." She extricated herself delicately. "You need sleep, Mother. Good night."

Lola walked with purpose to the back door, closing her ears to everything but her own quickening steps.

TWENTY-ONE

When it came time, Lola got up and went through the motions of a normal morning. She poured hot coffee down her throat and glanced at the liquor cabinet. She mechanically dressed in the outfit Elaine laid out: wide-legged pants in buff, tailored tweed jacket with waist belt, cream blouse, hunter green neck scarf. She pulled her hair back into a tight twist and decided against a hat. She ate her breakfast without tasting it, considered a bottle of scotch for a few moments but picked up the telephone instead. The appointment was made for mid-afternoon. Lola lit a cigarette when the call was done, and sat for some minutes, thinking over her options. The telephone rang.

"Lola, good morning. I'm glad I caught you," said Betta rapidly. "Listen," she continued after Lola had exchanged greetings, "A friend of mine just rang me back last night. She's been out of town, just received my message. She was at the Temple, same time as your friend."

"What've you got?" asked Lola, her heart racing at the idea of a new lead.

"I'm with patients all morning. Come by at lunchtime and I can talk at leisure."

They made arrangements for a lunch meeting and rang off. Lola smoked some more, made another telephone call and another meeting time. When she set the receiver on its hook, she had a rare sense of satisfaction. She caught her reflection in her bedroom vanity mirror and pulled up short. Instead of her own overly pale face and dark-ringed eyes, she saw the final expression on Arbogast's face, the mouth gaping and eyes wide with shock. Lola closed her eyes and shook her head.

"Are you all right?' asked Aubrey.

Lola hung her head, unwilling to speak. Finally, she heaved a breath, pushed herself up from the chair, and moved around the room. She stowed two knives and her gat, made sure she had cigarettes in her case, and walked out into the living room. She told Elaine, "I'll be out all day."

Elaine nodded solemnly. Lola grabbed her keys from the porcelain bowl sitting on the little table next to the door. She was in the elevator and down to the cars in a matter of minutes.

"Where to?" Aubrey asked.

Lola gritted her teeth against the nausea in her gut. She got into her beat up Buick, jammed it into gear. She forced herself to answer. "I promised an update." She waited for the onslaught of questions, but Aubrey was silent. Lola drove grimly southward. It was barely ten o'clock.

She found Jed Wing in his backyard this time, trimming his clematis vines. She knocked on his gate and the older man startled. He whirled around. Lola raised a hand in greeting and placation. Wing closed his eyes for a second, then motioned for her to enter his yard. He seemed rooted to the spot, a pair of shears in his bare hand, while she approached.

"Good morning, Mr Wi—".

The older man motioned impatiently. Lola stopped a few feet in front of him.

"What's happened? Did you find Bodewell?"

She didn't know how to soften it. She tensed, ready to catch the poor man if he needed it.

She said, "I'm sorry, Mr. Wing. Mr. Arbogast is dead."

Wing stood, motionless, his eyes riveted to her face. Lola felt her gorge rising once again, but she kept a tight rein on her expression. She watched Wing's face fill with fear. He said, "How? Did he...was it...suicide?"

"I'm sorry," she replied as gently as she could manage. "It was murder. The police are looking into it, of course." It was painfully inadequate even to her own ears. Lola waited for more questions, her jaw clenched.

"I suppose," said Wing, looking around at his yard. The shears in his hand caught his attention and he compressed the handle, making them *snik* as the blades scissored together. "I suppose they'll be asking me more questions again." He sighed and turned away. Lola stayed on the grass. Wing put the shears down on a small workbench. He took a few steps toward the back door before he turned back to Lola. "Thank you for coming by. I'll ring you with details for the service." He paused as a thought came to him. "Both services," he added. "I guess I'm responsible for them both, now."

"I'm sorry for your bereavement," said Lola, offering the ritual response. She clamped her lips against the bitter taste in her mouth.

Wing stared at her, clearly lost in his own thoughts. Lola nodded her goodbye and departed. As she walked around to the street in front of the houses, she breathed as deeply as possible, trying to calm herself. Her stomach was rebelling against the coffee, and her head was already beginning to pound. She remembered suddenly that she hadn't had anyone look at her head since she'd smashed it the previous night. That thought led her back to Arbogast's body and just like that, she was breathing shallowly, trying her damnedest to avoid vomiting right on Wing's pretty flagstone path. Lola staggered to her car and slid inside. She rolled down the windows and started the engine. Cool air streamed inside as she drove down the street.

"It'll get easier," said Aubrey. "Even if it never goes away."

"I barely knew the man," replied Lola. "Not sure you can grieve for a virtual stranger."

After a moment, the reply came: "I meant the guilt." Lola felt like she'd been socked in the gut. She breathed as best she could through the pain, kept her eyes on the road, and drove out of the little community of Southern Plains.

By the time she made it up to Ria's desk at the *Herald*, Lola was composed once more. She came right to the point.

"I'm making good on my promise. Clear?" She took a deep breath before speaking. "My client was murdered last night. I don't have a lead on the story for you, but you should start annoying a pair of DIs named Bednarski and Marks."

Ria scratched down the names with a pencil. "You spill on your client to them?"

"No choice," replied Lola lightly. She clutched the back of Ria's visitor's chair. "I found the body." Lola felt suddenly weak-kneed. She decided to sit.

Ria's eyes bulged. "Are you all right? Where was this? What happened? What were you doing there?"

Lola put up her hands. "I can't give you all the details right now," Ria screwed up her face, clearly ready to argue, "but I swear that I will, as long as you don't ID me in the piece," Lola finished quickly.

"Don't be a complete twit," retorted Ria. "I want to know if you're jake, you crazy broad."

"Sure," replied Lola. "I'm here, aren't I?" She swallowed hard past the thickness in her throat. "Anyway, I didn't want you crabbing that I didn't hold up my end." Lola stood up. "I gotta make tracks. Loose ends."

Ria eyed her suspiciously. "Whatever you say, angel," she said, clearly dubious. "Make sure you ring me, doll. You know I hate worrying about you."

Lola nodded, turned away, and threaded quickly back through the maze of reporters' desks. When she got to her car, she found two surprises waiting for her.

Thick tipped his hat. "She wants to see you."

"Now," added Thin with a smirk.

"Get off my car," said Lola. "I know the way."

The two men pushed off her car with exaggerated care. They smiled insincerely at her before sauntering toward their black Packard. It was parked immediately behind her Buick. Thick hesitated after he opened the driver side door. "After you, Princess."

Lola got in, started up and cut into traffic. It was a short drive across a few blocks of downtown. She stashed her car as soon as she found a spot along the block. She walked briskly down the sidewalk and up the grand front steps, now contemptuously familiar. Lola walked over the gleaming marble and plush carpeting underfoot, wondering if the thugs would show up behind her suddenly or if they'd already be waiting in the office. When she knocked on the anteroom door, she was surprised to see an assistant at the desk. The stocky young man grimaced at Lola and told her to go right in. Lola glanced behind her, but neither Thick nor Thin were in view.

She steadied her breathing, strode across and pushed open the inner office door.

Copenhagen greeted Lola with a sunny smile. "Good morning, Lola." She waved her over from the vantage point at a window. "Beautiful day, isn't it?" Sunshine streamed in and lit Copenhagen's red hair with orange fire. She smiled false sympathy with carmine lips. "Rough night?"

"Where're Mutt and Jeff?" replied Lola, stepping inside.

"Around," Copenhagen said. "You've kept me waiting all morning. I was expecting you first thing." She stepped to her desk and sat down. After a pause, Lola took the chair opposite and pulled out her cigarettes. Copenhagen moved an ashtray forward. "You owe me an explanation. I tasked you with finding poor Arbogast. I had no idea I needed to specify 'alive.'"

"That's callous, even for you."

"Don't translate your guilt into anger at me, Lola. I don't have his blood on my hands." Copenhagen leaned forward, pointed with one red-tipped finger. "You weren't up to the task. Deal with it." She sat back once more. "Mayor telephoned over this morning. I have a meeting with him this afternoon. He wants a full accounting from me personally of what Arbogast did for this department."

"You going to spill on the extortion ring?" asked Lola, eyes narrowed.

Copenhagen nodded. "Of course. It's the truth, after all."

"I doubt that, but I'm sure you've got all the proof you could make up to support your story."

"I do believe you're accusing me of lying," said Copenhagen. She waved dismissively. "No matter. I *do* have proof and I *will* show it to him. It's my duty."

"How convenient that the only people who can dispute your story are dead."

"That had nothing to do with me. They made their choices. Poor ones, to be sure, but that's not my problem. You see," she continued, "I don't bother with guilt. It's just another way to wallow in self-pity, another self-indulgence I don't need."

Lola took a pull on her cigarette, exhaled a blue plume of smoke. She kept her voice even. "Why drag his name through the mud? We both know he's not the extortion leader. Why lie?"

"I'm handing over the details of a large, City-wide criminal enterprise, uncovered due to a months'-long investigation I started and led. Of course I'm taking credit."

"Is that all this is? You're just looking for a pat on the back? A way to boost your resume?"

Copenhagen threw back her head and laughed. Her eyes sparked with contempt. "You really don't understand the civil service, Lola, if you think that's something to look down upon."

"You think you can claim the mayor's chair someday?"

Copenhagen shrugged. "Only if Mayor ever decides to retire, as it were. That could be a long time away, as I believe he chose Ghosthood exactly in order to hold office for eternity. No, I'm not interested in that. But Commissioner of Gaming, that's another story. Breaking up this extortion ring is just the way to get noticed."

"What if I had proof that says different?" said Lola. "What if I had another theory, just as provable?"

Copenhagen was already shaking her head. "You're a terrible bluffer. I know you've got nothing. There *is* no other possibility. I can easily prove that Arbogast ran that ring. I've got all the ledgers and statements I need, Lola. It's time to face facts. Arbogast has been pegged by over twenty mah-jongg parlours."

Lola clenched her fists, resisting the urge to use them.

She said, "You planned it well, I have to give you that. You made sure no one ever linked you to the ring. As the bagman, Arbogast was the only person those managers had regular contact with. I'd be willing to bet your two thugs were careful to stay separate from him as well. You made sure Arbogast entered those figures himself, while you watched. No one would suspect daily meetings between the Assistant Deputy and a department accountant. No one would ever suspect you of extorting money from gambling parlours of all things. Especially since you're also a wealthy heiress in your own right." Lola took another drag of her Egyptian. "Why would you possibly need the money?"

"I think you've disproved your own theory, Lola," replied Copenhagen. "Why would anyone believe that story? Without corroboration? Without any witnesses?" She shook her head. "If that's all you've got, it's pathetically little. I *will* make my case against Arbogast, Lola. You can count on it. I understand from my secretary that you have the appointment before mine with Mayor. If you're considering trying to persuade him of your little story, I suggest you think again. You'll only make a fool of yourself."

Lola cocked her head, calculating her next approach. "So this is what it's come to, for you? A shot at becoming Commissioner of Gaming?" She inflected the title with derision. "That's a far cry from being the best natural talent in Conjury in recent memory. Do you know that's what your instructors at the College had to say about you?"

"Beg your pardon?" said Copenhagen, her voice icy.

"You can't be surprised I made some inquiries," said Lola. "Your heavy-handedness all but guaranteed that."

Copenhagen narrowed her eyes at Lola briefly before her expression smoothed out. She smiled and re-settled herself. "I'd think you'd have more compassion for me, Lola. After all, we've both chosen the paths our fathers wanted for us. We've both made hard choices to do so. I had to turn away from Conjury."

"Did you?" Lola asked. "I wonder. There are two years of your life that no public record can account for. Two years is plenty of time to hone your Conjury skills. Why you chose to do so in secret is the most pressing mystery to me."

Copenhagen clapped her hands, once, twice. "I'm impressed you got that far. My private life is not on the public record, for very good reason. It's *private*. Whatever you think you know about me, I assure you, is wrong. I am a dedicated public servant, Lola. What you see is what you get." She gave a Gallic shrug. "Now, I've got some minor details to attend to. I suspect I shall see you again, this afternoon."

The door to her office opened. Copenhagen looked over Lola's shoulder and bared her teeth in a smile. "My assistants will escort you out."

TWENTY-TWO

Lola took a left and slid to the curb halfway up the street. She sat for a moment, waiting. Watching. There had been no sign of a tail from the Gaming Commission Building, but she preferred to be certain. After a slow count to fifty, she swung herself out of the Buick. She melded with the flow of people on the sidewalk and waited at the corner upstream. She and about half the horde stepped out before the light had turned red. At the familiar cut-out doorway, she took the ground floor entrance.

Sunlight streamed into the front room, barely held in check by flexible bamboo shades pulled across the large window. No one sat in the window seat, but a thin Chinese woman with iron-grey hair was in one of the chairs lining the wall. She looked at Lola with wary eyes, unsmiling. Lola knew better than to offer any smile of her own. The Chinese were suspicious of warm greetings.

A bulb glowed dull red above a doorway leading to the back. Lola went behind the counter and checked Betta's bookings for the day. Other than Mrs. Fung, promptly waiting for her noon appointment, Betta had nothing until half past two. Lola slid the book back into its place beneath the counter. She found Mrs. Fung watching her with open curiosity. Taking a page from her aunties' teachings, Lola gave neither explanation nor acknowledgement of the old woman's attentions. She picked up a newspaper and sat down at the end of the row, away from the sunshine.

At ten to noon, the red bulb blinked off and the door opened.

A stout man, neatly turned out in a cream suit, brown tie and sporty brogues, preceded Betta into the front room. They spoke in hushed tones while the man paid for his treatment. He made no other appointment. Betta greeted Mrs. Fung demurely and disappeared into the back room once more. Mrs. Fung waited for Betta's return a few minutes later before accompanying her within. The red bulb switched on again. Lola finished the international section, re-folded it crisply, and moved onto City news.

"This is bad, Lola," Aubrey said. His voice seemed tight, higher than usual.

"I think you'd better be more specific," murmured Lola.

Aubrey didn't respond for a few minutes. When he spoke again, his voice was calmer but still tense. "Copenhagen. She's involved in Arbogast's murder, Lola. I could feel it."

"We're in agreement on that," said Lola slowly. "What's the bad part?"

"No, you don't understand. The same disturbance, the trail that led me to Arbogast. I sensed it in her office. I didn't want to get too near her. I think she can see me. I think she's just been pretending otherwise. Maybe to hide her Conjury background, I don't know."

"So you didn't get near enough to her to what? Smell her?"

"You're missing the point," Aubrey said, impatient. "Copenhagen has the same disturbance around her that led me to Arbogast, which is the same disturbance that I sensed around Mayor."

Lola thought about that from a number of different angles. She couldn't figure out the connection between Mayor and Copenhagen. Did they know one another or didn't they? Did Mayor truly not know Arbogast? Why had Copenhagen gone to the trouble of hiring Lola on a bogus case? Just to renew their acquaintance so she could use Lola to bait Arbogast into giving himself up? But Lola didn't believe he'd been running that extortion ring anyway, so that couldn't be the reason. Copenhagen was the one running the extortion ring. Lola couldn't prove Copenhagen had anything to do with the two murders, but her instincts were strongly in favour of that being likely.

So, how did that tie in to Mayor? Why would he want Josephson and Arbogast dead? What would Mayor possibly have invested in the Gaming Commission? Like Copenhagen, he was also independently wealthy. He was already the most powerful being in the City. Was it a personal reason? Or a political one?

Aubrey must have been having similar thoughts. He finally said, "It can't be a coincidence, Lola, but damned if I can come up with a plausible reason for it." He made a frustrated noise. "The more I think on it, the more questions come up."

"I'm going to finish reading the news," murmured Lola. She snapped the pages out crisply. Aubrey grunted but said nothing more for a long while.

By the time Betta escorted Mrs. Fung to the front door, Lola was in need of a good stretch. "Your chairs leave something to be desired," she said as Betta turned back to her.

Betta smiled and retreated into her back room. Lola stood, working on the cricks in her neck and spine. She picked up the paper, once more in immaculate condition, and replaced it on the pile in the corner of the window seat. Betta came back out.

"Hungry?" she asked in her light voice. The smile brought out her crow's feet, made her eyes glitter. Her hair was pulled back in its usual neat bun.

Lola nodded. "You?"

"Sorry about the wait. Mrs. Fung was very insistent." Betta turned her attention aside, her face becoming sober. "Aubrey, is something the matter? You look worried."

"Just something on my mind," the Ghost replied. "Nothing for you to fret about."

Betta didn't reply, just looked intent for a few seconds. Finally, she sighed. "You two are more alike than you'll ever admit." She busied herself finding her purse and putting a cardigan on over her pale blue shirtwaist dress. "Let's go then. I'm ravenous." She swung a little blue hat with feathered hatband in her hand but didn't put it on.

Betta locked up the front door and swung her sign around. Lola followed her back through the storefront and out into the rear alley. The shorter woman slid her arm through Lola's and they walked that way down toward the mouth of the alley. Before they reached it, however, Lola turned left into a recessed doorway. She opened a heavy metal door and the smell of hot oil billowed out. Betta extricated her arm and walked down the dim hall until they came out into a crowded restaurant. Once within, Lola's mouth watered at the scent of frying food, boiling soup and strong tea. A waiter with shiny black hair, somehow simultaneously looking welcoming and harried, waved the women over to a table beneath an embroidered wall hanging of horses stampeding through a narrow mountain pass. Lola heard Aubrey's voice raised in polite greeting numerous times as they weaved through patrons and tables and bustling table-staff.

Lola was content to let Betta do all the ordering. The waiter set down a white porcelain teapot, used a lead pencil to scratch out their order on a pad of paper curling at the corners, and left in a whirl. Two steps away from Lola and Betta's table, he began shouting at a bus girl to clean up a table that had been abandoned a mere two seconds prior. Lola watched the chubby girl work feverishly, clearing dirty dishes in under a minute with loud clattering. Lola could tell the girl was no rookie, despite the two pigtails and smooth face, as she had managed to avoid even a single piece of broken pottery. The girl was back in about two minutes with chopsticks, bowls, tea cups and napkins. The table was barely ready when a family of four sat down and the mother began ordering while the waiter set down a plain white teapot. Lola could see a chip on its spout.

"This is exactly what I need after a morning of long silences," said Betta, smiling. "Thanks for coming by."

"Hey, when do I ever say no to lunch?" replied Lola, forcing herself to answer lightly.

"Well, I'm grateful, even if you're not being gracious about it," chided Betta.

Their food arrived. The waiter set down a steaming bowl of noodles, topped with pieces of barbequed duck, their juices sliding down to mingle with the soup. Another bowl contained wonton and noodles in clear broth. A plate of shiny green vegetables followed suit. Both women attacked their meals. By mutual and silent assent, the first mouthfuls were taken without interruption.

Lola waited until Betta had eaten half her meal before she spoke. "All right. That oughta take the edge off. So? What did your new informant have to tell you?"

"I'm pleasantly surprised you waited so long," Betta said, teasing. "Well, my friend painted quite a picture of your Amber Jade Stoudamire." Betta picked up a spear of *gai-lan* and delicately bit into it. Lola followed suit, relishing the *snap* of the slender green stem.

"What about her mentor, the one who died. What was his specialty? How did he die?"

Betta swallowed and took a sip of steaming tea. She considered Lola for a moment. "The feeling I had from my friend is that your Amber Jade was a phenomenon unto herself. Her mentor requested her. That was unheard of. He had exacting standards and high expectations of all his pupils. And that was when *they* begged to apprentice *him*."

"Did you know him personally?" interrupted Lola.

After a brief hesitation, Betta nodded. "I studied with him for my final year."

"He was a Healer?"

"No," answered Betta slowly. "He was a Spell Caster, a powerful one."

Lola cocked her head. "You studied to be a Conjurer?"

Betta shook her head. "No, I studied with him. I was never an apprentice. He occasionally taught seminar groups of three or four students. We had to interview with him to be accepted. It was a way for the Temple to force their tenured professors to expand their focus now and again." She ate a wonton. "Let's get back to your original topic. You asked about the mentor. He died in his sleep. It was a peaceful end. My friend was actually there. She saw nothing but an old man in an armchair by the fire. Of course, the grapevine was rife with the worst kinds of speculation." Betta paused. "Apparently, he'd been reading an old tattered Spellsbook. It laid on the floor where he'd dropped it when he passed. Mah's, Fourth Edition." At Lola's blank look, Betta explained, "Sorry, it's the classic text on higher consciousness among humans who are gifted with Conjury talents from birth. Like your Amber Jade."

Lola nodded. "Why was your friend there? Did she find him then?"

There was the slightest hesitation before Betta nodded. "She was his weekend housecleaner, paying her way through school."

Lola chewed thoughtfully. "What were the rumours, then? About his death. Reading that book when he died. Having such a gifted apprentice. My experience with Amber Jade was she didn't make friends. Sycophants aplenty, but no friends."

"As a matter of fact," said Betta, nodding, "even I heard plenty about his mysterious death being some sort of plot against the Temple. He'd been teaching at the Temple for decades. He was still active in Temple politics. Some saw it as a blow to the old guard, but truly, my friend is adamant there was nothing foul about his death. She's a powerful Conjurer now and was talented from birth as well. She'd have known something was amiss." Betta leaned back. "Of course, there were jealous students, jealous teachers even. Something like that is bound to bring out the worst in some people. But there was no police inquiry into his death."

"So his star pupil leaves the Temple shortly afterward and then swears off Conjury forever?"

"It was actually solstice break when he died. She simply didn't return to the Temple." Betta shrugged. "I imagine they had a close relationship. Perhaps your friend, in her youthful arrogance, believed no one else capable of guiding her studies."

Lola nodded slowly, taking an absent-minded bite of food. Betta waited her out. Finally, Lola said, "If you were a wildly talented Conjurer-in-training, what could you do other than be a Conjurer?"

Betta's reply was immediate. "Nothing."

"That's your expert opinion? Not supposition?"

"There's nothing else out there for people like us. We have a natural gift for communicating with Ghosts. The Temple teaches us

Spells and Wards. We become Spell Casters or Healers or Catchers." She paused. "Oh, I suppose monks and nuns, too. Although their specialty is really quite limited to funereal ceremonies."

"Let's talk about Spell Casters then."

"Not my area of expertise—"

"—but you'll bear with me."

Betta nodded, sighing. Lola continued.

"Is it possible that Amber Jade continued to study Spells and Wards away from the Temple? That she became something other than a hired magic-slinger?"

"Cute," said Betta with a half laugh.

"Surely these spells taught at the Temple exist in books? Books that people can copy or steal?"

Betta nodded. "Books, yes, but the Temple guards them closely. I've never heard of a theft there. Never, in their entire history."

"Well, I don't imagine that's something they'd advertise."

Betta's attention slid away then. Lola checked quickly over her shoulder, but saw nothing of alarm. She looked closely at Betta then and realized the other woman's gaze was directed inward. Lola waited, impatient but all but biting her tongue in order to stay quiet.

Finally, Betta spoke, her voice hushed and thoughtful. "Mayor taught himself to cast Spells and Wards." She grinned mildly at Lola's expression. "Don't look so shocked. I'd've thought you'd figured him capable of all sorts of nefarious deeds."

Lola ignored the jab. Instead, she said, "If the Temple guards their Spellsbooks closely, then how did Mayor get his hands on them?"

"The Temple must have given him permission," replied Betta. "He wouldn't have stolen them." At Lola's look, Betta explained,

"There are multiple copies of normal Spellsbooks, the ones used in the normal curriculum. They're readily available. Most every student buys her own copy. It's just easiest that way. But if you want to borrow one of those, you're still required to sign them out, so that the Librarian can keep track." Betta paused to take a sip of tea. "But the Spells that Mayor learned in order to become what he is now, those aren't in regular circulation. They're extremely powerful and dangerous to a student who isn't ready for them."

"Does anyone know if the Temple did loan him those books? He wasn't enrolled as a student, was he?"

Betta shook her head. "Not that I've ever heard. Here or elsewhere. I'm sure it would have made some headlines, if he had. And I've never heard of those particular kinds of Spellsbooks being loaned out from the Temple."

"It might have happened covertly," said Lola, thinking aloud.

"I suppose," Betta said, but she sounded dubious.

"So we're left with two options," said Lola. "Mayor may have had the sanction of the Temple, which loaned out those dangerous Spellsbooks to him."

Betta shook her head. "That would set a precedent, I think, possibly a dangerous one. Who would decide on access? What would the criteria be for assessing those deemed worthy?"

"Those in power don't necessarily require an ethical code," said Lola, her tone dry. "If someone *has* started a lending program, so to speak, it doesn't mean they're concerned with rules." Lola paused, gauging Betta's reaction.

She continued when the older woman didn't object. "Or, option two. Mayor found a way without the Temple's sanction to learn Spell Casting."

"Which sets another precedent, equally dangerous," said Betta. "The Temple teaches more than simply how to use magic. It teaches ethics, responsibility, morals. Casting a Spell requires more than saying some words and tapping the Ether. That sort of clumsy work's what we call 'slinging muck.'"

"Three options then," said Aubrey. "It could be another school entirely. The Temple may be the best in the world, but other schools would have dangerous Spells as well. Mayor could simply have gone elsewhere to buy his education."

"His European background." Betta considered it. "Perhaps he found schools in Europe willing to teach him, secretly."

Lola said, "Ria didn't find evidence of Amber Jade Stoudamire enrolled anywhere else in the world, but she may've simply used a false name. So Copenhagen could also very well be a Spell Caster." At Betta's confused look, Lola explained Amber Jade's current identity.

"But why are you investigating her?" asked Betta. "And what is the connection to Mayor?"

"I'm not certain," admitted Lola reluctantly. "All I seem to have now is the possibility that they're both self-taught Spell Casters. I don't know if they're enemies or allies—"

"—or weekly mah-jongg partners," finished Aubrey.

"There's something else." Lola lowered her voice. "What can you tell me about a Dispersal Spell for Mayor, specifically?"

Betta's eyes widened and she pulled back abruptly. "Where did you hear about that?"

"From Mayor."

Betta looked horrified. "*Mayor* told you? Why?"

Lola explained the previous night's events.

"I'm somewhat less than a threat to him," she finished.

Betta replied, "I wouldn't be so sure of that. You've got Aubrey, and any Ghost at close proximity is a threat."

Lola thought about that for a minute. Realization came slowly: "You mean, someone else could cast the Spell."

Betta nodded. "They would simply need Aubrey to be in close proximity to Mayor. Perhaps just in the same room."

"I thought Spells couldn't be cast through walls."

"They can't. Not the ones I know of, and that would include this Dispersal."

Lola remained silent. She asked finally, "How *do* you know about this Spell? It can't be common knowledge."

Betta poured them both more tea. "I have to get back," she said. She gathered her purse and hat, then murmured, "Let's pretend we never spoke about this." Betta looked intently into Lola's eyes, reminding Lola abruptly that Betta Ha was the most powerful Healer in the City for a very good reason. The strength of her will was startlingly clear in that look.

"Lola," said Aubrey, his voice heavy, "I think you'd best agree."

After a tense pause, Lola nodded once, curtly.

They exited the restaurant the way they'd come. In the alley once again, Lola walked ahead of Betta a few paces. She took the time and space to calm herself down. She could hear murmuring behind her but made out nothing of sense. She looked back, once, to find Betta scowling at the air. So Lola wasn't the only one whom her Ghost rubbed the wrong way. When the older woman caught her watching, Betta's features smoothed out and she made a shooing motion with her hands.

Lola turned back around and kept going.

Betta used her keys, and they were back inside her storefront. "Tell me one last thing" Lola said.

Betta became motionless where she stood at the front door. She held the Open/Closed sign in her left hand. She looked out as a teenaged couple walked past, holding hands, oblivious to the two women just on the other side of the door. After a pause, Betta turned to face Lola.

"If I can," she replied.

"Given what you were told about Amber Jade, do you think she could—"

"Mayor is an Adept, Lola. He would have extremely powerful Wards around himself. I can't say I understand the significance of Aubrey's sensing that poor dead man. But even so, I would guess Mayor and his Conjurers would know if something happened to weaken his ceremony last night." Betta stopped, a thoughtful expression once more on her beautiful face. "Even if she were as talented as everyone at the Temple believes, she would still need help to learn her Spells. And if she were to best Mayor, then she would require rigourous training and some very powerful Spells indeed."

"Is that a yes?"

"It's an 'I don't know,'" replied Betta. "Don't tempt Fate, Lola. Stay away from the lot of them."

"Fate," repeated Lola. "Right."

In the car, she got right to the point. "What did you talk to Betta about?"

"Something I can't discuss with you." Aubrey's voice held no rancour, nor surprise.

"About this case?"

"Lola," he said, "I have no choice in this matter. There are certain things we are forbidden to discuss with our Hosts."

"Ah, even Ghosts are entitled to their little secrets, I take it."

"It's for your protection, Lola. Trust me."

"What choice do I have?" she replied. Aubrey remained silent.

On the way up to the office, Lola shared the elevator with two pretty girls wearing dark glasses and red lipstick. Their dresses were strictly last Spring, but snug-fitting and flattering. Neither spoke to her. When the lift stopped, the girls, holding hands, headed straight for the surgeon's suites at the opposite end of the floor.

Lola hoped the studio was paying for the work.

There was no one waiting for her in the anteroom. She swept up her mail and opened her windows.

Aubrey spoke into the silence. "So we think she's a murderer and magical saboteur. To what purpose?"

"Mayor's Dispersal still seems the best play," replied Lola. "She wants him gone." She sifted absently through the envelopes as she sat. The entire pile went into the trash. She made a rude noise. "We don't even have any proof she knows about the damned Spell."

"He's well-known to be a strong Spell Caster," mused Aubrey. "She'd need some immense firepower to best him. Ghosts are just better attenuated to the Ether. It gives Ghost Spell Casters, like Mayor, an extreme advantage."

Lola stared at the wall. Aubrey continued his murmuring.

"There's got to be something in this Conjurer background of hers. She left the Temple two years before she joined the City corps."

"That doesn't necessarily mean anything." Lola kicked at the trash bin. It toppled with a clang that reverberated around the room.

"We've got nothing but conjecture. Just a big fat hunch that there's some connection between her and Mayor."

"With you squarely in the middle," retorted Aubrey. "If that doesn't constitute your business, I don't know what would."

Lola righted the bin, collected a few pieces of mail that had scattered. She slapped the unopened letters against her palm a few times. Coming to a decision, she tossed them into the bin. "I didn't say I was packing up my tent." Lola picked up her telephone.

"Monteverdi, City Desk" came the clipped answer on the other end.

"Me again. I'm coming in fifteen."

"Bring me some lunch and you can have me for an hour."

"That's my girl."

"Not so fast: Finklestein and Chang. Mustard duck on rice."

Lola made it in less than half an hour, carrying a medium-sized bamboo steamer basket. Ria grabbed her lunch and spun around on her heel. She was already carrying a pair of pale chopsticks. Lola followed her to a small meeting room. A round table and three chairs sat in the middle of the room. A single window was shaded against the harsh afternoon sun. Ria had the steamer lid off and was chewing on a sliver of duck by the time Lola entered. Lola turned on the small fan and pulled out a chair opposite. She pointed.

"Eat fast. You have to take me down to see Loverboy again."

"Ah, that imperious tone. The girl is jake once more." Ria scooped up some rice. She spoke as she chewed. "Still buzzing around Copenhagen?"

"Bzzz."

"Give me five minutes."

Ten minutes later, the women were downstairs in the *Herald* archives, and Dinwoodie Kwong was rummaging through the vast catalogue of the venerable newspaper. He directed Lola to the reading tables and started piling up past issues and bound books. Lola picked the earliest date and started skimming.

Ria slumped into a neighbouring chair and grunted. "You sure this is the right trail?"

Lola shook her head. "No clue. Just sniffing out an idea."

"Give, chum."

Lola barely paused long enough to glare. "If Mayor can teach himself Spells, who says someone else can't do the same? I've got a feeling Amber Jade used those two missing years for some very serious studying. She must have had some help. Betta thinks the Temple actually loaned their High Magic books to Mayor."

Ria's eyes widened. "But they hate him."

"So why'd they do it? Did someone put the screws to 'em? Did he have something on them?" Lola shook her head. "It doesn't make any sense."

Ria's eye roamed over the growing pile of papers and books. "So, did our little classmate have the same leverage?"

"Wait a minute." Lola sat back. "She wouldn't have needed it. Not the same way, I mean." She turned to Ria. "Listen, everyone there loved her. According to them, she was the best thing since jasmine rice."

Ria considered Lola's theory. "Did she have that much clout?"

Lola shrugged. "She had a great sob story. Picture this: our intrepid Conjurer, poised to become the most powerful Spell Caster in history, is forced to leave the Temple because of Daddy's political ambitions for her. How can she leave the one thing she's truly meant for?"

Ria picked up the tale. "She doesn't. She continues her studies in secret, with the best mentors and all the books of the Temple at her disposal." Ria sat up straight. "To what purpose? Why would the Temple groom her if she has to keep her skill a secret? Surely, the greatest Conjurer in the Temple's history would be someone they'd want to celebrate. At the very least, they'd parade her everywhere they could. Enter her in international competitions. Flout their success in training her."

Suddenly, Ria looked around. "What about you Aubrey? Any ideas? Know of any *secret societies* that would need a hidden Conjurer in their back pocket?"

"Ah…no. Outside my bailiwick."

Lola thought he sounded strange, but she relayed Aubrey's response without adding her own doubts. Ria threw up her hands. "Great theory, chum, but we have absolutely no proof."

Lola gave her a grave look. "I don't need proof. I've got charm."

Ria snorted and checked the large wall clock above their heads. "Time for me to earn my keep." She pulled Lola up with her and thanked Dinwoodie Kwong with a dazzler of a smile. Back upstairs in the so-called bullpen, Lola used Ria's telephone. No answer at her mother's house. She rang off and tried another exchange. After some trouble, she got Bednarski on the line.

"Look, are you boys done with my mother yet?"

"As a matter of fact, no. I just came out to get her a cup of coffee." The cop's tone was blandly polite.

"Is Locke with her?"

"Superintendent Locke has been in to see Miss McCall."

"How much longer will you keep her?"

"Well, Miss Starke, your mother's here of her own free will. She can go any time. She knows that."

"How much longer, Bednarski?"

"Can't really say. These things are unpredictable."

"Yeah, well, thanks." She dropped the receiver onto its cradle.

"Off again?" Ria was sifting through a pile of message slips. She scratched a few notes on a pad.

Lola nodded. "Gotta see a man about a thing."

"Be good," said her friend, looking up at her.

"Not a chance," replied Lola.

"Then make sure you let me know how bad you've been." Ria pinned her with a glare. "You still owe me a headline."

TWENTY-THREE

Mayor had three assistants: Miss Chang, Miss Delgado and Miss Li. Any one of them could be lighting up the silver screen, with their lush black hair and seductive almond-shaped eyes. No one would be faulted for thinking they'd stepped onto a film set. Dark wood paneling, chair rails, plush Persian carpeting underfoot, heavy furniture and a trio of exotic beauties. The script was clear: this was the anteroom of a powerful man.

The women smiled at Lola in that professionally impersonal way of the very best administrators. Miss Delgado came around her desk. Her eyes flickered quickly over Lola's outfit. To tell by her expression, she thought nothing of what she saw, nothing at all. Three other people in the room stood as Lola entered. They were robed in mustard yellow and they ignored Lola completely. She edited the script: the man had become a Ghost and he was more powerful than the mere man had ever been. The Conjurers watched Aubrey with sharp-eyed suspicion.

"Problem?" asked Lola. She kept her tone casual.

Miss Delgado glanced at Miss Chang. The other woman shrugged. Delgado replied, "No, Miss Starke. Mayor is expecting you." Then she led Lola through a doorway. Lola had already taken five steps into it before she realized it was an empty room.

Lola stopped and looked around her. It was smaller than the anteroom. A single door in the opposite wall. No decorations on the walls. No windows.

Miss Li was suddenly standing in the room as well. She briskly closed the door behind her. She smiled politely at Lola. "Your purse please, Miss Starke. This shan't take long."

Lola waited a beat, then complied, a tight smile on her lips. Li opened it up and took out Lola's gun. "I'm sorry but this is for the protection of our Conjurers. I'm sure you understand." Li smiled impersonally. "We'll have this waiting for you when your meeting is done."

Lola nodded once, sharply. Li returned the purse. Lola reached into her jacket pocket and extracted her switchblade. "You'll probably want this too."

"Thank you." Miss Li nodded at Miss Delgado, then exited back into the outer office.

Miss Delgado was at the other door. She gave another neutral smile. "I'm sure you understand the irregularity of being allowed your Ghost during your meeting with Mayor." Lola startled as a yellow robe brushed past her right elbow. The Conjurer gave no indication of having noticed Lola and continued until she was beside Miss Delgado. The Spell Caster's face looked slack but her eyes were focused enough as she watched Aubrey.

"I'm sure I do," murmured Lola.

"Shall we?" said Delgado. She allowed the Conjurer to open the door, but she gestured for Lola to go within. "Please enter."

The Conjurer moved a split second before Lola did. The woman, shorter than Lola, nevertheless raised a hand at Lola's approach. Lola stopped within touching distance. The hand did not move to close the gap. Instead, the Conjurer waited, her head suddenly cocked to the right. The woman nodded and Lola heard Aubrey smoothly offer thanks. The hand disappeared within the robes. The way was clear.

Lola stepped inside.

The room was classically decorated in what the Europeans called "chinoiserie": large black lacquered desk, two floor-to-ceiling calligraphy banners on opposite walls, an enormous carpet patterned with phoenix-and-dragon. Two entire walls were windows; lightweight bamboo blinds were pulled down against the sun, filtering light to a pale yellow. Buildings and trees were still visible as outlines through the slats. Mayor sat at the desk, his back turned to the windows. Behind his chair stood two more Conjurers in yellow robes. Mayor wore his customary dove grey suit and dark striped tie.

"Thank you, Miss Delgado. Lola, Aubrey, come in." He scrawled something on a document and put it aside. Lola found it an odd sight: Ghosts weren't meant to manipulate objects. Hells, Ghosts weren't meant to be visible. The door behind her closed softly. She checked. Delgado was gone, but the Conjurer remained.

Mayor continued, "Any progress on your client's murder?" He stood up and walked toward a sofa upholstered in pale gold. The character for "longevity" was hidden among tiny sprays of violet flowers embroidered into the fabric. Mayor sat down and gestured for Lola to do likewise. She did, warily noting the movements of the Conjurers. The woman moved away from the door and stepped closer to Lola. Her two colleagues remained motionless. Six pairs of eyes followed Aubrey.

"You're an expensive Ghost to maintain," said Aubrey.

"Apparently, the taxpayers agree I'm worth it," replied Mayor with a smile.

"Let's hope you get volume discounts," Aubrey said.

One of the Conjurers, tall and pale, narrowed his eyes, but said nothing. Mayor sat at his ease, his smile neutral and polite.

Lola decided to start easy. "Tell me about my mother's involvement in your ceremony."

Mayor blinked once. "It's straightforward enough. I require her physical presence while intricate spells are woven to Ward me."

"She doesn't do anything?"

"She stands in a specific place, relative to myself."

"Are you vulnerable during this casting?"

Mayor paused. "Your mother is in no danger whatsoever during the ceremony," he said finally. "Any Spells that would be used to disrupt the Warding would not affect her."

"Could someone harm her to disrupt your ceremony?"

He shook his head. "A Warding circle is specially created and maintained by two Conjurers who do not participate in my warding." He smiled wolfishly. "We are hardly amateurs at this."

"No," countered Aubrey, his voice deeper than usual, "but your main concern is for yourself, not for Grace."

"True," agreed Mayor, "but her safety is integral to my interests."

Lola said, "You must Ward more than once a year."

"Monthly, in fact, but they are of lesser intensity."

"Who knows of your annual ceremony?"

"My assistants, Conjurers, security, Grace—and now the two of you." He smiled enigmatically.

"No other City departments or officials? Police? Councillors?"

"I'm not in the practice of confiding in my enemies," Mayor replied, "nor in my potential enemies."

Lola pushed on. "The Gaming Commission."

"Yes. I spoke with the Commissioner. His office found a record of Mr. Arbogast's employment, but more than that, he couldn't say. He certainly did not know the man, not even by sight."

"Did you speak with Assistant Deputy Commissioner Copenhagen?"

"We have a meeting after this one."

Lola waited for him to elaborate but instead, Mayor remained silent, considering her.

Finally, he said, "I've done a little sleuthing myself. ADC Copenhagen is indeed a City official, as was your Mr. Arbogast, but he was not officially assigned to her for any work. If they knew one another, it was not in a formal capacity."

"Any reason the Commissioner would lie?" asked Lola.

Mayor gave her question some thought. "Not about this."

Lola nodded. "No, I don't suppose this would concern him."

"That's not entirely true. An employee of the Gaming Commission was found murdered in my house. I still have some questions for Commissioner Deng."

"You ought to get acquainted with the Assistant Deputy while you're at it. I'll get you started." Lola extracted the black ledger from her purse and tossed it onto the sofa next to Mayor.

He read through the book carefully. The Conjurers at the desk stirred, catching Lola's attention. She saw their eyes slowly follow Aubrey, back and forth, back and forth.

Mayor looked up. "Aubrey, stop pacing, if you please. You're making the Conjurers quite nervous." He waited a few beats, then returned to the ledger. Lola lit a cigarette. In the silence, she heard the faintest hint of traffic below. No noise came from the rest of the building.

"You had your office proofed against sound?" she asked.

"A remnant of Mayor Leung's special brand of ostentation," replied Mayor absently.

A few more minutes passed. Lola tapped her ashes and waited.

He looked up again.

"How did you get this?"

"It's not important."

"What do you make of the contents?" asked Mayor.

"It's meant to prove extortion." Lola shrugged. "I became suspicious of my client's motives, so I followed Arbogast one afternoon. I saw him visit five of those parlours. I confronted him. He gave up the story. He was the bag man. His lover, Josephson, was also involved."

"Are you always so suspicious of your own clients?"

"If I have reason to be," replied Lola. "The point is, Arbogast is the obvious suspect for this extortion ring, and I had proof that would put the coppers onto him quick and easy. But he was more afraid of his boss than of me." She paused, allowing her words to sink in. Then, "Aubrey is certain Copenhagen is involved in my client's death."

Mayor shifted his attention. "How?" he asked, narrowing his eyes.

"The disturbance in the Ether," said Aubrey. "As I told you, it was strong on you when you came into the ballroom. I sensed the same, although weaker, around Copenhagen this morning."

"Do you still sense it? Here?" asked Mayor.

"No." Aubrey's reply came reluctantly.

Mayor said, "So she was there, somehow." He turned his attention to Lola. "How well do you know Copenhagen?"

"We attended the same high school. We were never friends," said Lola.

"How did you become reacquainted?"

"She had her thugs kidnap me and then she hired me." Lola met Mayor's gaze straight on. "My suspicious nature may just serve *you* well, when this is through." Lola outlined her investigation into the other woman's background.

"It appears she may very well still be a Spell Caster of some sort," continued Lola, "if not officially ordained by the Temple." A stirring among the Conjurers in the room, but nothing was said by any of the three. "I was led to understand you taught yourself Spells, so it should be possible for others. There are two years of her life that no one seems to know about. They happen to be the years after she left the Temple and before she reappeared as a City official. That oughta be enough time, even for a halfway decent student to learn some useful things. I'm told Amber Jade is easily your match when it comes to a natural ability in Conjury."

"You think this old school chum of yours is out to kill me?" Mayor's mouth quirked in an amused smile.

"You seem interested in taking precautions, just on principle. Why ignore this possibility? Amber Jade was widely acknowledged as a powerful natural talent in Conjury years ago." Lola paused, weighing her audience's possible credulity. With a shrug, she continued. "Listen, I haven't got a thimbleful of proof, but what if she did complete her training? What if she is a highly skilled Conjurer, Bound and Ordained by the Temple in secret? Or, for all I know," added Lola, "by some other organization?"

Mayor looked over at his two Conjurers, behind the desk. Neither man met his gaze. They continued to follow Aubrey's every move with focussed, hostile eyes.

Mayor faced Lola once more. He said, calmly, "And your ideas on her motives?"

"If she's a hired gun, then someone on that long list of enemies of yours has a reason." She assessed his expression.

"This isn't a legal case, Mayor. Motive is for convincing juries to make sense out of senselessness. Does it matter what her motive is? I think she's out to get you, and I think it's worth your while to know about it."

Mayor smiled, then, slightly. His eyes remained as lifeless as the rest of him. They were the same empty grey holes one saw in his newspaper photographs. This time, though, it was no trick of the light, no deficiency of the medium.

"I'm suspicious of you, Lola." Mayor folded his hands and laid them on his lap. "I also don't believe in coincidence. You have fastidiously avoided me for years. Yet here you are, now, you and Aubrey, the second time in twelve hours. You appear during a most important ceremony for me, and you bring a dead man as a house gift. A dead man, who also happens to be involved in an extortion ring *you* believe is being run by the Assistant Deputy Commissioner of Gaming."

"I'm not interested in killing you," repeated Lola.

"Not knowingly, perhaps," retorted Mayor. He leaned back against the cushions. "But I'm not afraid of you, nor of Aubrey. Death Moon is a dangerous time, yes, but today is a day of renewal and strength." Mayor held up a hand. "I'm no fool. I see the threat. However, Spells are well within my purview, as you've admitted. What are you looking to gain, coming here?"

"I want justice for Bodewell Arbogast and Joseph Josephson," she replied.

"Ten rounds in the ring, as it were? Bare knuckles? No holds barred?" He shook his head. "I can't condone vigilantism, Lola."

"You have a strange mind, Mayor. No one said anything about hangin' 'em from the nearest branch."

"You were being coy."

"No, I was being honest. The cops don't care about Joseph Josephson. They only care about Bodewell Arbogast because he happened to spoil a spot of floor in the Mayor's mansion."

"So guilt is behind your apparent altruism. Guilt," Mayor repeated, "is never a reliable substitution for logic, Lola. I'm sure your father would have agreed, yes?"

"He probably would have, but he's not here now. I am. So deal with me, Mayor." Lola paused, took a breath. "I want to speak with her alone, after the cops are done with her. How you get her to the cops is your business. I've done my civic duty by you."

"I suppose that's fair," said Mayor. After a pause, he continued: "You may not like it, Lola, but we have begun a relationship of sorts, you and I. I believe strongly in a foundation of trust for any lasting association. By coming here, by warning me, you've gained a small measure of that from me."

Lola stubbed out her cigarette. "Should I be flattered?"

Mayor smiled. "I've never dictated to my citizens as to their feelings."

"Good policy." Lola stood. "Let me know when it goes down." She turned away.

Mayor chuckled softly. "Does it bother you that I'm dead? You know, it's not healthy, as a Host, to resent your Haunting. Makes life for both you and the Ghost miserable in the extreme. Or is it simply that you object to poor Aubrey, your long-suffering companion? Would you have been happier, say, with your father Haunting you?" His dead eyes flickered between Lola and Aubrey.

Lola stopped, faced him again. "My father would never have Haunted me without asking first. And if he had, I would've said no."

Mayor looked surprised. He began to laugh softly.

Lola continued calmly. "As for you. You bothered me more when you were living."

"Ahh, we're back to your mother."

"My concerns were for my father," retorted Lola.

"I was not the cause of their divorce, Lola. That was in the works before I met Grace. Ah. You think if I'd not kept her in Europe, she'd have returned to him." A small smile played at the corners of his mouth. "Again, I'm compelled to contradict you. Grace was determined to pursue her career. I placed no pressure on her to stay. Your Ghost can speak to that, can't you, Aubrey?"

Lola's Ghost kept his mouth shut and his feet moving. Lola watched the Conjurers tensing up as their eyes tracked Aubrey's pacing once more.

Mayor continued speaking as he got up and returned to his desk. "That was all a long time ago. A lifetime ago. Butch never seemed bitter about it." He sat, shifted his eyes briefly. "Not when I knew him..." His voice trailed away. He assessed Lola in silence. She would almost swear she could see the gears grinding within his head.

"Ignore him, Lola." Aubrey's voice was close at her ear. "He doesn't understand the first thing about your father."

"He was a forgiving man," Lola said to Mayor. "I'm not like him."

Mayor said, "So you've said. Well then, as I was saying. Trust is a key element of our relationship, Lola. I'm about to tell you something that no other living person has ever heard." He aimed a smile at Aubrey.

"Stop," growled Aubrey. "This is not her business."

Mayor shook his head. "That's where you're wrong. Again. She has nothing to fear from them. I can protect her easily."

Lola strode back across the room. She stopped directly in front of the beautiful black desk and the smiling Ghost behind it. "Tell me."

"No, Lola. They'll kill you. It's a death sentence—"

Lola sliced the air behind her with a hand. She kept her gaze on Mayor. "Tell me."

"She's a grown woman," said Mayor, expression smug. He returned his attention to Lola. "I suspect you're nothing like your cautious father, after all."

Lola squelched the unease that sprang up at his cruel smile. She forced herself to listen carefully.

"There is a group of Ghosts who call themselves The Council. They fancy themselves a governing body for all Ghosts, everywhere. I won't go into the logistics nor even the most superficial description of their powers. Suffice to say that they rule through fear and intimidation. They collect tithe from Ghosts, in the form of energy. Your energy, in fact." Mayor smiled grimly. "In effect, Aubrey over there is a parasite. He survives only because he feeds from your life force. That feeding binds him to the Ether and to the Council. All the elaborate Spells of the Crossing Ceremony ensure that this binding lasts until the end of your life. When your life ends, poof—your Ghost is gone."

Lola pushed words past a rigid jaw. "But that doesn't apply to you."

Mayor nodded slightly. "Exactly. The Council and I disagree, you see. I made myself without being tied to a single Host. I will survive as long as I so choose. And I do this all without giving that pack of hyenas an iota of stolen energy." He smiled.

Lola was silent a moment, her eyes on the shadowy skyline behind Mayor's chair, as she thought, hard. Then: "So Copenhagen might play assassin for this Council?"

Mayor nodded. "If she is truly as much a natural talent as you say, she would be the perfect choice for their dirty work. It would have taken someone with prodigious skills to penetrate my mansion Wards and murder a man without any one of us knowing."

"Stop talking," shouted Aubrey, "Lola, please. Stop listening to him. It's time to leave. Now. It's not safe for you here."

"On the contrary," said Mayor. "The best place for your precious girl is under my protection. Don't allow your petty jealousy to blind you to the obvious."

"I'm hardly going to entrust her survival to your arrogance," Aubrey spit back.

Lola ground her teeth for a few moments.

"This doesn't change my demands. You'll have plenty of time to grill her after you catch her. I don't give a good goddamn about this Council you're so afraid of. I just want my twenty minutes with her once you're—."

The door to the outer office blew inward, banged against the wall. Mayor's Conjurers split up. The woman Conjurer ran toward the doorway, hands raised, shouting incoherently. Lola stared at the doorway, caught a glance of a booted foot. It quickly disappeared into the gloom of the empty space beyond.

The sound of a gunshot from the outer room.

Mayor's Conjurer was thrown back by the impact of the shot. Her body landed with a sickening sound. Lola averted her eyes from what remained of the woman's face. One of the other Conjurers screamed. The rage in his cry rang in Lola's ears.

Someone flew through the doorway, knocking the door open again. Gunshots roared inside the room. Screams of anger and pain reverberated around the space.

Lola felt intense pressure on her back, Aubrey's shouts unbearably loud in her ears. Turning back to the desk, she saw Mayor vanish. In her peripheral vision, she saw the remaining Conjurers crumple, dark stains spreading across yellow robes, wet matter sprayed across desk, chairs, rugs.

Lola dove over the heavy black desk and mashed herself back against the drawers. Bracing herself on one knee, she reached down. She pulled out a snub-nosed revolver from the ankle holster and held it close, waiting.

There was only silence now, ringing with the echo of violence.

TWENTY-FOUR

Show yourself, traitor," Copenhagen shouted.

Lola held her breath.

Copenhagen laughed. "Come on, come test me, haunt."

Lola slowly crept forward, awkwardly duck-walking. She manoeuvered until she could see past the desk leg. Copenhagen stood against a wall, her eyes narrowed and watchful. A small smile played on her lips. Next to her, the door was pushed shut once more. Between Copenhagen and Lola's vantage point was the larger of the two sofas. Lola set herself more firmly, pulling her gun forward. Before she could squeeze off a shot, Copenhagen caught sight of her. She swung her own gun up and fired. Lola fell back, but momentum carried her leg forward past the cover of the desk. The other woman found her mark. Lola cried out as the bullet passed through the meat of her calf, leaving a gush of blood behind. She scurried backward. Tearing at her neck, she messily pulled away her neck scarf and tied it tightly around her injured leg.

Copenhagen laughed. "Lola, predictable as ever. Well, thank you for being punctual."

"Pleasure's all yours," replied Lola, gritting her teeth.

Aubrey was suddenly at her ear, whispering: "I can feel it again, the disturbance, stronger than before. She's Warded the room. No one gets in or out. You have to stop her, Lola. If she catches either of us, she'll use the Dispersal spell and we'll both be dead."

"Mayor?" whispered Lola.

"He's trapped too. And there's no telling if he'd help us anyway."

"Be easier for him to kill you first," muttered Lola in agreement. She thought for a moment, listening hard with one ear for movement from Copenhagen's side of the office. Finally, she squared her shoulders. "I have a proposal," Lola shouted.

"Next time, I aim for your head," replied Copenhagen. "Enough of this, haunt," she suddenly shouted. "Show yourself and you won't have to watch your lover's only child die."

"Aubrey can see him," countered Lola.

"Of course," Copenhagen laughed. Lola felt her skin crawl at the delight in the woman's voice. "You don't owe him anything, do you?"

"But first, a trade of information," said Lola. Carefully, she eased up onto her haunches. Her calf collapsed under the strain and she fell down, cursing under her breath.

"Time's a-wasting, Lola," Copenhagen said. Another shot rang out and chips of lacquered wood flew from the desktop. "Tell me where Mayor is, Aubrey, and I won't kill you both."

"Actually," called out Aubrey, "I'm curious why you can't locate him yourself. Is he better at this than you, after all?"

"I can always find you, Aubrey. *I can see you.* Don't forget that."

"That's not much of an answer," he replied.

"That's because it's a threat," said Copenhagen. "You can't hope to match Spells with me, Aubrey. You're a zero in this equation."

Lola interjected, "But you need him for your Dispersal. You need me alive for that, at least. So why don't you put up the gun for now?" Lola slipped her revolver into the back waistband of her slacks. "We can talk like civilized adults."

"How's the leg?" countered Copenhagen.

Lola glanced down at the widening patch of blood.

"No go," said Copenhagen with finality. "I'm not here for you, Lola. I want the traitor. Help me and you won't suffer."

"Why does the Council want him dead?" asked Lola.

Copenhagen laughed harshly. "*Brava,* Lola. You might have made an investigator after all."

"You cornered Arbogast. You killed him and Josephson. You—"

"Yes, yes, and I had their cozy little home tossed to the hells and back. What of it?"

"Tell me why, tell me all of it, and I'll give you your haunt."

"She's lying," came another voice. Lola swiveled to get her bearings, but it seemed to emanate from everywhere around her.

"Parlour tricks won't save you now," spat Copenhagen.

"She's lying," repeated Mayor. "Aubrey is even less of a Spell Caster than you. He cannot see me."

"Show yourself and we'll put your claim to the test," challenged Copenhagen.

Aubrey was once again at Lola's ear: "I can get you a clear shot. Be ready."

"Wait," Lola whispered fiercely. "She'll see you."

"I think she won't use me until she can pinpoint him first. Be ready."

A laugh broke out from across the room. "Testing my Wards, haunt?" asked Copenhagen. "Do I get full marks?"

"Your masters are thorough, if nothing else," said Mayor.

"You'll discover that firsthand soon enough," said Copenhagen.

"You can't hope to Detect me, killer. Subtlety is not your strong suit."

Lola grunted, pulling herself onto her haunches once more. She bit her lip, drawing blood, as the wound in her leg pulsed painfully.

She crouched awkwardly, waiting for Aubrey's signal. He said, "Shift over to the left end." She obeyed, careful to keep her body out of Copenhagen's line of sight. "She saw me. She's moving toward the desk," hissed Aubrey. "Coming at two o'clock. Be ready."

Lola gripped her revolver surely.

"Don't do anything foolish, Lola," Copenhagen called out.

"Wouldn't dream of it," shouted Lola as she sprang up and started firing. Something connected and Copenhagen fell over with a grunt, her upper body then hidden behind the smaller sofa. Lola ran around the desk and toward the fallen woman. Her leg buckled. She tumbled onto her right side, the gun beneath her. The landing jarred her shoulder and her trigger finger squeezed reflexively, sending a bullet through her own forearm. Lola's head snapped back, her face pulled tight in pain. She tumbled onto her stomach.

"Lola," cried Aubrey.

Suddenly, Copenhagen was up again, the wound high on her left shoulder. She hobbled over to Lola, raised her leg and stomped down on Lola's back. Then she kicked her in the ribs and turned her over. Lola grunted heavily and tried to scramble away. The revolver was just out of reach. Copenhagen kicked it away. Lola looked up in time to see Copenhagen pointing her own gat at Lola's head.

"Offer's off the table." The killer grinned. "You *will* suffer."

Lola jabbed with her foot, kicking out Copenhagen's leg just below the knee. Copenhagen fired as she collapsed. Lola heard the whistle of the bullet as it passed her left ear. She jumped up, unevenly, and lunged for the other woman's pistol. Copenhagen swung wildly with a fist and caught Lola on the neck. Lola coughed harshly, still reaching for the gun, but she miscalculated and fell short. Copenhagen reared up and punched down, landing a fist into the side of Lola's head. Lola heard ringing and her vision filled with white spots. She grabbed blindly but her opponent brushed her hands aside and scrabbled away. A kick landed squarely in Lola's solar plexus. She convulsed, gasping for air.

"I'm happy to beat it out of you, Lola. Surely you know that by now." Copenhagen was slightly out of breath but in far better shape. Lola looked up in time to see the gun in Copenhagen's hand, swooping toward her head. It connected with a sickening crunch and Lola buckled. She toppled over and curled into herself.

"I hope you're watching, haunt." Lola's eyes were clamped shut, but the smile in Copenhagen's voice was clear.

Lola heard the shuffle of feet and managed to pry her eyes open to slits. Copenhagen approached again. Lola felt a trickle of blood seep toward her eye. She blinked heavily and tried to get up. Copenhagen planted her leg and swung the other back for another kick. Lola held her breath and raised a hand out to deflect the blow as best she could.

A mist abruptly coalesced in between the two women. Lola caught a brief glimpse of Mayor's grim expression before he turned away to face his would-be assassin. The other woman was caught off guard, overbalanced, and fell back. Mayor grabbed Copenhagen by the shoulders and slammed her into the floor. She squeezed off a bullet, but it passed through Mayor and lodged into the ceiling. Lola heard a distinct cracking noise as she watched Mayor land a punch and break Copenhagen's cheekbone. The assassin's hands slackened and the pistol fell away. Mayor picked her up and held her off the floor. She hung motionless for a few seconds, then suddenly, she began thrashing.

Aubrey cried: "Get up Lola! Get—"

Lola felt a blast of air pass on her left, where Aubrey had just been shouting. She staggered, feeling the pull of that invisible wind. Her skin was crawling with unseen insects, every hair on her body standing up on end.

Mayor disappeared from view. His grip remained firm, though. Copenhagen was held up in midair, her face puffing up and darkening from the broken bones. Her eyes were glittering as she stared intently at the space in front of her. Her lips moved rapidly and she glared fiercely at her now-invisible opponent.

The wind, grown twice as strong, buffeted Lola until she stumbled. Her hair, torn from its twist, flew madly around her face, obscuring her vision. She tried to move forward, her body leaning into the suddenly solid air, but she could make no progress. A scream pierced the thick atmosphere and Lola looked up. She scrabbled at the strands of hair covering her eyes.

Copenhagen's mouth was agape, eyes bulging. A second scream died as it barely began. The pain on her face came into sharp relief. The dark bruising of the broken cheekbone stood out starkly against the paleness of her skin. Her limbs and head were suddenly flung back, her body forming an unnatural curve. She thrashed wildly, her arms and legs carving terrible arcs in the air, pin-wheeling unnaturally in midair. Then she seemed to pull back into herself and the convex became a concave. A sharp, wet tearing sound filled the room.

The wind died, Copenhagen fell.

Lola's weak leg gave way once again. She faltered and landed on her side. After a moment, she raised herself up on one arm. A sudden intense chill accompanied the silence. Lola was enveloped in a fine cloud. She coughed, trying to work some moisture into her dry mouth and throat. Her eyes watered, rejecting all of her efforts to blink away the tears. When she finally managed to wipe them away, she felt the cold lifting. The cloud was no longer around her. Instead it had formed above Copenhagen's motionless body. Tentacles of icy grey fog crept along an invisible thread, down to the woman's back. The mist seemed to pulse, once. Lola heard a soft sigh. She blinked again. The cloud was gone.

TWENTY-FIVE

A delicate young woman sat next to the hospital bed, her dark hair pulled back into a loose bun at her nape. The harsh lights overhead did nothing to diminish her soft features. Lola looked at her with grit-filled eyes and a grim mouth.

"Are we done here?" she asked, her voice ground down to a nub.

The woman shook her head. Her expression remained bland. "Your Ghost must explain again why he aided in the Dispersal."

"I didn't," came Aubrey's weary reply. "I was trying to get my Host to safety when I was pulled into the Spell. I had no choice. At the time, I didn't know what was going on."

"And yet you still exist," said a fourth voice, the smoothest in the room. Lola felt the hairs on her neck stand up. She rubbed at them, irritated at their slavish constancy even after all these hours. She really ought to be used to hearing the invisible Ghost by now. The disembodied voice continued. "You should not have survived the Spell."

"Something happened she didn't expect," said Aubrey. "I don't think Copenhagen completed the Spell properly."

"Yet Mayor is now gone," countered the voice reasonably.

Lola jerked her arm involuntarily, setting the handcuff rattling against the metal rail of the bed. The young woman watched her with neutral eyes, then returned her gaze to Aubrey.

"You obviously know more about that than I," replied Aubrey. "As I've said, I'm no Conjurer's Ghost nor am I a Spell Caster."

A long pause followed Aubrey's angry assertion. Lola collapsed against the pillows behind her, wincing at the stab of pain in her side, the pounding of her headache. It was difficult to breathe through the tight wrappings around her middle. She reached for her cigarettes then remembered she had none. She kicked her leg in irritation, then sucked in a harsh gasp at the pain in her injured calf. Lola breathed shallowly for some long seconds. She refused to allow her physical infirmities to overcome her.

The other woman sat as she had for the entirety of the interrogation, composed and still.

The other Ghost's velvety voice said, "Let's hear it again, please, from the top."

"Let's not," Lola ground out. She rattled her handcuff again in agitation. "Telling it a tenth time won't get you the answers you want to hear. You've heard the truth from us. Make up your own damned lies."

"Lola," said Aubrey. He spoke precisely, coolly. "Lola, please, calm down. Ms. Heung and Mr. Liao are just doing their job. If they need to hear it again, I'll tell it again.

"Mayor's warding ceremony was infiltrated by Copenhagen, when she murdered Arbogast. The particulars of that, I'll leave to you lot, but my intuition says the poor man's soul was the disruptive force in her Spell. She created a vulnerability in Mayor's Warding by killing Arbogast and using his soul." Aubrey explained the disturbance he'd felt, how that taint had led them to Arbogast's body, and how it had also swirled around Mayor as well as Copenhagen. "We thought it certainly possible, given our investigation into Copenhagen's Conjury background, but Mayor refused to consider it as a possibility. He was convinced he was invulnerable. We think Copenhagen used that against him. He let us in, far too close for safety, but he was so sure we were no threat. She knew Lola had an appointment so she knew when we would be in the same room with Mayor.

"Lola and Mayor were discussing the results of her investigation into the extortion ring when Copenhagen attacked. She killed Mayor's Conjurers. Shot them all. Lola tried to hit Copenhagen, to disarm the threat, but Copenhagen shot Lola and tried to kill her. Copenhagen would have shot Lola in the head, but Mayor intervened. He and Copenhagen struggled, while my Host lay beat and bleeding on the floor. I urged her to get up, to leave immediately, but then I was torn away. We, Lola and I, we knew Copenhagen had intended to use me in her Dispersal spell. But to be honest, I'd forgotten about that. I just wanted to get my Host to safety. I struggled when I felt the Spell being Cast, when I was pulled into it, but I'm no Spell Caster and Copenhagen was strong." His voice trailed away.

"What did you feel?" asked Heung without inflection.

"Please be specific," added the other Ghost.

Aubrey's voice was quiet. "I felt as though she plunged her fingers into me and spread me out. She was wrapping me around Mayor, tightening a noose, a net, a rope, something deadly. I felt myself dissipating. He cut through me, then, sharp as a cleaver. I might have cried out, I don't recall. I ... thought of Lola, and her mother, I tried to hold on to myself, my...Essence. She still had a grip on me. He stabbed and slashed until he came free. I floated in tatters between them." Aubrey's voice was dull now.

"But you were still conscious of yourself?" asked Liao. "You knew who you were?"

"Yes."

Lola sighed.

"It seems damned clear to me. Copenhagen used him to Disperse Mayor, but the old hack got to her before she could finish. He tore out her soul," she concluded, her face suddenly tight. "And Aubrey pulled himself together, out of harm's way."

"I was lucky," said Aubrey.

"And Mayor simply disappeared?" asked Heung.

Lola nodded. Her throat was raw with exhaustion. "That's what it looked like. She tried to tear him apart. He tore out her soul. I thought I saw a mist of some sort, afterward. It might've been him. It disappeared, but Copenhagen, her body was on the floor...beside me."

The silence lengthened. Heung sat calmly and searched Lola's face with her flat, dark eyes. Finally, Lola said, "You considered yet that Copenhagen tried her Spell with Josephson and his Ghost first? Maybe she couldn't get them close enough to Mayor. Maybe they weren't cooperating. I don't know. A junkie and his Ghost might have been simply too unreliable."

Aubrey broke in. "It's just as likely Lucille convinced her brother to leave town on the promise of another score."

"Whatever the reason," Lola said, "Copenhagen needed another plan. So she looked for another option."

"And found you," said Liao, his voice low and thoughtful.

Lola shrugged, suddenly weary again. She dropped back against the pillows, grimacing as the metal cuff scraped her wrist bone.

A knock at the door. Heung closed her notebook and stood. "We appreciate your cooperation, Miss Starke. This is a most unusual situation. Your Ghost posed some interesting suppositions regarding the magics involved, which we will be following up. We may require your Ghost's presence at another interview. In the interim, it's in your best interest to stay in Crescent City."

Lola pulled at her arm, handcuffed to the bed. She let its rattle express her ire. She stared wearily at Heung's crisp blouse and creased slacks. "Who's next?" she asked.

The door opened and in stepped two familiar figures.

"Ah, the same old dog-and-pony, I see," Lola said. "Any chance of a cigarette? Now that the oh-so-sensitive Conjurer's off?"

Heung nodded cordially to the two detectives and swept out into the hall. Lola heard footsteps, voices, squeaky carts, rattling dishes—all the sounds of a busy hospital—from the hall until Marks closed the door. Beneath his neutral demeanour, Lola sensed exhaustion. She almost snorted. It was nothing compared to how she felt. Bednarski pulled over the chair Heung had sat in. He reversed it and straddled the seat. Marks remained standing at the foot of the bed.

"Seems the staff Conjurers are satisfied for now, Miss Starke."

"I'm so happy for them."

"It's far-fetched enough to be the truth," commented Marks. He slid a hand into a breast pocket and re-surfaced with a packet of cigarettes. His expression bland, he offered them. Lola's cheeks reddened.

"Those always give me a headache, and the shape I'm in," she swallowed past an abruptly tight throat. "No thank you."

Marks shrugged and shook one out, lit it with a shiny metallic lighter.

Bednarski said, "We just have a few more questions and then you can go back to sleep."

"But don't leave town, right?" asked Lola. She rattled her cuff again.

"What can I tell you? You're the sole surviving witness in the murder of the City's highest official. By your own admission, you were an instrument in his demise."

"Did you just say 'demise', Bednarski?"

"—although an unwitting one," he finished.

Marks chimed in: "But ignorance only gets you so far."

"Some farther than others," Lola replied. Before Marks reacted, she sat forward, determined to ignore the pain, and asked Bednarski, "So now what? You need me to connect the dots for you too?"

The big man nodded, "Something like that, sure."

Lola looked from him to his partner. Neither man looked any fresher than she felt. She sighed. "Your guess is as good as mine, gentlemen."

"That's not much help, Starke."

Lola shrugged at Marks's scowl. "Did you think we had a civilized chat in there? That she conveniently explained her murderous scheme to me before she was going to kill me? What kind of dime-store novel you think this is?"

Bednarski raised his hands appeasingly. "We just want to know what she said, if anything."

"Oh gosh, Inspector," gushed Lola, "she said she was going to torture me slowly until Mayor showed himself, at which point, she was going to use Aubrey to kill him, thereby killing my Ghost in the process and then, hopefully, she was going to kill me as painfully as she could."

"Yeah, yeah," said Marks, "but why? Why target Mayor?"

Lola shrugged. "Since you're so desperate as to be asking an ignorant gumshoe like me, I'll take pity on you. I'd suggest taking a look at those two years before she hired on with Gaming."

"Tell it now, Starke," growled Marks.

"Got nothing to tell." Lola turned her face away. "I couldn't dig deep enough."

"Now *that* I believe," replied Marks.

"That's enough," said Bednarski. He rubbed his face, his stubble rasping against his palm. "I'm calling it a night."

"Don't leave town," said Marks. He pointed a long finger at her.

Lola clenched her fists. The cuff pressed into her wrist.

"I apologize for the cuffs, Miss Starke," said the big man. "Like I said, you're a possible suspect and material witness. The Staff Conjurers'll check into your story. We'll check into the physical stuff. We'll let you know as soon as it comes clear." Bednarski replaced his chair and went to the door. Lola waited for the door to close with a soft thump before closing her eyes and collapsing against the pillow again. She considered calling for the nurse but was asleep before she could remember where the button was.

"Miss Starke, your mother is waiting to take you home. You're free to go."

Lola rubbed at her bandaged wrist. Three days with that gods-damned cuff on her hand. No wonder it was raw. She nodded her thanks to the nurse, a grey-haired woman with gentle eyes. The nurse helped her into the wheelchair.

"I prefer to walk," Lola said, her voice tight.

"Hospital procedure, Miss Starke. Wouldn't want you to have a mishap on your way out."

Lola grunted. The nurse held out a cane of dark wood with a silver cap. Lola hesitated before accepting it. She laid it on her lap, its silver-tipped end resting on her feet, her hand clasped firmly around the cap.

The nurse pushed Lola down the hallway, around a corner and out into the reception area. Lola saw her mother immediately. Just behind her stood St. John, his face neutral but Lola recognized the tightness in his stance, the set of his jaw, sure signs of his disapproval. Beside him, a few feet away, stood Bednarski and Marks.

Grace McCall wore a tailored midnight blue dress. Its square-cut décolletage highlighted her delicate collarbone. A tear-shaped diamond hung against her porcelain skin. She repeatedly slapped one glove against the palm of her other gloved hand, the very picture of elegant, steely disdain. As soon as Lola was within reach, she gently took her daughter's arm. Before turning away, however, she gathered herself up. She tipped her chin up and looked down her nose through the small veil of lace cascading down from her hat.

"Tell Superintendent Locke I shall be expecting him tomorrow afternoon," she said coldly.

"Yes, ma'am," replied Marks.

"The next time you wish to reach my daughter, you shall do so through our solicitor." Grace gestured at St. John, who proffered a simple card to Bednarski.

"Thank you, ma'am," said the large man.

Lola used her cane to push herself up out of the wheelchair. The nurse helped her up with a hand on her elbow and the other gently on her back. Lola nodded to the homicide detectives and held herself straight-backed, thinking of her maid Elaine. She thanked the nurse and allowed her mother and St. John to guide her out of the hospital. They walked carefully to the car, miraculously waiting at the curb.

St. John opened the door and helped Lola in first. Then Grace slid in. The door closed with a soft click.

"Home, St. John," Lola said. After a beat, she added, "please."

The car started up and silence fell within.

Lola closed her eyes, leaned her head back, and listened to the purr of the Packard. She dozed eventually, and came to just as the car pulled to a stop in front of her apartment building. Rubbing uselessly at her eyes, Lola prepared to get out. She looked down and realized her mother was holding her hand.

"Darling," Grace hesitated, "I'm leaving in two days." Another pause. "Is there anything else I can do for you?"

"No thank you, Mother. I'll be fine. The Aunties will take care of me. And Betta." She paused. "Thank you for the cane."

Grace opened her mouth to protest, then shut it firmly. Her face fell by degrees. "I'll come by tomorrow, after I see Locke."

Lola nodded. She gently extricated her hand, turned away. She hesitated before pulling the door latch. Relenting, she said, "He died well. If that's any consolation."

Grace seemed to shrink inward. "No," she said faintly, "actually, it's not."

EPILOGUE

"It's not safe for you to drive," he says. "You've only been out of hospital five days."

"You sound too much like Vivian." I glance at the cane on the passenger's seat. The silver cap is smooth but pitted. I've found myself rubbing it soothingly too many times since my mother gave it to me.

"She happens to be right this time." Aubrey, talking again. Right.

I shrug.

"Where are we going?" he asks.

"I'm going to the Jade Sparrow. You can make your own plans."

"Another frivolous night?"

I pull out into a slackening rain. A light smattering on the top of the car. Barely enough moisture to scrape across the windshield.

He speaks again, suddenly. "Could you tell I was gone? When you woke?"

I shrug again. "Barely felt a difference."

"Even you know that's not true."

As if I'd tell him about my first taste of freedom in twelve years.

"I was summoned by The Council," he says.

I check my mirrors, gauge traffic. "What's the damage?" I ask finally. "Should I expect a summons of my own?"

"They've promised to leave you alone."

"Their price?"

A long pause. Too long.

Then: "An increase in my tithe." His answer is all but lost in the increased tapping of the rain.

I grip the wheel, hard, and maneouvre around a taxi letting his fares out. "What does that mean for me?"

I can feel his hesitation, like a shove. He really doesn't want to tell me. "They've chosen an additional Host," he whispers then.

My gut tightens painfully. I take a guess. "Mother."

His silence is answer enough.

"How did you tell her? What about The Council?"

"I did what I had to do. You'd be dead otherwise. You and your mother." I can hear the tremor running through his voice. I think about that as I navigate through the City at night. Cars are everywhere, filled with glittering, marcelled girls laughing as their white-tie beaus dart and race through traffic. I catch glimpses of people on the sidewalks, waiting in line at the cinemas, or walking in groups. Everyone seems to be going somewhere.

It comes to me, then, clear as day. "You didn't tell her. You bastard. She doesn't even know."

"I know it's difficult for you to accept, but I'm thinking of your best interests. It was the only way to protect you. And Grace. They didn't give me a choice of Hosts. They'd already decided."

"Let me guess." A bitter taste twists my mouth. "I can't tell her either."

He sighs. He actually sighs, damn him. "I had no choice. You can accept that, or not. You can be angry for the rest of your life. It won't change one bloody thing. It certainly won't change the past."

"Ah, how convenient. Done and dusted. No need to consider your actions, then."

"My conscience is clear."

"Mine isn't," I shout. I take a few, concentrating on the streets, other cars, the pedestrians. I try to calm down. My heart is racing, though. This is madness. I can't let it happen. "Let me talk to this Council then. I'll bear the burden alone."

"It's too late, Lola. Grace is already...tethered."

"You don't even sound bothered." I clench my jaw shut. The traffic thins as I keep driving. Past the Jade Sparrow, past all the rest of the houses and buildings in East Town. Past the City limits.

I'm driving too fast, but I can't stop.

"You have absolutely no idea what I'm feeling." His voice is as cold as the night air streaming through my window now. "I saved us the best way left to me."

"So the end result is worth any amount of duplicity, is that it?" I'm sickened by his righteous tone. Doesn't he understand how deeply he's deceived my mother, his childhood friend? The sheer magnitude of the betrayal stuns me.

And he's roped me into it.

I clamp my teeth against the pressure building in my chest, the scream battering to get out.

"Someday," he says, his voice cutting, "you'll be faced with a choice between your vaunted principles and the safety of a person you love. We'll see which you choose."

My eyes fill with tears, I'm clamping down so hard against the scream. I feel my gorge rise, swallow against it. I gnash out each word carefully:

"You. Don't. Love. Me."

My knuckles show starkly white in the darkness inside the car. I loosen my grip on the steering wheel. "Get it straight, haunt. You don't know me. I don't owe you anything. You tricked me into this

Hosting. I haven't discovered why, but I will. The day it happens, be ready for a reckoning."

I drive eastward, toward the flats and the stark, black mountains. The rain's stopped completely, leaving a light greasy film on my windows. Behind me lie the lights and glitter of the City. Ahead, nothing but empty road and the dark chill of the desert night.

I drive until my face is numb and I'm deaf from the roar of the wind.

I drive until I'm sure I won't throttle the first person to speak to me.

Then I stop.

The sky is limitless out here. The black shapes of mountains brood in the far, far distance. Their vastness pushes at me even from afar. I swipe at my eyes, get out of the car. Stars, mere pinpricks of light, blink among the tatters of pale clouds. The moon hangs its crescent horns in the black sky.

Bracing for it, I think of Arbogast, his last words to me and his smile when he introduced himself and explained his name. I think of Mayor, as he spoke of my parents. And then his expression before he tore a woman's soul away.

I remember my father, his handsome face, kind and intelligent.

In the distance, the City pulls at me. Its neon lights pulse against the cold desert sky. I recall my plan: hard drink, easy tiles and a date with a stranger.

Back in my car, I gun the engine and take a deep breath.

There's plenty of night before the dawn.

ACKNOWLEDGEMENTS

This novel was first published as an ebook in 2013 by Carina Press. I'm grateful to Angela James and the whole Carina team for the work they put into that original manuscript. I especially thank Krystal Gabert, my original editor, for championing Lola in all the ways she did. I'm so proud that the book was a finalist for Best First Novel in the 2014 Arthur Ellis Awards for Excellence in Canadian Crime Writing.

This print edition, though, the one you hold in your hands, this one's my baby. As such, it also had its midwives, as it were.

Thanks Heather Little, of little h design works, for the super cool cover for this print edition. I couldn't have done it without you.

Thanks Jodi McIsaac, Minister Faust, Alexis Kienlen, and Nicole Luiken for answering my various urgent and convoluted questions. Going indie was a lot easier with your help.

Thanks Kate Boorman for being such a love and a smartie to boot. You always make me laugh. In a good way.

Thanks Janice MacDonald and Randy Williams for your warm support, inimitable humour and incredible generosity. YEG would be a smaller, darker place without you two.

Thanks, always, to my brother Gary and my mum Susan. I think Dad would be proud of us—in his usual cantankerous way.

Finally, as ever, thank you Kevin, E, and Wubby with all of my full, full heart.

ABOUT THE AUTHOR

SG Wong lives in Edmonton, Alberta, with her family and a whole lot of LEGO. She writes the Lola Starke novels and assorted Crescent City short stories in a lovely blue office where she can often be found staring out the window in between frenzied bouts of typing.

Connect with her via Facebook, @S_G_Wong on Twitter and at www.sgwong.com.

CPSIA information can be obtained
at www.ICGtesting.com
Printed in the USA
LVOW12s1015231016
509928LV00003B/581/P